BRESCIA COLLEGE LIBRARY
3 6277 00005888 5

STORMING BABYLON

STORMING BABYLON

Preston Manning and the Rise of the Reform Party

SYDNEY SHARPE

AND DON BRAID

KEY PORTER BOOKS

To Laurent (Jeff) Dubois, J. Patrick O'Callaghan, and Franklyn Sharpe, for their wisdom and inspiration.

CONTENTS

Canadian Cataloguing in Publication Data

Braid, Don, 1942–
Storming Babylon : Preston Manning
and the rise of the Reform Party

ISBN 1-55013-412-4

1. Manning, Preston, 1942- .2. Reform Party of Canada. 3. Canada - Politics and government -1084- I. Sharpe, Sydney. II. Title

JL197.R34B7 1992 324.271'0983 C91-095398-8

Key Porter Books Limited
70 The Esplanade
Toronto, Ontario
Canada M5E 1R2

Printed and bound in Canada
on acid-free paper

92 93 94 95 96 6 5 4 3 2 1

ACKNOWLEDGMENTS

THIS BOOK would not exist without the encouragement and assistance of many people. Colleagues at the *Calgary Herald*, as always, were understanding and helpful. Our children, Gabriel and Rielle, were infinitely patient with their overworked parents. The Reform Party leader and party officials remained courteous and professional throughout. Many dozens of people consented to be interviewed; those who agreed to be named are cited in the text. Our publisher and editors contributed vastly to any quality and depth that enriches the book. If errors escaped their diligent scrutiny, the responsibility is ours.

We would also like to thank the staffs of various libraries and archives which house precious information on the Mannings and the history of western populism. The Alberta Provincial Archives, and the University of Alberta Library and Archives, were indispensable. The Alberta Legislature Library, not for the first time, chased down publications and tolerated tardy returns. Also helpful was the Library of Parliament in Ottawa. In every case, the staff people were friendly, knowledgeable, and highly professional.

Many friends provided invaluable encouragement and moral support, especially Jim Stanton and Lisa Grand, whose hospitality at a crucial point was invaluable.

CHAPTER ONE

STORMING BABYLON

"I have to laugh when I hear people say he's new to politics. After all, this is Senator Manning's son!"

– Historian Desmond Morton

"I'm building a kite and I need wind for it to fly."

– Preston Manning

IN A REMARKABLY short time, the Reform Party has come charging out of the West to assault all the towers of "Old Canada" – the three traditional parties, a federal system that costs too much and delivers too little, politicians who try to placate Quebec, the discredited champions of bilingualism and multiculturalism. Reformers see all these forces as agents of a corrupt, bankrupt system that no longer represents their traditional faith in family, frugality, the rights of the individual, and one united but decentralized nation. They hear a Babel of Canadian voices, too many new voices, all contradictory, many incomprehensible, none saying what they want to hear. They yearn for a simple, clean-cut Canada with homespun verities at its heart. To achieve their "New Canada," they are ready to storm the federal Babylon and throw out the unbelievers. Their increasingly powerful siege engine, an organization with more than 100,000 members by the beginning of 1992, is not so much a political party as a populist movement unlike anything Canada has seen since the 1920s and 1930s.

The leader of these political shock troops is Ernest Preston Manning, age 49, the son of Ernest Charles Manning, who was Social Credit Premier of Alberta from 1943 to 1969. Preston Manning seems fresh to many Canadians because he is new on the national scene, but he has been active in politics for 25 years, and he has been preparing himself for leadership all that time. "I have to laugh when I hear people say he's new to politics," says University of Toronto historian Desmond Morton. "After all, this is Senator Manning's son!" (Ernest Manning, the enemy of almost everything the federal Liberals stand for, accepted a Senate appointment from Pierre Trudeau in 1970 and served until 1983.)

Preston Manning seems to be the very opposite of a slick and seasoned politician. He could easily be mistaken for the shy, modest proprietor of a religious supply store in rural Alberta. When he appears on a podium or a TV screen, he has the darting, big-eyed look of a nervous owl ready to pounce on some misplaced fact. His nickname among friends – "Press" – is as plain as his appearance, and his family life appears so uneventful that one relative calls Preston and Sandra Manning "Mr. and Mrs. Perfect." But this meek demeanour masks a political will cast in iron, skills as polished as a tap dancer's shoes, and beliefs so radical they would entirely change the nature of Canada.

The deep religious convictions of the Manning family, rooted in evangelical Christianity, are central to Preston Manning's political beliefs. For many years he appeared on his father's evangelical radio show, "Canada's National Bible Hour." He believes that every word of the Bible is true and knows that he has a calling to translate those words into political action. Every one of his policies, from his views on capitalism to privatization, can be traced in a straight line back to his vision of the proper Christian society. He is convinced that Canada is hell-bent for damnation but can be saved by turning sharply toward the heavenly beacon of the Reform Party's New Canada. Ernest Manning once said, referring to Social Credit, "No other philosophy in the world today offers anything but ultimate slavery." Today the Reform Party espouses much the same philosophy and Preston Manning believes the stakes are just as high.

Anyone who gets close to Manning senses at once his intensity and his burning devotion to the Reform cause. In conversation he can be restless and fidgety, often squirming impatiently when he hears something with which he does not agree. His manner is pleasant and his responses are always polite, but behind them lies a strong mind that settled on most of the answers long ago. There are very few political issues Preston Manning has not studied and pondered deeply. His attention to detail is almost obsessive, his concentration legendary among friends. He once spent an entire day honing a single sentence of a policy definition. His brother-in-law, Phillip Stuffco, remembers stopping his car a few feet from where Manning was sitting behind a picture window. "I blew the horn and the guy didn't even hear me," Stuffco recalls. "He was writing a paper or something."

Manning's personal sense of duty and obligation, implanted by religion and family example, is both his strength and his burden. His father served in the Alberta legislature and the Senate for an astounding total of 47 years. Now 83, Ernest Manning still preaches damnation and salvation on the radio twice a month, his powerful voice reminiscent of the charismatic Social Credit founder William "Bible Bill" Aberhart. Many sons would run from a model so daunting, and Preston Manning may once have tried in his quiet way to escape. For his first two years at the University of Alberta he studied physics and considered a career in pure science, far from the world of politics. Then he switched to economics and embraced political life, propelled by duty, aptitude, and perhaps by a trace of guilt, for there was a quiet tragedy in the Manning family. Preston Manning's older brother and only sibling, William Keith Manning, was afflicted by cerebral palsy and institutionalized for much of his short life. From his youngest days, Preston Manning felt responsible for his brother, and his sense of loss was immense when Keith Manning died in 1986. Fundamentalist religion and his father's impressive service created in Preston Manning, the lucky healthy son, a profound sense of obligation and mission. As his father would say, Preston Manning felt a call from the Lord. The call from his family circumstances was just as loud and compelling.

Manning is the polar opposite of Prime Minister Brian Mulroney, the leader whose regime he challenges so fiercely. Mulroney has always been far more interested in people than policy. He knows nearly every important decision-maker in Canada and counts his friends and acquaintances in the hundreds. As John Sawatsky shows in *Mulroney: The Politics of Ambition*, the prime minister is an extroverted charmer who measures success by his influence over people. Manning, on the other hand, is a true crusader whose main interest is the mission. Despite his deep faith in the individual, he does not have the born politician's burning desire to win over every person he meets. He tends to be shy and even awkward with strangers. Ron Nicholls, a Calgary Tory and friend of Mulroney's, once encountered Manning in a store in Arizona while both were on holiday. "I'd never met him," Nicholls recalls, "so I introduced myself and said, 'I used to be president of the provincial Tory party in Alberta.' I might have been a convert just ripe for convincing, but he didn't seem very interested. He just sort of said 'hello' and drifted off." Mulroney has always made a point of cultivating key people in other parties, but Manning hardly seems interested. (In Nicholls' case he should have been; the Calgary architect wrote a report for Mulroney on the Reform Party's prospects in Alberta.) Very few people know Manning well, and the vast majority of decision-makers in Canadian politics and business have never met him. While Mulroney was climbing the ladder in the Montreal business establishment, making contacts all over the country,

Manning worked in Slave Lake, Alberta, trying to pull a small town up by its bootstraps. His relatively limited circle of friends and acquaintances tend to work at the policy-making levels of business, government, and consulting.

His zeal for the cause has never diminished. Over the years, Manning was quietly involved in many political causes and ventures, always waiting for just the right moment to found a new federal party. His timing was excellent; he moved in the spring of 1987, just before English Canada's discontent began to explode into a true fury over Meech Lake, the national debt, the Goods and Services Tax, Quebec's law against English signs, the rise of the Bloc Québécois, and criminal charges against Tory politicians.

From the start Manning hoped that his new populist movement, once firmly rooted in the West, would become truly national. He did not want just another western-based party that would shout briefly at Ottawa and fade away: no Western Canada Concept or West-Fed for him. "I'm building a kite and I need wind for it to fly," he told Quebec journalist Michel Vastel in 1987. In this sense too, his timing was impeccable. Pollsters began to notice in the late 1980s that "western" issues were becoming "national" issues. The same things that bothered westerners for so many years – high taxes, the seemingly unending focus on Quebec, the feeling that the federal system is a foe rather than a friend – were now common perceptions in Ontario and Atlantic Canada as well. At the same time there were lingering memories of outrages such as the Liberals' 1980 National Energy Program and the Mulroney government's decision in 1986 to award the CF-18 fighter maintenance contract to Montreal rather than Winnipeg. For all these reasons, Manning's ideal of taking a regional party to the national stage was suddenly possible.

Roger Gibbins, one of Canada's leading experts on regional alienation, does not see the Reformers as a regional movement at all. "Two things have happened," says the University of Calgary professor. "The western Canadian electorate has been nationalized in the sense that their concerns are not parochial any more. And second, the primary issues the Reform Party is addressing are not really regional. It's a much more broadly based movement."

The party also taps into powerful international currents that are eroding old systems far from Canada. The death of the Soviet Communist party, the defeat of socialism in Sweden, the redrawing of borders along ethnic lines in Eastern Europe, all fit the Reformers' belief in the bankruptcy of "collectivist" government. So does the growth of populist, anti-establishment parties in nearly every country of western Europe. Like many of those groups, the Reformers want decentralized government, state functions in private hands, social needs met by free enterprise, and more citizen control over politicians. They are even ready to contemplate Canada's ultimate ethnic split, the cleavage of Quebec from the rest of Canada, if Quebec will not accept their vision of the country. They believe that local control is better than central control in everything from politics to economics. Now they are convinced that the world is moving their way.

Manning sees his movement as part of these international trends, and he identifies with the leaders in eastern Europe. He was powerfully impressed by a meeting he had with the Polish, Hungarian, and Czechoslovakian ambassadors to Canada. "These guys are trying to change the system on every front," Manning said in an interview. "They're trying to convert from a Marxist economy to a market economy. They're trying to go from a totalitarian system to a democratic system, and they're trying to get beyond this left-right stuff. These are populist type things, they're bottom-up, democratic, and market-oriented. The difference, of course, is that in Canada we have all this freedom. These guys can't understand why if Canada wants to make systemic changes it shouldn't be about the easiest thing in the world."

As an avid amateur historian, Manning is also attracted to the populist tradition in Canada. The Reform Party echoes the great western populist movements of the 1930s: the Progressives, the Co-operative Commonwealth Federation (CCF), and Social Credit. Some of Reform's rhetoric, especially about Quebec, is powerfully reminiscent of the One Canada speeches of the late Tory Prime Minister John Diefenbaker, the last leader whose western voice found wide national appeal.

But the main parallel lies deeper in the past. The left-liberal Progressives, led by farmers and workers, who won 65 seats in the 1921 federal election, are the tactical model for the Reformers as they march onto the national stage. The rightist Social Credit movement, which ruled Alberta from 1935 to 1971 and elected many federal MPs, provides the strategic goals, the grand design for Canada. Most of the ideas espoused by the Reform Party today, in fact, were developed by Manning and his father in the late 1960s as they tried to keep the populist spirit alive in a form appealing to modern Canada.

Populism can have its dark side, as Manning knows very well. Alberta Social Credit was often blatantly anti-Semitic, and today there are racists among the Reformers. Manning admits this is a problem but argues that his party can purge extremists merely by growing beyond them. Meanwhile, though, some people in the party come very close to the perceptive definition of American observer Kevin Phillips: "Populism likes flags, criticizes welfare as well as Wall Street, and keeps a gun in the pick-up truck."

All Manning's careful planning, mixed with good timing and even better luck, propelled the Reformers to national attention with shocking speed. In May of 1987, 300 disgruntled westerners went to Vancouver for the Western Assembly on Canada's Political and Economic Future. By November of that year in Winnipeg, the same group created the Reform Party of Canada with Manning as leader. The new party had fewer than 1,000 members, a vaguely crackpot image, and money in the bank only because rich donors believed enough to give. Soon the Reformers gained just the kind of national attention they needed in the 1988 federal election, especially from

Manning's unsuccessful run at Joe Clark in Alberta's Yellowhead riding. In 1989, Reform candidates in Alberta won both a byelection and that province's peculiar provincial election to choose a Senate candidate.

The real surge in Reform support came after the collapse of the Meech Lake Accord in the summer of 1990, and the passage of the GST at the end of that year. The party began 1990 with 27,000 members and finished the year with 54,000. By the end of 1991, the membership had nearly doubled again, to about 100,000. Similarly, the party collected $200,000 in donations in 1988, $1.1 million in 1989, and more than $2 million in 1990. For 1991 the figure was expected to top $4 million. Canada has not seen a new federal party grow so explosively since the Progressives burst out of the West and Ontario to finish second to Mackenzie King's Liberals in the 1921 election.

Nevertheless, the Reformers are not the Progressives or anything like them. Above the genuine populism at the grass roots sits a modern political apparatus that operates out of the party headquarters on 4th Avenue Southwest in Calgary. Nearly every day, computer operators open sacks of mail and pour out new membership applications, each with $10 enclosed. By fall of 1991 the party had launched a major drive for corporate donations, headed by Reform chairman Cliff Fryers; hired Frank Luntz, a Republican pollster and campaign planner who used to work in Ronald Reagan's White House; engaged national pollsters; and signed Hayhurst Communications, a sharp Calgary-based advertising firm, to sell its image. (The contract was sensitive for Hayhurst: the company first asked all its other clients if they had any objections to the Reform account.)

The party's original slogan, "The West Wants In," disappeared with expansion into Ontario. So did the red-white-and-blue logo, to be replaced with green, the hot colour of the 90s. "For us [green] denotes growth and vibrancy and freshness," said Manning's new executive assistant, Diane Ablonczy. The old logo was also too close to Tory colours for comfort. Yet many of the party's structures, including Reform Fund Canada, draw heavily on Progressive Conservative models. This is only natural, Manning says, when 70 per cent of Reformers in Alberta are former Tories. "What they know about constituency organization is mainly from the Conservatives. Reform Fund Canada is exactly the same as the PC Canada Fund." When the party assaults the towers of Old Canada in the next election, it will fire the same weapons as the occupants.

Not surprisingly, some westerners see these changes as compromises with the very system that the party is trying to change. Elmer Knutson, founder of the Confederation of Regions Party, accused Manning of selling out to Ontario power brokers. On September 24, 1991, the day after his party had won eight provincial seats in New Brunswick, Knutson told *The Edmonton Journal*: "He said at first he was a western-based party. . . . Then he wasn't going to go beyond the Manitoba-Ontario border. [Westerners] are now seeing that Manning is taking his orders from Bay Street." Later Knutson added: "He's a wimp if I ever met one."

The accusations did not seem to slow Manning in the West or anywhere else. The major reason for the growth of Reform, beyond doubt, is deep discontent with all traditional politicians, and especially with the governing Tories. "Very little of the Reform Party would have come about if it had not been for the blundering of this awful Conservative governnent," says NDP icon Stephen Lewis, with only slight exaggeration. This bitterness against the Tories is so powerful, as Roger Gibbins points out, that the content of Reform policies is almost irrelevant. "There is a lot of anger and discontent searching for a home," he says. "The Reform Party provides the vehicle. That opportunity for people to express themselves is going to be more important than any of the policies the Reform Party has . . . . With the almost total collapse of the Conservatives, literally hundreds of thousands of people are looking for something else, and that doesn't involve a very careful search among the alternatives." Yet the Reform Party does have a full set of proposals for Canada: radical ones. If they were all implemented, this would be a vastly different country, and very likely a country without Quebec.

The Reformers want a nation at once united and decentralized, a country without public debt where all people are declared equal but no individual receives special help. They believe that women should make their way without affirmative action or any federal programs to lift them up. "They have a very traditional view of women, if they think of women at all," says longtime women's advocate Doris Anderson.

The Reformers apply the same thinking to special groups within society such as recent immigrants, people of colour, other "visible minorities," and, of course, Quebec. There would be no official multiculturalism, sharply limited bilingualism, and no funding for any private group to preserve its identity. The provinces could develop their own policies in these areas but without federal money. Provincial governments would also have full control over medicare and most social programs. Ottawa would become a federal referee, an impartial arbiter of constitutional rules with a negligible role in social issues. All this brings fierce charges that the party is racist and right-wing because it would ignore minorities and the underprivileged.

The point of all these policies, the broad Reform Party goal, is to create a Canada where citizens shed their hyphenated identities and everyone has equal opportunity but no state guarantees of equal outcomes. Collective values, such as the principle that the state has the major responsibility for helping the poor, would be virtually wiped off the slate and replaced by the Reformers' brand of frontier individualism. Indeed, this belief in the individual is the Reformers' core value, and for their leader it has a religious root. All people must be as free as possible, Preston Manning believes, in order to find God in their own way.

On this point alone the Reform Party and modern Quebec are

fundamentally incompatible. While Quebec politicians increasingly try to foster *la collectivité* (the francophone majority), the Reformers always stress the rights of the individual. The Reform Party has no intention of reconciling these disparate visions. If Quebec cannot accept the Reform view of Canada, the party says, it should seriously consider leaving. The Reform Party invites Quebec to consider these ideas, then come back and talk after "New Quebec" has defined itself. Yet there is no indication that Quebec is ready to accept either the invitation or any of the Reform Party's prescriptions for Canada. Reform is the only national party that makes no effort to accommodate Quebec within Canada. Its policy boils down to: "Here's our view of the country, take it or leave it." The unilingual Manning's view of himself as a skilled conciliator, based mainly on his business record, does not extend to his attitude toward Quebec.

"He says he wants to show Reform is not a redneck party," notes Vastel, who followed Manning through western Canada for 10 days in 1987. "Yet he uses anti-Quebec feelings to make points in his speeches. . . . He doesn't look like he's full of himself but you get the strange feeling that he might be a demagogue. He scares me a bit. At the same time, I kind of like him."

Political institutions would also be very different in Preston Manning's New Canada. Every province would have the same number of senators, those senators would be elected, members of Parliament would no longer be under the thumb of their party leaders, and federal election dates would be fixed rather than decided by the prime minister. The voters could start petitions to kick out their MPs, launch new legislation through citizen initiatives, and generally have much more direct influence over the system. These policies respond to the deep conviction that politicians no longer represent the people. Yet, when taken together, they would radically change Canada's system of representative democracy to an unfamiliar hybrid of representation and direct democracy.

Combine all these policies, and the result is a truly radical blueprint for Canada. Many Reformers do not seem to be aware of this, however. A good number who join the party are not familiar with the full range of policies, but seize one or two that appeal to them. As a result, many newer Reform Party members are more moderate than the leader or party officials. Those who joined Reform at its inception, on the other hand, are often more radical than the leadership. Manning's cautious statements as he tries to walk a line between these groups show how tricky life can be for the leader of a populist movement.

The Reform Party's appeal is also uneven in the regions of Canada: it is very strong in British Columbia and Alberta, less so in Saskatchewan and Manitoba, powerful in pockets of rural southern Ontario, but limited in Toronto and other big cities. For obvious reasons the party will try to field candidates in every riding in Canada, except in Quebec.

By late 1991 support in Atlantic Canada was weak at best, so Manning set off on a tour of all four provinces to win converts. Ever the optimist, he told people in Nova Scotia that his party is not a western interloper, but a natural heir to the great Nova Scotia reformer Joseph Howe. On an earlier trip Manning held a news conference under Howe's statue, and did the same in Ottawa under the monuments to Robert Baldwin and Louis-Hippolyte LaFontaine, early reformers of central Canada. Preston Manning knows his history and uses it to advantage.

There is a powerful reform tradition in all of Canada, not just in the West, Manning insists. But he allows that Atlantic Canada will be hard to crack because under his policies the region would have to accept less help from Ottawa. The Reform Party's appeal, he concedes, "is offset by this psychological depression that accompanies the economic depression in Atlantic Canada. People believe you can't change the system. They read our *Blue Book* [on policy] and say, 'That's right, we've got exactly the same views.' But when it comes to political actions or doing something about it, it's a harder sell."

Yet some Maritime observers, including Nova Scotia author and playwright Silver Donald Cameron, feel the sell could be easier than many believe. "Until now, Maritimers have been content to take care of themselves from within the power structure," he says. "But the Tories seem to be saying, 'you're on your own.' That will release a tremendous rage and the Reform Party could do quite well." Only two days after Cameron made the remark, the September 23 provincial election in New Brunswick seemed to bear him out. The Confederation of Regions Party won eight seats with 20 per cent of the popular vote, showing clearly that some Maritimers are just as discontented as westerners and Ontarians. Many CoR attitudes, especially annoyance at official bilingualism, echo precisely the feelings of Reformers.

Few experts now doubt that the Reform Party of Canada will have a major impact on the next federal election. Its powerful momentum, born of anger, enthusiasm, and fierce dedication to a cause, shows no sign of abating. "They'll be spoilers at least," says Patrick Gossage, a Toronto media consultant and former press secretary to Pierre Trudeau, reflecting a common view.

Preston Manning is a veteran leading a party of newcomers. Many of his followers, including party executives and organizers, had never attended a rally or joined a party before they found his Reform movement. But they are speaking out now, most for the first time in their lives, through a swelling party with its cerebral and pious leader. They have become the surging, bitter voice of a growing group of tradition-minded Canadians who feel excluded and ignored.

Great numbers of Canadians obviously welcome this assault on the bastions of the old Canada. Others echo the dark thought of a newspaper editor in St. Catharines Ont., who wrote after Social Credit swept into Alberta in 1935: "The whole thing is a chimera, a nightmare that passeth all understanding." Supporters see Manning and his followers as popular heroes led by a new prince of democracy, while enemies paint them as maddened, irrational rednecks storming the ramparts with pitchforks. There is truth in both images, for little about this movement is as simple as it seems. One thing is clear: Preston Manning and his party will continue to provoke deep and bitter controversy as they storm the old federal order, Canada's Babylon.

CHAPTER TWO

UPON THIS ROCK

> "There was a whole generation of people who settled the West, broke the ground, and had a deep fear of politicians, bureaucracy, and government. If they could manage it, they sent a son away to school to be educated, hoping that the son would come back to protect them from the profiteers and politicians. In a symbolic way, [Preston] Manning is that trustworthy son, the one who will protect everyone."
>
> – Filmmaker David Cunningham

THE BOND of trust between Preston Manning and his party is unique in Canadian politics today. He proves this time and again by performing a feat of on-stage magic that shows how eager his followers are to trust him even against some of their own cherished beliefs. He actually convinces his audiences that they should support the Goods and Services Tax, while leaving them with the impression that it was their idea. The way Manning does this shows a good deal about both his technique and his astonishing political skill.

A classic example is his performance one night in June 1991 before an audience of about 1,300 in Peterborough, Ont. When a written question about abolishing the tax is read to him, the audience jeers at the mere mention of the GST. But then Manning says:

"We have done a lot of study on this. If we were in the 1993 Parliament and this question came up, would the GST be ripped up or revised in some way?"

Then he answers his own question. "Well, one option is to rip it out. We opposed it when it was instituted. But if you rip this thing out, you'd also have to rip 25 billion dollars' worth of expenditure out of the federal budget.

"The [other] option is to revise it, reduce the exemptions, make it more visible, and dedicate part of the proceeds to reducing the debt. Now I won't hold you to it, but I want to take a little straw vote. If you were advising your MP, how many would favour revising it?"

At this point, amazingly, a large majority raise their hands, first slowly and then in a spreading wave. Manning nods with satisfaction. "Yeah," he says brightly, "We've asked this question I don't know how many times at meetings, and usually the vote is about two-thirds in favour of revising it." His audience has agreed not just to keep the tax but to make it more onerous by reducing exemptions.

Manning manages to do this even though most people in his audiences hate the GST, and a good many joined the Reform Party because they thought he did too. Their impression is certainly justified, since Manning was ferocious in his opposition to the tax before it was passed in December 1990. In a Calgary speech two months earlier, he called for the election of Reform Party candidates "who will rip out the GST if it has been imposed against the will of the people." Every poll then and afterward has shown that the vast majority of Canadians opposed the tax, so there cannot be much doubt about the public will. Yet less than a year later the loyalists at Reform Party meetings never seemed to sense a touch of hypocrisy in Manning's remarkable change of heart. In Peterborough, he pulled the audience along with him at the very time many Ontarians were voting against high taxes with their wallets by shopping across the border in the United States.

Manning manages this feat, in part, by following the populist tradition of letting the audience decide for itself. He carefully weights the dice toward his point of view, but the decision belongs to his listeners, not to him. This seems to be an exercise in the kind of pure democracy the party promises. On important matters, Reform policy states, the people in a constituency will instruct a Reform Party MP how to vote. If the member cannot live with the voters' instructions, Manning says, he or she is obliged to quit before the next election. The party's *Blue Book* states: "We believe in the accountability of elected representatives to the people who elect them, and that the duty of elected members to their constituents should supersede their obligations to their political parties."

Yet Manning's own reversal on the GST, and his success in getting his followers to agree with him, shows how flexible such principles can be in the hands of a canny leader. Manning has decided that the national debt is more important than the atrocity of the tax, but he does not even have to explain this. His bond with the party runs so deep that members accept inconsistencies from him that they simply would not tolerate in another politician. They trust his motives and honesty absolutely. As a result, he has the authority to exercise enormous control over everything from party policy to tactics.

Shrewd observers of Alberta Social Credit noted long ago that the Socred movement was not truly populist, but a massive delegation of trust by voters to revered leaders, first William Aberhart and then Ernest Manning. The same dynamic appears to be at work today in Preston Manning's leadership of the Reform Party. Audiences hang on his words with rapt attention, applauding every point and laughing at every joke. No other politician in English Canada today faces such uncritical crowds, partly because Manning knows how to relax his listeners with humour. For instance, he often delights Reformers at rallies by saying:

"Canadians cannot afford to be in the position of Christopher Columbus when he started out for the New World. He had no map.

When he started, he didn't know where he was going; when he got there, he didn't know where he was; when he got home he didn't know where he'd been; and he was doing it all on borrowed money." The crowds always hoot with appreciation at this witticism from the leader, unaware that Social Credit politicians in Alberta used the same story 30 years ago.

Members of the Reform Party's executive council unconsciously repeat Manning's precise words and cadences. ("We need to get our parliamentary house in order, our fiscal house in order, our constitutional house in order," says rookie council member Danita Onyebuchi of Winnipeg, sounding exactly like Manning.) When Reformers describe Manning, the same adjectives pop up again and again: modest, humble, sincere, honest, direct, no-nonsense, courageous. They cherish his very ordinariness because it brings him closer to them, and sets him apart from traditional politicians. After the seemingly endless barrage of betrayed trust from political leaders, Manning's antidote, a straightforward persistence, invites confidence and faith. "He's able to talk to people in words and language they can understand," says Ron Wood, his loyal press aide. "There's none of the standard hyperbole – no waving wheatfields and shining mountains and the beautiful Great Lakes. He just talks about the problems and solutions."

Everything about Preston Manning seems average: his plain, softly pointed face with slightly crooked teeth, his sixties-style aviator glasses, his lank slicked-back hair, his neat but nondescript suits and jackets, his clunky oxford-style shoes, his partially pigeon-toed gait, his gangly posture. As he sits on a platform waiting to be introduced, his eyes seemingly search for the easiest exit, while his nervous face forces a hopeful smile. He looks at once vulnerable and earnest, like a Sunday school teacher reluctantly ready to preach the first lesson. He is a caricaturist's delight. If Manning were a Saturday morning cartoon, he would be Alvin in "The Chipmunks' Adventure."

Psychologically, he does not crave or especially enjoy the spotlight. The man who spent 20 years in business striving to disappear behind his clients does not relish celebrity any more today. "If he isn't a recluse, he's the nearest thing to it," says his good friend Deborah Grey, the party's lone Member of Parliament. "I'm sure his preference would be to stay home and read books and policy papers. It's hard for him to get up and speak. I'm very public. That's the way I am. But he's just the opposite. This is a real mission for him." Part of Manning's appeal comes from this impression that he cares about the mission more than his own ego.

Sometimes, when Manning talks to an especially large group, a careful watcher can catch the tell-tale signs of real stage fright; the hands clutching at the sides of the podium, the dry-mouthed swallowing, the darting panicky eyes that say: "I don't belong here! What the heck am I doing?" Before he started speaking to a huge crowd of 6,000 at Toronto's International Centre in June 1991, Manning looked simply terrified. He always fights down the dread when he begins to talk, but stage fright is never far away. As his father told one of the authors: "He has a shy disposition. He's developed a good platform presence, and once he gets into his work it doesn't bother him. But he's not motivated by a desire to be in the limelight." This obvious shyness separates him from blowhard political orators who live for the odour of their own ham cooking in front of a big audience.

Nevertheless, nobody should mistake Manning's retiring nature for a weak will, or his apparent ordinariness for lack of appeal. When he steps behind a podium after the audience sings "O Canada" (always in English only), something astonishing often happens. Crowds are at once soothed and electrified by this blend of conviction and plainness. Manning's nasal, piercing voice, with its distinctive western twang, reaches easily into every corner of the hall. The voice is folksy but it has been carefully schooled during years of preaching on "Canada's National Bible Hour." Many of Manning's anecdotes and phrases have a Biblical, church-like cadence. "I command you to go forth," he told the party Assembly in 1991, with a trace of self-mockery. Like many a preacher, he relies on almost numbing repetition to drive home his points. In some speeches his repetitions seem like a gospel chorus inviting the audience to sing along, as he recites the words "A balanced, democratic federation of provinces." His peculiar intonation, more a family quirk than a regional accent, draws out and hardens vowels, turning "federal" into "fa-deral" and "democratic" into "da-mocratic." He drops his Gs and often stammers in his rush to get his ideas out. Sometimes he sounds like a country and western singer chatting up the devotees between songs. But he shows his trust in the intelligence of his audiences by going far beyond slogans into the details of policy.

Edmonton filmmaker David Cunningham comes as close as anyone to pinpointing Manning's remarkable bond with western crowds, which always include many people older than he is. "There was a whole generation of people who settled the West, broke the ground, and had a deep fear of politicians, bureaucracy, and government," Cunningham says. "If they could manage it, they sent a son away to school to be educated, hoping that the son would come back to protect them from the profiteers and politicians. In a symbolic way, Manning is that trustworthy son, the one who will protect everyone." Lately, the connection seems to work not just in the West but in Ontario as well. Even in the Maritimes people are curious about the son, although not yet ready to embrace him as a protector.

As a burgeoning leader in Canada's political scene, Manning is careful to avoid any hint of the perks, patronage, or special treatment that he so often criticizes in other politicians. He almost always carries his own legal-sized briefcase, bursting with documents. Before a party volunteer meets him at an airport, Manning's office issues a firm order that the car not be luxurious. Air travel is always economy class, a gesture that delights veteran air travellers who often fume at the sight of Members of Parliament spread out comfortably in executive class. Meals in restaurants are small and simple, often with coffee but rarely with anything trendy like cappuccino, and certainly never with alcohol. A culinary pleasure for the Manning family is the homemade cinammon buns at Edmonton's Highlevel Diner. His wife Sandra has been known to send their buns and muffins to her daughters travelling in Toronto. In private or in public, that is about as extravagant as life gets for Preston Manning, and his followers love him for it.

With party officials and executives, Manning always plays the conciliator who coaxes people to agree. Discord unsettles and rattles him. Answering his own questionnaire for party candidates, Manning makes a startling admission. "I would say that I am used to long hours of work, travel and the standard stresses and strains of political life," he writes. "I would add, however, that I find internal bickering and quarrelling among our own Reform Party people, usually over minor issues and personality conflicts, to be far more stressful to myself than any attacks or stress caused by external opposition or the challenge of meeting contemporary political issues." Above all, Preston Manning is a man who wants his friends to get along.

He is also more bothered than he admits by personal attacks. During his Ontario trip in June 1991 Manning had his first taste of big-time demonstrations and an aggressively hostile press corps. Sometimes he grew impatient with the criticism and brusque with reporters, to the point of once brushing past them with disdain. Callers to radio phone-in shows attacked Manning and called the party racist. He could only repeat his stock answer that his party's policies are "colour blind." The main purpose of the Ontario swing was to refute charges of extremism, and Manning was clearly upset at having to deal with the accusations. Usually Manning's style is an extension into politics of the modest, frugal, and friendly way he has always lived his private life. To that extent, it is genuine. But at another level he surely knows that his ordinariness is an asset to be cultivated and used. It is no accident that in the questionnaire Manning lists himself as strong on media skills. After many years of watching his father, and after helping to shape the humble image of Ernest Manning's successor as Alberta premier, Harry Strom, he knows what people respect and like. His emergence on the political stage in 1987 coincided perfectly with the beginning of Canada's age of reduced expectations. Humble he may be, but he is shrewd and ambitious too.

His whole political background, in fact, is far from ordinary. Manning grew up at the side of a premier who knew all the key people in Canada's political elite, from Mackenzie King to John Diefenbaker and Pierre Trudeau. He had far more early political training than most MPs in Ottawa, but he strikes people as fresh and unspoiled largely because he is new to the national media and because his party itself seems fresh. Yet he is not saying anything that he and his father have not worked on and repeated for years. None of this bothers Reformers. As one said after a meeting in Calgary, "I don't care whether the message is old or new, it reflects what I believe and I like it. It's about time somebody started saying these things."

The shift in Manning's GST policy is minor compared to the huge change in emphasis that came when he led the party onto the national stage in April 1991. A majority of Reformers at the party's Assembly in Saskatoon voted then to expand from the four western provinces into Ontario and Atlantic Canada (but not Quebec). This was a contentious issue within the party, whose motto had been "The West Wants In." Some members believed expansion would make the party seem hypocritical and cost it support in the main power bases of Alberta and British Columbia. Others worried that western interests would be buried, in true Canadian fashion, by larger numbers from Ontario. A smaller group wanted to use the energy and money to create provincial parties in the West (in Alberta, a provincial party with a credible leader would have been an instant government-in-waiting).

All these groups had a point, because the party's early rhetoric, and Manning's, had been almost purely western. After the party was formed in 1987, it built support quickly by playing on deep feelings of alienation and rejection among westerners. It tapped their dislike of bilingualism, their disgust with the federal Tory obsession with Quebec, their dismay at the prime minister's attempts to paint opposition to the Meech Lake Accord as somehow un-Canadian. The Reform Party's rhetoric was in the grand old barnstorming tradition of western protest movements from the United Farmers to the CCF and Western Canada Concept. Manning regularly blasted away at the standard anti-western atrocities: the federal decision to give the CF-18 jet maintenance contract to Montreal rather than Winnipeg; Pierre Trudeau's 1980 National Energy Program; and Tory delays in killing the last trace of the NEP, the Petroleum Gas Revenue Tax. The Tories had condemned the tax while in opposition, Manning liked to say, but they used it between 1984 and 1986 to squeeze another $2.5 billion out of Alberta's oil patch. The NEP itself was "a deliberately planned rape of the West for the short-term benefit of the federal treasury and eastern consumers."

Manning could, and did, cite chapter and verse of western grievances from the time of Métis leader Louis Riel. He was not above using resentment of Ontario and Quebec power to increase support. "The system is unfair," he said in 1988. "Don't blame your MPs. Blame a federal constitutional structure which allows the populous centres of Ontario and Quebec to call the shots." His main goal, expressed time and again, was for a band of Reform Party MPs, loyal only to the West, to hold the balance of power in a minority government. They would vote for purely western interests without having to answer to party caucuses dominated by Ontarians and Quebeckers, he said.

Manning's very first speech to the budding movement, delivered to the Western Assembly on Canada's Political and Economic Future, was called "Choosing a New Political Vehicle to Represent the West." The traditional parties were useless to the region, he told a group of 300 at the gathering held in Vancouver in May 1987. "Their top political priority continues to be to maintain and hold seats in Ontario and Quebec. The West needs a party which makes western concerns and western aspirations its number one priority." To the old parties he threw out this warning: "If you seek to engineer another raid on the resource wealth of the West such as was done with the NEP, you will initiate a constitutional and political crisis in Confederation that will make the past turmoils in Quebec look like a Sunday school picnic." The remark earned him a long standing ovation. Later in the speech he said, "A new party that captured 30 to 40 seats across the West would have a better than 50-50 chance of holding the balance of power in the next federal Parliament."

But Manning's preference was for national expansion, and he was honest enough to make this clear. In listing his "specifications" for the new party, he said it should give itself plenty of "room to grow" beyond its region of origin by developing a broad enough ideological base to appeal to large numbers of people everywhere. All past western movements were "too narrow" to be truly national, Manning contended. Louis Riel's support was too ethnic, the CCF was too ideological, and Social Credit was too rooted in the Depression. Even the Progressives, the western protest movement that expanded most explosively beyond the region, relied heavily on farm support and had little appeal in the big urban centres of Ontario. Manning argued that in order to break this pattern, the new movement should exhibit "a hard head and a soft heart" by mixing free enterprise economics with a strong social conscience. Unless it could take support from the Tories, the Liberals, and the NDP, he said, there was no point in starting a new party at all.

Manning was offering exactly the same recipes he had set down with his father in the book called *Political Realignment* in 1967. This was updated Social Credit passed on to the new Reform movement, but it hit this little band of 300 reform-minded westerners like a perfectly aimed missile, scoring a direct hit on all their western hopes and frustrations. After listening intently to Manning for 40 minutes, the listeners leapt to their feet to applaud.

Indeed, Manning's speech was remarkable for its display of foresight and planning. He had considered every detail, from the arguments people would raise against a new party to the problems of getting ready for the 1988 election. He showed the audience both a coherent vision and an intimate knowledge of working politics. His speaking style was sometimes a bit jittery and unpolished, just like the Reform Party videotape that preserves it today, but the overall impact was startling and powerful. There was nothing surprising about any of this, since he had been working toward the moment for more than 20 years. But the people in the audience, many of them hearing Manning for the first time, seemed to sense the creation of a leader. Manning would face an opponent, Stan Roberts, when the party held its founding convention that fall in Winnipeg. In reality, Manning probably sewed up the leadership that spring day at the Hyatt Regency Hotel in Vancouver.

Even before the Vancouver meeting, Manning impressed influential westerners who were already beginning to talk about a new party. In Calgary, lawyer Doug Hilland had phoned around to his friends in the fall of 1986 to press the need for change. He recruited several people, including fellow lawyer Robert Muir and the late Marvin McDill, the man behind two Canadian challenges to U.S. domination of the America's Cup yachting title. In Vancouver, economic consultant Stan Roberts worked toward the same goal with philanthropist Francis Winspear, now one of the largest individual donors to the Reform Party (he gave an early donation of $100,000, and $5,700 in 1990).

Manning worked with close friends in Edmonton, and by October began to travel and meet the others. "I was sure impressed," Muir recalls of his first meeting with Manning. "He had helped his father with that book [*Political Realignment*]. He obviously had studied this business of a new party for years and years. He has a deep knowledge of western history and politics. As far as I was concerned, he was head and shoulders above anybody in sight to be the leader of this party." After all these meetings, the group agreed to call itself the Reform Association of Canada and hold the exploratory meeting in Vancouver. Nearly everyone seemed to assume that if the delegates agreed to form a federal party, Manning would be the leader.

There was some very messy business to get through before that happened, however. Manning's opponent would be Roberts, a flamboyant former member of the Manitoba legislature, ex-head of the Canadian Chamber of Commerce, and past president of Simon Fraser University. Roberts was also a Liberal who somehow convinced the Lachine riding association in Quebec to nominate him for the 1984 federal election, even though he was living in Vancouver at the time. Roberts, 61, was handsome, sandy-haired, square-jawed, competent in French, and an excellent public speaker. Despite his being a Liberal, his western credentials were impeccable. In the 1970s he was president of the Canada West Foundation, the Calgary think tank that studies western issues.

In 1987, like Manning, Roberts was an economist with his own consulting firm. Unlike Manning, he had shown that he could be elected during his six years as a Manitoba MLA. In addition, he lived in Vancouver, a definite advantage since many Reformers were beginning to worry that Albertans would dominate the movement. On the surface Roberts seemed to be at least the equal of Preston Manning, his friend for many years. They had worked together when Manning's company prepared a study on Confederation for the Canada West Foundation.

But Manning prepared his ground carefully over the months before the Winnipeg meeting, while Roberts failed to campaign or line up delegates. Robert Muir recalls that three weeks before the

Winnipeg meeting, Roberts told him he did not intend to run. He failed to declare his candidacy until little more than a week before the convention. At that gathering Roberts stayed in the public halls pressing the flesh while Manning worked in the background. In the crucial hours before the vote, Roberts noticed that many of his friends and supporters were not in the room. He tried to get the leadership decision delayed for six months. When the convention refused, Roberts withdrew his name and walked out, accusing his rival of stacking the room with Albertans while excluding as many as 100 of his supporters from B.C., Saskatchewan, and Manitoba. Manning was turning "a western party into an Alberta party," Roberts charged. He raised unfounded suspicions, never proven or taken seriously by party members, that $50,000 in party money had disappeared. "This party was founded on the principles of honesty and integrity and those principles appear to have been compromised during this convention," he told the delegates, his voice breaking.

Manitoba public relations expert Jo Hillier, Roberts' good friend and an organizer of the meeting, called this startling twist her worst nightmare for the party. Just as the Reformers were trying to fight off the crackpot reputation that clings to many bickering western fringe groups, they appeared to be exactly that. The lingering image of the fracas tainted Manning's victory and slowed the party's growth, especially in Manitoba. He would need more than two years to put it behind him.

David Elton, the current president of the Canada West Foundation, still finds the whole episode puzzling. "I knew both of them very well," he said in an interview. "They were both very much on the same wavelength, both on the same team, up until the decision to run for the leadership. I didn't see all that much difference in their outlook, even though Stan had that Liberal background and Preston came out of Social Credit."

At the convention, Elton said, "Stan wasn't himself. He seemed to be going through some kind of upheaval. It wasn't the Stan

Roberts that I knew. I saw what he did as a face-saving exercise on Stan's part." Less than two years later Roberts died of a brain abscess. He was controversial even after his death: a Vancouver brain surgeon, Dr. Ian Turnbull, later claimed that a biopsy was delayed because of cuts in provincial funding to hospitals. If it had been done on time, he said, the abscess could have been drained and the patient saved. Roberts' son, Kim, wrote in a letter of complaint to B.C. medical authorities: "The only conclusion I can reach is that the delay in obtaining a biopsy killed my father." It was a sad end for a passionate and dedicated Canadian.

After Manning won the leadership, he carefully guided the growth of the party in the West but he always kept his eye on national expansion. He made several forays into Ontario and Atlantic Canada to test the waters. By mid-1990 letters from Ontario were pouring into Calgary headquarters urging the party to expand. An eager group of Ontarians, led by current provincial organizer Reg Gosse, spent most of 1990 organizing furiously, hoping to show the 1991 Saskatoon Assembly that Ontario was fertile ground for the party. In any party debate, Manning made it clear that he favoured expansion. He somehow managed to do all this without offending too many of the people who disagreed; as always, he convinced a good number of Reformers that the decision was all theirs. He had a formula handy to ease fears that new Ontario members would swamp the party: Ontario would have only four members on the party's executive council, just like all the other provinces. This was the Triple E Senate solution at work within the party, and it seemed to soothe some western Reformers.

By the time of the Assembly in April 1991, the groundwork had been laid with all of Manning's usual attention to detail. The Ontarians were ready with their argument, which amounted to a resounding "Let Ontario In." Requests for membership from outside the West were piling up, and Manning had denied his interest in western provincial politics so many times that people finally believed him. The vote was a cakewalk: once again, the populist leader had guided his party to a foregone conclusion.

In an interview, Ontario organizer Reg Gosse showed how delicately the movement to expand into Ontario was handled. "The first time I saw Preston on TV I called out west and said, 'We need to have you folks down here, you need to be in Ontario.' They said 'We're not ready yet.' They said they'd get back to us. So on June 1 [1990] I got a call from the then vice-chairman of the party, Gordon Shaw, who was heading up expansion. He came down and met twelve of us from Ontario and the Maritimes. They said, 'If you can find mainline people, and do not use the resources from the West including money and people, see what you can do. If you really want in, prove it.' We went out there and met the executive council and had some speaking engagements. We had to be sensitive to how the membership in the West felt about it."

Manning and the council had the go-ahead from the membership to study expansion, but the effort went far beyond mere study and became a full-blown membership and organization drive long before the final approval came. Reg Gosse did not merely drum up support, he put together riding associations. By the end of June 1991, 85 of Ontario's 99 ridings were organized. Harried party staffers back in the Calgary office were dumping out mail bags every day with 200 to 300 membership applications from Ontario, each with $10 enclosed. Computer operators who entered the membership data fell a week behind. When Manning toured Ontario centres from Thunder Bay to Ottawa and Toronto, several thousand more bought memberships on the spot. Gosse, after working almost full-time as a volunteer for a year, was hired as constituency development and election readiness co-ordinator for Ontario. Some of Manning's critics, including Elmer Knutson of the Confederation of Regions, see this as evidence of betrayal. Yet the faint murmurs of criticism in the western wing of the Reform Party eventually died away, killed by success. Once again, Manning had shown remarkable timing.

The Ontario expansion brought other benefits that many Reformers did not anticipate, although Manning surely did. It helped to make the party more credible even in the West, and especially in Saskatchewan. "People in Saskatchewan hate Alberta political movements," says Dale Eisler, columnist for the *Regina Leader Post* and *Saskatoon Star Phoenix*. "The benefit of expansion is that it takes the Alberta label off the party." The same observation is probably true of Manitoba and, to a lesser degree, of B.C. as well. Support from Ontario gives the party legitimacy even among westerners who would never admit it.

Nevertheless, the Ontario expansion, although it offers a real chance of electoral success, raises some serious ethical and practical problems for the party. Manning's entire early strategy, the one that earned him so much support, was based on the prospect of western MPs holding the balance of power in a minority government in Ottawa. This was the only way they could force changes favourable to the West, he insisted. That idea went out the window with expansion. However much Manning talks about provinces being equal within the party, Ontario still has more federal ridings than all the western provinces together (99 to 86). His party is now vulnerable to the same central control that has made the Tories and Liberals so unpopular in the West.

When expansion came, Manning's rhetoric about regionalism and western power ceased (actually he had shrewdly toned it down several months before the final decision was made). He no longer talks about Ontario's domination of the country. Manning began to focus far more on his "national" issues: New Canada versus Old Canada, Quebec, and fiscal responsibility. He started to fight more strenuously against charges of racism that might hurt him in big urban areas like Toronto. He talks less about the Triple E Senate (although he does not ignore it either). At least in tone, the new national Reform Party sounds far different than the old western one did.

Manning's point man for expansion was Gordon Shaw, a retired Imperial Oil executive who was in charge both of the move east and of keeping crackpots out of the party. He "made sure we didn't have any kooks and loonies," Robert Muir says. Shaw stays out of the limelight, but his role in the early party was crucial. A computer specialist when he was with Imperial, he helped set up the party's state-of-the-art data system in Calgary. He also recruited Deborah Grey to run in Alberta's Beaver River riding after he spotted her reading Reform Party literature in an airport waiting room. Today the Vancouver resident is the party's Director of Special Projects, and one of his more delicate jobs is dealing with two potential embarrassments, the Reform Party of British Columbia and the Reform Party of Manitoba. Manning and Shaw worry that both of these tiny provincially registered parties, which have no connection with the federal outfit, will try to exploit its popularity. The Reform Party of Canada is already in court with the Manitoba party, challenging its right to use the name. This shows Manning's near-obsession with cleansing the party of its fringe image. "Any new light is bound to attract bugs," he has said. Gordon Shaw, the leader's loyal fly-swatter, describes his job as "making extremists feel as uncomfortable as possible."

The people attracted to the Reform Party are pretty much the same no matter where Manning finds them. As countless journalists have noted, his audiences are mainly white, male, middle class, and pushing the far side of middle age. Non-white faces are rare enough to be an event. At three meetings in Ontario, attended by a total of at least 9,000 people, there were fewer than 10. Not much has changed since early 1990, when a party poll leaked to the *Edmonton Journal* showed that 72 per cent of the party members were men, 48 per cent were over 60 years old, and 38 per cent were retired. The party says that it does not keep figures on ethnicity, but it doesn't have to. The answer is in the sheet of white faces staring raptly at Preston Manning.

The faces are not all that different from those that gazed at his father over 20 years ago. The Social Credit Party was "greatly overrepresented" by people over 50, and "greatly underrepresented" by those under 30, wrote Owen Anderson in his 1972 unpublished doctoral thesis, "The Alberta Social Credit Party." A Social Crediter was likely to be a white Anglo-Saxon Protestant male, married with a large family, living in his own home on a farm or in a small town. Women were "greatly outnumbered" by the men, although this was also true for the other political parties, said Anderson, who has been a close friend of Preston Manning since the 1960s.

Reform Party followers echo many of the same sentiments as those populist precursors. They are fed up with the arrogance of traditional national parties. They have had enough of MPs who represent their party and their leader rather than the people who voted for them. They will no longer abide politicians who tell them what is best instead of asking them. They came to loathe the prime minister for his smooth talk and mistrust him for the GST, his Quebec roots, and many other grievances, real and imagined. They want politicians who will talk for them against Quebec, not for Quebec to them. Most of all, they hate public debt and its inevitable outrider, high taxes. In many places, but especially in Ontario, their support for the Reform Party expresses a growing tax revolt.

Many of these Reformers do not see the party as particularly new or radical: for them, it expresses values and ideas they have always believed in. "It's just common sense," they say again and again. Governments, like families, should never spend more than they earn. Politicians should not provide money to private ethnic or cultural groups. (No more cash for "black lesbians from Dartmouth," said the late Reform Party Senator Stan Waters, in the most outlandish expression of this feeling.) Every Canadian is equal regardless of race, creed, or colour, so why give government support to ethnics and coloured minorities? A simple expression of equality will do.

Most ominous for the old parties, many people are joining the Reform movement because they like bits and pieces of its policies enough to ignore the parts that do not appeal to them. In Ontario, for instance, Reform's insistence on a Triple E Senate does not seem to hurt. "A lot of people find it a little bit funny because they're worried about losing the representation Ontario has now," says Ontario riding executive Mati Saar. "But they don't see that as a deciding issue. They look at all the parties and give us support based on what they like about us."

Torontonians Raymond and Kim DiCecco, a couple with young children, were first attracted by Manning's "positive attitude," but ended up agreeing with the Triple E Senate because "it's only fair." Dick Sanderson, a Burlington riding executive, says there is too much media focus on the party's Quebec policy. "I joined Reform because of other things, principally taxation. I'm sure you'll find that it's taxation that brings this group together. It's not things like Quebec or abortion," he adds. Manning's insistence that the party state its views on all important national issues seems to be paying off. Many people are so disillusioned with the old parties that they find one thing they like about Reform policy and hang on for dear life.

Although the crowds still shade heavily toward middle age, more young people are showing up at meetings. Often they are thoughtful, articulate, and well educated. Jan Headrick, 31, a high school social science teacher who went to an Ottawa rally, says he joined Reform because the "federal Tories and Liberals, and provincial NDP, have not done a good job of delivering on their campaign promises." Even though the Reform Party needs fine-tuning, he says he is "willing to give them a chance because it's either Reform or Rhinoceros, and that's not much of a choice."

Car salesman Blair Barrett, 30, says at the same Ottawa meeting:

"For the last two elections I've worked for the Conservatives, but they're not being true to their roots, and I'm here to find out what these guys are all about. I haven't made up my mind yet, but I like what I've heard so far." By the time the meeting is over, Barrett has decided to vote Reform. Kevin Patrick, an Ottawa radio reporter on his day off, says he used to be a Tory but is now a keen Reformer. After working in Calgary, northern Ontario, and now Ottawa, he sees "Tremendous potential for the party in Ontario. As far as I can see, the attitude in northern Ontario and Calgary and the West is exactly the same; they all feel excluded by government in just the same way."

Yet the Reform Party is not simply a home for disillusioned Conservatives. To a startling extent it is a party of newcomers and outsiders, of Canadians who have never been involved in politics before. These people show similarities to Richard Nixon's "Silent Majority": for years they have watched governments do things they do not like, growing ever more frustrated until they could keep silent no longer. Over and again one hears the same refrain: "I've never been active in a party before, but something has to be done."

Outsiders are the majority, not just in the party rank-and-file, but at the highest executive levels. Gordon Shaw always voted Conservative but was never active. Reg Gosse, the Ontario organizer, voted Liberal and Conservative at various times without being involved with either party. Most of the party's council members show the same type of profile: a bit of political interest here and there in the past, but never before this intense, passionate commitment.

Gordon Shaw tells a fairly typical story of how he found the party. "In January of 1987 I wrote a letter to [Deputy Prime Minister] Don Mazankowski saying why I was so fed up with Mulroney and the Conservative party," he says. "I don't know exactly why I wrote the letter, I guess I'd just had it. A couple of months later I read a little item about this Reform Party getting together in Vancouver. I went to the meeting without any intention of getting involved. Then I went to the Winnipeg meeting, still not intending to devote much time to it." At that gathering, he was elected vice-chairman.

"It's a kind of creeping commitment and now it has consumed our lives. My wife and I are both involved 12 to 14 hours a day. I feel that for the first time in my life, I'm doing something for my country. But it has as much to do with Preston Manning as anything else. I am so convinced he has got to become the leader of this country. He is the only man with the integrity and the intellect. I don't think most people know that yet, but they will."

Reg Gosse had a similar sudden conversion to Reform. "I was debating selling my business in Kitchener and moving to the States. With four children and seeing what was going on in this country, I said 'We've either got to resolve the problems here or the country's going to be destroyed, and if that's the case my kids won't have a future.' So my options were to go to the States or form our own federal party. I concluded that starting your own federal party was impossible, and then I heard that somebody had already done it! I saw Preston on TV and I thought, 'Boy, that sounds a lot like what I'm feeling and I'm thinking.'" Within months, Gosse had met Shaw in Toronto and had become the party's organizational boss in Ontario. At 43, this accountant who ran his own publishing business with his wife, a man who had never had a moment's political experience, found himself piloting the hottest burst of political growth in Ontario in years.

On the party's elected council sits Gordon Duncan, of La Salle, Man., who has been at various times a Mulroney Tory, an Ed Schreyer New Democrat, a Trudeau Liberal, and an ardent supporter of bilingualism. By 1987 he was convinced bilingualism had failed and became an original Reformer at the Vancouver meeting. "Most of us felt that the chances of forming a successful new party were very slight," Duncan recalls. "But we really could see no alternative. The growth since then has been phenomenal. I don't think there's any question that the genius of Preston Manning is at the heart of the party's success."

Lee Morrison, a council member from Eastend, Sask., echoes many of the same feelings. "I'm an old bugger so I've kind of been all over the map politically. What drew me was their statement that it should be the duty of the member to represent the constituents rather than the party or the prime minister. I helped to organize the constituency in my home riding, so with that as a background I drifted into the national part of it."

Even the two people who have won elections for the Reform Party, Deborah Grey and the late Stan Waters, had virtually no previous political experience. Grey was quite happy as a high school teacher in Alberta's Beaver River area before Gordon Shaw recruited her. Well known and popular with her students, Grey spent her time teaching, holding prayer meetings in her home, playing Scrabble with friends, visiting her relatives in her native Vancouver, and helping to raise six native foster children. She is a big, hearty, witty woman most people like on sight. Shaw saw her political potential instantly. They arranged to sit together on the flight from Calgary to Vancouver, where she was travelling for a brother's wedding. He invited her to meet Manning at a rally in Edmonton the following week. She did, was convinced, and on March 14, 1989, she won the Beaver River byelection with a large margin. Today she is an invaluable asset to the party. For one thing, Grey is a woman in a party noticeably short of females at the upper levels (only one woman, Danita Onyebuchi, sits on the 17-member executive council). She is also a first-rate public speaker who regularly warms up audiences for Manning. Most of all, she takes the Reform Party's outsider ethic to Ottawa and plays it to the hilt.

"The behaviour in the chamber just drives me wild," she said in an interview in her House of Commons office. "I taught Grade 8 for too many years to think this kind of behaviour is cute. My worst class ever, in all the years I taught, didn't come close to touching it. I was talking to a lady and she said, 'I forbid my children to watch the Parliamentary channel.' Yet they just carry on. When I had a kid act like an idiot on one of my teams I just suspended him. I'd say 'We need you, but we don't need you that badly, so sit out for the game.'" She refuses to play Ottawa's social games or to seek acceptance from other MPs by flattering them.

Stan Waters stumbled into the party too. After he retired early from the Canadian Forces with the rank of lieutenant-general, Waters was a consultant in the oil field business, an executive with Calgary's Loram Group of Companies, and an occasional volunteer for the Conservatives. By 1988, like so many Albertans, he was fed up with the Tories. "My wife and son both went to the original [Reform Party] meeting in Winnipeg," Waters said in an interview taped three months before he died of brain cancer on September 25, 1991. "They brought back all the literature and said: 'You're in the wrong party.'" Waters was inclined to believe them, partly because he knew Ernest Manning well from their years on the advisory board of the National Citizens' Coalition in the 1970s. After he met Preston Manning, the Reform leader urged him to get involved and later talked him into running for the party's Senate nomination. "He said, 'We'd like to get some high-profile people to stand for nomination and you'd be doing the party a favour doing that,'" Waters recalled.

It was easy to understand why Manning wanted him. Waters was a genuine war hero and a legend to many older Canadians inclined to support the Reform Party. As the leader of a commando unit, part of a joint force with the Americans, he was the first Allied officer to enter Rome the day it was liberated. At 23 he was already a major, he said, "Simply because I survived." Back in Canada he rose until he was the commanding officer of all Canadian land forces. "He was always able to inspire people by his presence," recalls Jim Stanton, an Ottawa public relations expert who once served as Waters aide-de-camp in Calgary. "He was called Stan the Man. The common soldiers loved him and the officers respected him. . . . He never hesitated for a second to make a decision because that was his job. He was brought up to be responsible for his actions, and Stan's values were unchanged from the 1930s. It's the Biblical stuff, the Ten Commandments, people having a responsibility to be certain of their direction."

Waters defeated three other candidates for the Reform Party nomination, then won Alberta's Senate election by a landslide on October 16, 1989. It was one of the most peculiar elections in Canadian history because the voters really had no legal right to make a decision. Only the prime minister is empowered to choose senators. Nevertheless, Alberta's Conservative government had passed a bill making it possible for Albertans to express their preference. The idea was to advance the idea of the Triple E Senate by defying Ottawa to refuse the voters' choice. Unfortunately for the Conservatives, their candidate, Bert Brown, was buried by Waters and the Reform Party. (Even the Liberal candidate, Bill Code, finished far ahead of the unfortunate Brown, the dedicated founder of the Triple E movement. Although still a provincial Tory, Brown has now joined the federal Reform party.) Premier Don Getty was then in the awkward position of pressing the prime minister to appoint somebody from another party. Brian Mulroney did, but only after a long delay: he finally agreed to name Waters after private talks with Getty during the Meech Lake negotiations of June 1990.

The whole soap opera gave the Reform Party a tremendous burst of national publicity. As a senator, however, Waters was often a mixed blessing. Sometimes, in fact, he seemed to be one of the right-wing radicals Manning tried so hard to purge; witness his remark about funding lesbians. At the meeting in Red Deer where he was nominated, Waters blasted the government for picking on the South African regime. In the taped interview, he made slight apology for any of this.

"My God, that thing haunts me," Waters said, referring to the remark about lesbians. "I was using it as an example of special interest pleading. I said the Canadian government is the kind of organization that would fund the black lesbians from Dartmouth. I made a mistake saying that because everybody leapt on it. But I'm still opposed to all this special funding to interest groups. They should raise their own money and make their own promotions and not use the taxpayers' revenue."

As for his stand on South Africa, he said: "I happen to be right. There's no question about that. I went out to South Africa, met [President] de Klerk, was convinced he was moving in exactly the right direction at the right time. Sanctions were ineffective. I felt we had a knee-jerk reaction on South Africa, particularly from Clark and Mulroney, who really hadn't been sensitive enough to the changes."

Waters denied, however, that he was a right-winger on anything but fiscal policy. "I get brassed off on social matters," he said. "The only people who think they have any heart on social matters are the NDP and that's a lot of crap. All of us are concerned about the aged and infirm and those who can't look after themselves. What we're concerned about is that we've started all these programs we can't afford and we're going to have the most awful bounce on the floor pretty soon."

Waters admitted he was not a polished politician, and it was difficult to disagree. His words in cold print never conveyed the warmth and good humour that often accompanied them. His death cost the party the highest-profile Reformer in Canada besides Manning.

Traditional politicians should not take too much comfort from all these tales of inexperience. The party shows remarkable competence for its stage of development, and what it lacks it makes up in pure enthusiasm. Meetings are invariably well organized and smoothly run. The tickets are sold and the money collected. The tables selling membership and buttons are staffed by hordes of eager volunteers. The meeting at Toronto's International Centre, with about 6,000 tickets sold at $5 each, was one of the most successful political events in the city in years.

There is also a good deal of hard-headed political skill and traditional arm-twisting at the top. In this vein, the story of how Manning and his father recruited Doug Main to run for the party in 1988 is very instructive.

Main was then the popular TV news anchorman on Edmonton's ITV, a station owned by the late Dr. Charles Allard, the wealthy developer of Second City and other popular syndicated shows. Manning came to the station one day to tape a program about the Reform Party and brought his father along. When the three men talked afterwards, the Mannings tried to convince Main to run for the party. Main said he later agreed but pointed out that leaving his job to campaign would pose financial problems. According to Main, Manning said: "Why don't I ask my dad to call Dr. Allard?" The elder Manning did, Main says, with the result that he was paid his full salary during the campaign. (He lost, but later ran for the Alberta Tories and became provincial minister of culture.) Main, who calls himself "a Bible-believing Christian," still considers Preston Manning a close friend.

The Reform Party obviously runs on a delicate blend of populist enthusiasm surging up from below, and careful steering from above. Preston Manning, after his years of study, is aware of every trap that a new or rising party can stumble into. The worst danger of all, he feels, is the temptation that such parties offer to opportunists and outright crooks who simply want a free ride to power and a fat pension. The Tories fell victim to this problem in 1984, he feels, and he does not want it to strike the Reform Party. He has come up with a remarkable device to keep this from happening.

His answer is the "Candidate Information Sheet," surely the most rigorous examination of prospective MPs ever imposed by any federal party. Manning produced this gigantic questionnaire in the spring of 1991 and promptly set a very high standard by filling it out himself. The form asks some pointed and penetrating questions. Candidates for nomination are expected to say whether they have ever undergone treatment for alcoholism or drug abuse, have been refused membership in any kind of club or organization, have participated in an illegal strike, or have been jailed or charged with an offence. They are asked to authorize a credit check by the party, not just for the aspiring candidates, but for spouses as well. They are quizzed in detail about debts, business failures, income, and assets. They are asked about their deepest values, whether they adhere to party policy, and whether they agree with a Code of Ethics drafted by the party. A 20-point description of the ideal candidate calls for a salary history "in the high half of job holders in that particular occupation" (a requirement that seems to rule out union members). If married, it continues, the Reformer should have "a family that understands the demands of the job and which will support the candidate in fulfilling them or, at the very least, a family that will not be a source of embarrassment." The questionnaire is so complex that Manning's reply runs to 32 full pages.

After reading the replies, members of riding nominating committees are expected to interview the candidates and make one of three rulings: urge the person to run, ask him or her to "get further experience and knowledge," or reject the applicant outright. To some westerners with long memories this sounded like another version of Alberta Social Credit review panels that sometimes rejected candidates already chosen by party members at open meetings. (Gordon Taylor, a long-serving Alberta Socred MLA and later a Tory MP, remembers that such a panel refused to give him a nomination when he first tried, even though he had polled the most votes at a public meeting. He was replaced by the second-place finisher.)

When the questionnaire appeared, it was instantly criticized as anti-populist, authoritarian, nosy, and likely to favour rich white males. "It bothers me a hell of a lot," Calgary Reform member Dave

Wylie told the *Calgary Herald.* Gerry Maloney, a candidate in 1988, said the information was none of the party's business. The whole process seemed to be a violation of grass-roots democracy.

Manning replied that candidates have no obligation to fill out the form (although their chances for a nomination would then seem slim indeed). It was simply a device, he said, for educating voters about the candidates, and making the candidates aware of their own strengths and limitations. By helping everyone make an informed choice, he claimed, it was truly a populist measure.

"A lot of people criticize populism because they say it's emotion-driven, it's not reasonable," Manning said in an interview. "This is to try to protect the populist process from those sorts of charges by saying 'Look, the rank-and-file can think about these kinds of things, can become themselves a screen.'"

"The questionnaire is intended to get people to think through the implications of running for the federal Parliament. Just add up the people who've got conflict of interest charges, the number of MPS in Ottawa whose political careers result in family breakup, alcoholism, or financial problems. The conventional wisdom is that one in three of western MPS has one of those problems: financial, family, or alcohol. If a guy's got that type of thing before he goes to Ottawa, you can just count on the fact that if it wasn't a problem before it's going to be one after.

"We also know there's a lot of opportunists who want to go after our nominations. . . . The more we can get people asking those things in advance of someone seeking the nomination rather than after, the more we can protect ourselves." Manning says that the questionnaire does not favour wealthy candidates with no debts, because people would have questions for a rich candidate as well as a poor one. They might suspect a rich man of conflict of interest and a poor one of wanting to pad his income, the leader argues. Besides, the candidates can always ask to have their answers kept confidential. Public response has been very positive, he insists, because people realize they often know very little about the members they send to Ottawa. As he likes to say in his speeches, "Some communities spend more time picking their rink manager than their Member of Parliament."

Again, the criticism quickly faded. Reformers have a bond of trust with Preston Manning, and upon this rock they build their party.

CHAPTER THREE

YOUNG TURK

> "If the Canadian political situation continues to degenerate . . . a wholly new political party committed to the social conservative position will find an ever increasing number of advocates and supporters."
>
> – Ernest Manning, 1967

FOR AT LEAST 20 years, Preston Manning waited patiently for his moment to plunge into federal politics, always hunting for the mixture of anger and frustration that produces major new populist movements. He was tempted many times along the way. He could have jumped in as early as 1972, when westerners were already fed up with the Trudeau Liberals, or in 1979, as Joe Clark's Conservatives stumbled and fell. An even more promising time came after 1980, when fury at those same Liberals gave rise to western separatist parties with a strong populist flavour. Yet Manning still waited.

When he finally decided to move late in 1986, circumstances seemed less auspicious. The Tory government was only halfway through its first term and most westerners were not yet thoroughly disillusioned. Meech Lake was still an obscure pond outside Ottawa. The Goods and Services Tax was only a dark whisper in Conservative circles. The Tories, moreover, were the champions of free trade, a cause Manning embraced ardently. The Conservative government would win western support again, in 1988, largely on the strength of that issue.

But Manning and other astute westerners sensed something powerful brewing by late 1986. People were beginning to grumble about government MPs who did not represent them, about Ottawa's failure to act on some of its promises, about the national debt, about taxes, about a total failure of national leadership, and about many other grievances. For the first time since the 1930s, there was a building national feeling that no government could fix the problems because the system itself was at fault. If the Conservatives could not make fundamental changes with all those powerful western cabinet ministers in Ottawa, who could? Yet separatist parties had been tried and discredited as a solution for westerners, and this was fine with Manning. He has always believed that the answers for westerners lie within Canada, not outside it.

Manning also sensed by late 1986 that the new round of constitutional talks would end in catastrophe. This became likely in August of that year when the provincial premiers agreed to hold a "Quebec round" of negotiations without "linkage." By pledging not to discuss other national problems, Manning suspected, they were inadvertently setting the match to a national brush fire. The rest of Canada was bound to ignite if Quebec alone had priority for too long.

So Preston Manning and his friends decided to move, first with their exploratory meeting in Vancouver in May 1987, then at an Assembly to found the Reform Party of Canada in Winnipeg that November. Preston Manning, dismissed as "Junior" and "Presto," at first looked like an awkward fellow trying to relive his father's glory. The party's showing in the 1988 election was respectable for a new party but not terribly impressive: Manning, after all, did not manage to beat Clark in Alberta's Yellowhead riding. Nevertheless, he knew that this disappointment was caused largely by the free-trade issue. Many westerners who favoured the deal did not want to split the conservative vote, so they held their noses and voted Tory. This masked the growing support for the Reform Party.

After the 1988 election, the country's disasters quickly became the party's building blocks. Meech Lake turned into a national English-French conflict unlike anything since the Conscription Crisis of the Second World War. The Conservatives insisted on ramming through the GST against the will of 85 per cent of Canadians. The national economy went into a deep dive, with mighty Ontario suffering most. Yet politicians of the three major parties clung blindly to party discipline and old formulas even as public rage mounted against them all. Western-style discontent with the entire political system was spreading quickly into Ontario and Atlantic Canada. The Bloc Québécois suddenly sprang up in Quebec, the perfect foil for a party that frankly says that it represents English Canada. The conditions were right not just for a new party, but for a powerful populist surge, a true movement of the kind that swept the Progressives to Ottawa in 1921.

The leader who would ride this wave of discontent had spent his whole adult life preparing for the moment. He was, as his father suggested, perhaps the best-prepared politician of his generation. He had virtually constructed himself to the proper specifications.

Preston Manning's upbringing was Christian, stable, and as normal as it could be for a premier's son. Born on June 10, 1942 in Edmonton, he spent his early years in the Garneau district on the city's South Side, near the University of Alberta. Manning attended Garneau School until he was 12, when his father bought a 900-acre dairy farm near Horse Hill, 11 miles northeast of Edmonton on the banks of the North Saskatchewan River. The area near the farm, now within Edmonton's city limits, is known today for the Manning Freeway and the Edmonton Institution, one of the toughest maximum security prisons in Canada.

By all accounts Preston passed the rest of his youth there quite happily, working on the farm, playing with friends, and going to school. He was a top student at Horse Hill High School, an eager and talented athlete, a good rider, a tinkerer with farm machinery, and a bit of a boyish adventurer. Manning and his pals used to shoot their BB guns at each other's horses, reports Ray Speaker, his friend for 30 years. He once tried to modify the flywheel of an irrigation motor to throw baseballs, without success. Manning's Grade 12 class graduation picture, taken in 1960, still hangs in the library of the school.

His proud father told the authors in an interview: "He was always a joy to us. He was very interested in sports when he was young. He played hockey and football and was very interested in all the general sports. And he was always good at his studies."

Preston Manning's mother, the former Muriel Preston, is a tall, striking woman who met Ernest Manning at William Aberhart's Prophetic Bible Institute in 1927. She is a talented musician who became nearly as famous as her husband when she accompanied him at the piano on "Canada's National Bible Hour." Preston Manning says his father was always trusting, while his mother tended to be more intuitive – or suspicious. "If she met somebody she didn't like, she'd say, 'He's a rat no matter how nice he seems,'" he recalls. Today Manning feels that he resembles his father while his wife, Sandra, has the same wary tendency as his mother.

Like his father, Preston Manning is a workaholic. His wife tells friends she would rather take him skiing than horseback riding because he can think about work while he is riding, but doesn't dare when he is zooming down a ski run. He learned to apply himself as a hard-working farm boy, just as Ernest Manning had 30 years earlier on the George Henry Manning homestead outside of Rosetown, Sask. At Horse Hill, Preston milked the cows in the morning and evening, helped seed and harvest the crops, and hauled away the manure. "My first job was driving a 'honey wagon' at a nickel a load," he told John Howse for *Maclean's* magazine. "Seventy Holstein cows can produce a lot of that stuff." The family had virtually no contact with the media. "My father was from that school that kept public life and private life completely separate," Manning said to one of the authors. "In those days the media respected that as long as you didn't try to play both ends, if you didn't try to use the family as some kind of a publicity thing."

Today, Manning likes to suggest that neighbours considered his family as a happy band of simple farmers. "My father was thought of in the community as Mr. Manning who kept a dairy farm in the valley and went into town during the week to run the government," he told Ian Pearson in *Saturday Night* magazine. In fact, the family was very famous and everyone knew his father as both the premier and the best-known religious leader in Western Canada. But Manning Jr. recalls that "The only impact his job had on me was when the legislature opened. They used to have a tea party where they made all these fancy little sandwiches. I could usually get a bunch of these afterwards and take them to school. They were always objects of wonderment as to why people would cut sandwiches so small." As he grew older he wasn't so naively innocent of his father's line of work. People in the government, he said, "would show me a paper that explained how a decision was made. I guess I was always more interested in government than politics. My dad was too, even though he was pretty good at the political end."

Few journalists ever had a glimpse of this private farm life, but Arthur Hailey was an exception. In 1964, on assignment for *Maclean's* magazine to write about scandals in Ernest Manning's government, he asked for an interview with Muriel Manning. To his great surprise he was invited to the farm. Hailey described the scene with the flourishes of the budding novelist who later wrote such international best-sellers as *Airport*:

"We chatted in the gracious cedar-paneled living room of the

Mannings' ranch-style bungalow. Sunlight streamed in through a double corner picture window overlooking rolling grassland. . . . Throughout the living area there is moss-green broadloom, with other furnishings in soft pastel shades. The effect is of restrained good taste. . . . The books in the Mannings' collection lean heavily to religious subjects. There is some biography, little fiction. . . . She spoke warmly of their younger son, Preston. [He] has been distressed, Mrs. Manning said, by the number of fellow students who have abandoned their faith. 'He has a call – not through anything we have urged upon him – to do something in religion.' But he will not enter the ministry, nor does she believe he will follow his father into politics. . . . Mrs. Manning does not tell me, but I knew, that her eldest son, Keith, has been afflicted since birth with cerebral palsy. It has been one of the great sadnesses of the Mannings' life."

Preston Manning's brother, William Keith, was born May 2, 1939 with brain damage that led to cerebral palsy. Although Keith spent much of his early life at special schools, Preston Manning took considerable responsibility for him when he was home. Later, when they were young adults, Manning and his friends always tried to include Keith in their outings.

"I'd talk to Keith when he'd be home on weekends," recalls Ray Speaker. "He'd be with Preston and go to picture shows, things like that. He was a quiet fellow, well mannered. The family was very caring and understanding. He was just with you when you were in a group, and it was a normal activity. He was a nice guy." Phillip Stuffco, Manning's brother-in-law, recalls Keith as "a big, friendly giant. Preston was always caring for him." Later Keith Manning lived in an institution in Red Deer where he met and married a woman who suffered from epilepsy. He died in Edmonton in June 1986 of cardiac arrest at age 47. "Preston took it very hard," Stuffco says. "It was a very difficult time for him." Some years earlier, after Stuffco's own brother died of electrocution, Manning had spoken movingly at the funeral. After Keith's death he told Stuffco: "Now I know how you feel." The service for Keith was at Edmonton's Fundamental Baptist Church, the family's church for many years. It seems likely that Preston Manning's sense of duty, his feeling of being called for a mission, stems in part from the tragedy of his brother's life.

Preston Manning met his wife-to-be, Sandra Lillian Beavis, at the same Fundamental Baptist Church. Her father, J. Gordon Beavis, sang in the choir for "Canada's National Bible Hour," recalls Ingrid Speaker, Ray Speaker's wife and one of Sandra Manning's best friends. "I don't know if Preston ever dated anybody else. I couldn't say when their first date was, but it was probably when they were high-school age. Sandra's comment always was that Preston didn't know there was a girl on the map." Sandra Beavis, two years younger than Manning, was pretty, lively, and traditional in her notions about marriage. Like Muriel Manning, she was also a gifted musician who used her talents at the family church.

They married in 1967. Sandra Manning gave up her nursing studies and they moved to California for a year while Preston Manning worked for TRW Systems Ltd. Over the years they had five children: first Andrea, and then Avryll, Mary Joy, Nathan, and David. In late 1991, the children ranged in age from 23 to 12.

The Mannings remain very close both to the Beavis family, often visiting them at their lakeside home in Slave Lake, and to the elder Mannings. For many years Preston and Sandra Manning lived on an acreage outside Edmonton, fairly close to his mother and father. Because their older girls were enrolled at the University of Calgary, the Mannings moved to Calgary in 1990. (Also, Calgary was clearly the most fertile ground for the Reform Party in Alberta, and the site of its national head office.) Manning's parents were not far behind. Within a year, Muriel and Ernest Manning sold their house in St. Albert, north of Edmonton, and moved to Calgary, even though both were in their eighties.

The most important presence in Preston and Sandra Manning's world is God. Next comes family. Manning describes his wife as "a fort-holder," and she repeats the phrase cheerfully. He needs to know that she is handling "the base," he says, "because that way you can accomplish a tremendous amount." In conversation, Sandra Manning is energetic, enthusiastic, perceptive, and deeply interested in her husband's political career. His approach is driven much more by goals than by ambition, she says. She has opinions on everything from Saskatchewan NDP Premier Roy Romanow to the views of Reform Party delegates, and she does not hesitate to express them.

Mostly, however, Sandra Manning stays in the background, looking after the family. Her husband seems as determined as his father was to shield them from media view. When Preston Manning filled out a section of the candidates' questionnaire that asks how his riding association could help the family, he replied: "Respect privacy and needs of family members." The authors met Sandra Manning by chance while speaking to her husband in an Edmonton restaurant. The conversation was pleasant, but all subsequent requests for an interview with her went unanswered. Encountered later, she said: "I don't know what I could have added."

Sandra Manning has no shortage of friends to praise her and her family values. "Her first and foremost goal is being a mother," says Ingrid Speaker. "She gives 100 per cent of her time to being mother and wife. Herself, she's at the bottom of the pole and she doesn't mind that. She's not like one of these people who has to put time away for herself. She just thoroughly gives all her time for her family, and enjoys doing that."

For years much of Sandra Manning's time went into her daughters' passion for synchronized swimming. All three are experts, and Andrea Manning, once a member of the national team, is now a coach as well as a student in pre-law. In tones approaching awe, Ingrid Speaker explains Sandra Manning's devotion to her family. "Her hours were taking them to swimming at 5 a.m. and sometimes picking them up at 10 at night at the pool. A lot of people would have said, 'Well that's not going to continue forever.' But she did it with every one of them." Now she ferries the boys around to hockey, baseball, and golf.

One of Sandra Manning's greatest boosters is brother-in-law Stuffco, who married her younger sister Marian Beavis. "I don't think I've ever met anybody who is as genuine and kind as she is," he says. "We call her the soft touch because she will do absolutely anything not only for her own children, but for her friends and her family, to a point where I think that she's almost too nice. . . . She will drive all night. She will go get a part-time job if she has to, to see her kids travel. . . . She's always doing bingos and charity work. Her home was always open for visits or free meals. When I first met her sister I was just a university student, and I was over there freeloading all the time. Free meals, borrow vehicles, money, it didn't matter – what she had she gave.

"For example, if she takes her kids to her parent's home in Slave Lake, she will take food for everybody, not just for her family. I had a water ski boat and she'd bring the gas to pull her kids. She would share her clothes with her sisters. It's a bit of a family joke, but she's Mrs. Perfect and a perfect match for Mr. Perfect. . . . I can't find any fault with either one of them, and I've known them for 20 years. You try to find something wrong so you can pick an argument with them, but you can't. It's frustrating for the rest of us mere mortals to be around them.

"She always tries to find good in a situation. Her motto is 'We'll turn bad into good.' It doesn't matter whether it's pouring rain or whatever, she always tries to be happy. She's a genuinely happy person."

Ingrid Speaker warns enquiring media types that "They'll have trouble finding any holes in that marriage. Preston and Sandra really have a very close, extremely trusting relationship. Most political marriages come under close scrutiny. Because people are apart a lot, and because their lifestyle takes them into bars and that type of thing, before long they have problems. Because their lifestyle isn't like that they have such an advantage."

Sandra Manning is certainly willing to sacrifice for her husband's crusade. She signed a party declaration acknowledging that as a politician's wife she might lose respect, might have to move, might have to endure resentment within the family, and might be separated from her husband for long periods. The only section the Mannings disagreed with was a statement that the family might become secondary to the job. "Neither they nor I accept this proposition," Preston Manning wrote under his wife's signature.

Without question, religion guides the roles Preston and Sandra Manning choose to play. They believe in the literal truth of the Bible, which is full of references to the subordinate behaviour expected of women. "Wives submit to your husbands," says the Book of Ephesians, "for the husband is the head of the wife as Christ is head of the church." Proverbs declares: "The woman Folly is loud; she is undisciplined and without knowledge." Corinthians says: "As in all the congregations of the saints, women should remain silent in the churches. They are not allowed to speak, but must be in submission, as the Law says." In the family's Calgary church, women are not exactly silent, but they are certainly deferential and do not play leading roles. In the Manning family there is a sense that men and women know their places and are content with them. They share this feeling with many other Reformers, and their views are clearly reflected in the party's attitude that women need no special help to improve their lot in society.

From his early 20s, Preston Manning's political ideals have been inspired by his father. At the same time, the son has had enormous influence on Ernest Manning. The foundation of Reform Party thinking today rises from a unique father-son collaboration that began about 1965, when Preston Manning and a small circle of his young friends began to write most of the major policies espoused by the Alberta Social Credit government. So completely did this group come to dominate the government that old-line cabinet ministers and party members derisively called them the "Young Turks."

"We were 20 years ahead of our time," says one of the group, Manning's friend Owen Anderson, as he notes the similarities with today's Reform Party. Social Credit insider John Barr wrote: "[Erick] Schmidt and Preston Manning maintained a more intimate association with Manning in the planning of new directions than most of Manning's own cabinet ministers." Even today both Mannings often unconsciously say "we" when they describe what they did and thought in those days. "We already had a long whack at the provincial thing and it didn't seem to advance the interests of the West," Preston Manning told Ian Pearson of *Saturday Night* magazine in 1990. "And we never had an ally in the federal field that would have helped those efforts."

Today, Manning prefers to downplay the family connection. In his disclosure statement to the Reform Party, he states that he made "major contributions to the Alberta government's *White Paper on Human Resources Development* and a book entitled *Political Realignment: A Challenge to Thoughtful Canadians.*" He does not mention that only his father's name appears on both documents. This is perhaps understandable: many Reformers, especially older westerners who remember Alberta Social Credit, believe that Ernest Manning, even at 83, pulls the strings. The reality is that Ernest and Preston Manning depend on each other.

Manning showed his interest in politics very early when he ran as a federal Social Credit candidate in the 1965 general election. "He was very young at the time," his father recalled in an interview recorded for the University of Alberta Archives in 1982. (These interviews, taped between 1978 and 1982 but never published, are an invaluable source of information about the Mannings and their politics.) "But he put up a good campaign – he came in second!" Although Ernest Manning enthusiastically backed his 23-year-old son in an open letter to voters, and Preston called himself by his full name, Ernest Preston Manning, the young candidate edged out the Liberal for number two spot in Edmonton East. Tory incumbent Bill Skoreyko polled 13,596 votes to Manning's 6,762. Edmonton East is a heavily ethnic riding held today by the only NDP federal member from Alberta, Ross Harvey.

According to the account Manning usually gives of his career, he then withdrew from active involvement in politics. In an interview with one of the authors he said: "I was quite conscious, and so was my father, in the 1960s, that the whole populist movement of the Depression was over. It was over for Social Credit and it was over for the CCF. That's what the whole NDP thing was about [the creation of the NDP from the CCF in 1961]. And rather than get in on the tail end of the Depression ones, my own impression was it was better to wait until it happened again. . . . I wasn't just sort of lying awake at night waiting for that to happen. But it was the only type of political thing I was interested in directly."

Yet there were many other "political things" that attracted Manning. In 1968, after his father made it known that he planned to retire, he became one of the leading contenders for the job of Social Credit leader and premier of Alberta. His circle of friends – including Schmidt, Anderson, and Don Hamilton – began to lobby quietly on his behalf. One person they approached was veteran Social Credit minister Gordon Taylor, who planned to run for the leadership himself. "I told them I didn't believe in the divine right of premiers," Taylor recalls. Taylor and other veteran Socreds were not impressed by the idea of passing the torch to the young man just because he happened to be a Manning.

Socred chronicler John Barr paints this sympathetic picture of the potential candidate: "The party was going to need a strong and imaginative leader, and Preston, his worldly inexperience notwithstanding, had many of the right attributes. Fair and slight, like his father, on the platform he was transformed into an even better speaker than his father – he had the Manning voice and technique of marshalling his arguments, but more forcefulness. More important, he was young . . . and a prolific generator of ideas. . . . he had a host of ideas on how modern systems analysis and management theory could be applied to overhaul politics and government."

Those who know Ernest Manning have different impressions. They say that Preston Manning, although taller, appears somehow less imposing than his father. Reverend Ed Checkland, a professor at the University of Alberta, remembers Manning Sr. firmly standing on the platform, appealing to his audience, always "with a sense of authority." Ernest remains "a shadow over Preston," he says.

The Preston-for-premier drive was ultimately spiked by his father, who believed that his son would have too much trouble establishing his own identity and controlling a cabinet of older men. He was certainly right, given the hostility of Gordon Taylor and others. Preston Manning and his friends decided that he would not declare himself a candidate. Instead, they would support Ernest Manning's personal choice, Harry Strom. A friendly, ineffectual man, Strom would lead Social Credit to a resounding defeat at the hands of Peter Lougheed's Conservatives in 1971.

The Young Turks worked actively on Strom's campaign, with Don Hamilton as general manager and Manning developing a plan. They put out a brochure which made it clear that their motives for backing Strom were partly religious. "Harry Strom is an active Christian layman who believes that Christian principles are relevant and applicable to politics and public affairs," the pamphlet said. "He has held executive and teaching positions within the evangelical Free Church and has long participated in the work of other Christian organizations and service groups." They then added the same kind of disclaimer Manning uses today to soothe people's fears about his own religion. "His personal faith will not be expressed in terms of inflexible positions on such matters as Sunday movies, Sunday hunting or liquor regulations (he believes that these matters must be decided by plebiscites in accordance with the will of the majority)."

It would be wrong to assume that Ernest's rejection of his son's candidacy means there was jealousy between them. An astute judge of the political climate, Ernest knew that Preston Manning would face a turbulent ride and create a rift in the party. Whatever the young man's hopes for the leadership may have been, he accepted the decision and remained extremely close to his father.

In fact, his influence on his father at this crucial time was simply remarkable. Manning was just out of university with an unlikely background in physics combined with economics and political science. Ernest Manning was nearly 60, had been premier for 24 years, had dealt with every prime minister since Mackenzie King. He was so respected across the country that a few Ontario Tories were courting him to run for the federal Conservative leadership. Yet the father had immense regard for the son's opinions and political ideas, and not simply because they reflected and amplified his own.

Preston Manning has an impressive record of intellectual achievement. He won a national Governor General's medal for scholarship in Grade 9, graduated from Grade 12 with a 93 per cent average, was offered three scholarships, and excelled in his University of Alberta courses. Proficiency in French was not one of his achievements, however. He took the subject in school but did not become bilingual. He now says he has no pressing desire to learn.

Never one to take his ability for granted, Manning concentrated on his studies in his first years at university. His friend Ray Speaker remembers dragging him out to the annual model Parliament to sit as a Socred. (Joe Clark was then leader of the student Tories.) "He was there to study physics," Speaker says. "Preston had a commitment to do a certain thing, he had a target, the goals were clear. He'd set out to achieve a certain degree of accomplishment in physics, and that's where his attention was. He didn't want to get diverted over to politics that soon. I'd say by the third year I was there on campus, Preston became more involved in our meetings and social activities, and more involved in the model Parliament."

This coincided with an academic switch from physics to economics, a move which Ernest Manning explained in the archival interviews in 1982: "He used to come home . . . and he'd say, 'This is wonderful stuff, but if you're really going to go all out for this you've got to get off in a laboratory somewhere and forget there's a world outside.' Well, that was contrary to his nature altogether. He was very interested in people and very concerned about resolving problems people faced. That was something he was very intense about from the time he was just a young person." It may also be that science looked appealing for a while because this was one area where his father cast no shadow.

The young Manning became, as Barr suggested, a careful, systematic political thinker. He worked his ideas through with extreme care, often bouncing them off dozens of people before taking a position. At the University of Alberta he loved "teach-ins", day-long sessions on issues from space travel to federalism. Later he carried this concept inside the Alberta legislature, where his band of Young Turks developed government policy. For hours, they would sequester in a small room to refine complex ideas into short sentences and phrases.

Ray Speaker, by then a Socred MLA (and today a provincial Tory minister in Alberta), recalls how Manning would apply himself. "Preston and I, and Erick Schmidt and Don Hamilton, once spent hours with a blackboard writing one sentence on the definition of Social Conservatism. We just kept honing it until we thought it was pretty good." Speaker sees this steadfastness as admirable. "Preston's persistent and he's consistent," says this loyal friend. "Whatever he has done he has thought through, spent a lot of time working at it, honing his ideas. He is very clear on what his position is, and once he's got that position he sells it and doesn't deviate from it.

"He has ultimate honesty and integrity," says Speaker. "He's very unselfish. Right now, what he is doing is not for Preston Manning, Preston Manning's aggrandizement, or Preston Manning's ego. It's because he really believes that what he is selling can change the lives of Canadians. He really believes that, and he's worked on it all the years we've known each other – 30 years."

What Preston Manning wanted then, and still wants now, is nothing less than the wholesale transfer of major Social Credit ideals into a new party that can win the allegiance of modern Canada. The CCF made such a change when it transformed itself into the New Democratic Party in 1961, ensuring that an outdated agrarian movement adapted fairly successfully to new realities. Social Credit, the political and religious response to Prairie socialism, simply died, or seemed to.

In fact, Manning and his father were striving desperately to create a similar resurgence on the right in the 1960s and 1970s. Over the years, Manning Jr. approached many western Conservatives, including Joe Clark, former MP Doug Roche, and former Tory David Kilgour, now a Liberal MP. Always he wanted them to reform the Tory party, even change its name, so it would be a powerful conservative alternative to the NDP and other forces of collectivism.

A former Ernest Manning cabinet member, Alf Hooke, noted derisively in his 1971 memoir that both Erick Schmidt and Preston Manning were at the September, 1967 Conservative Leadership Convention won by Robert Stanfield. John Barr adds that both Manning and his friend Schmidt had attended a Conservative Thinkers Conference a month earlier in Quebec, but returned home disappointed at the lack of interest in their proposals. Perhaps this shows they were still rather naive; any established party resists radical ideas, even at meetings allegedly devoted to thinking.

Now Preston Manning has finally succeeded, as leader of the Reform Party, in riding his own populist storm.

Populist parties are like oil wells, tapping reserves of pent-up energy. Every generation or so they release the anger of Canadians in a geyser of frustration directed mainly at the country's political and economic elites, the people who claim to know best. Populism is always angry, often negative, and never friendly to the status quo, but it is ultimately useful because it forces politicians to get back in touch with the people. The Reform Party has already had a profound impact on government policy. In the constitutional package of September 24, 1991, the Conservatives promised to entrench property rights, reform the Senate, shift control of culture and other matters to the provinces, and strengthen the economic union. All these ideas come straight from the Reform platform. The Tories are hardly the first governing party to steal policies from a populist movement.

Populism is a western tradition because of the frustration people feel toward a perceived colonial power structure in Ottawa. Louis Riel, the founder of Manitoba, led both the Red River Resistance in 1870 and the North-West Rebellion of 1885 against an indifferent and callous government: for this Prime Minister John A. Macdonald saw that the rebellion was crushed and Riel hanged.

Early western politicians were very different from their cousins in eastern Canada. They refused to recognize the party system at the local level, even though members of the elected Northwest Territories government (comprising Manitoba, Saskatchewan and Alberta) belonged to federal parties. In 1903, for example, NWT Premier Frederick Haultain sharply defended the non-partisan approach of his cabinet: "But the policy of that [Conservative] party and those principles have nothing whatever to do with my position in this House or with the business of this House." Later, in 1911, Haultain, who was by then leader of the Conservatives in Saskatchewan, still refused to kneel to Ottawa: "I am not prepared to sit at the feet of any of these Eastern Gamaliels and study loyalty." Westerners have always sensed that party loyalty in federal politics works against them. The Reform Party struggles with the same tension today as it strives to reconcile service to local voters with loyalty to the party in Ottawa.

The reaction to federal party politics gained momentum as anger and betrayal consolidated into another movement for reform. In 1914, farmers' associations called for a non-partisan "progressive party" with "no platform other than 'vote the desire of your constituents.'" After the First World War, this agrarian revolt elected farmer-led governments first in Ontario, then in Alberta, Saskatchewan, and Manitoba. In 1921, the farmers went federal as the Progressive Party under the leadership of disgruntled Manitoba Liberal MP Thomas A. Crerar. They won 65 seats in the West, Ontario, and New Brunswick, second only to Mackenzie King's governing Liberals. The Progressives refused, however, to assume the role of Official Opposition.

The Progressive movement was not simply an agrarian revolt over inflation and debt, but another clarion call against the injustices created by the National Policy and its system of tariff protection for commerce. Paradoxically, its causes ultimately sounded its death-knell. In his classic 1950 work, *The Progressive Party in Canada*, W. L. Morton explained that "Any political movement which draws strength from transient and remediable causes is, to that extent, subject to the influence of anything which operates to remove those causes." That "anything" was Prime Minister Mackenzie King.

Crerar and Alberta Progressive MP Henry Wise Wood were often at each other's throats, and King exploited this disunity while adopting the Progressives' social and tariff reform policies. The resurrection of the Crow's Nest Pass Freight Rate and the implementation of the Natural Resources Transfer Act probably would not have occurred without pressure from the Progressive Party. (The latter bill finally transferred resource control from Ottawa to Alberta and Saskatchewan, which had been denied this right since their creation as provinces in 1905.) Preston Manning says that these changes alone justified the brief existence of the Progressives. Nevertheless, he must have mixed feelings today, as he watches the Conservatives plunder his policies in just the same way.

During the Dirty Thirties, populism again rose across the country with the formation of the CCF in Saskatchewan, the Social Credit movement in Alberta, and the Union Nationale in Quebec. The CCF was a social democratic party with roots in both the progressive farm and labour organizations. Its response to discontent was massive government intervention, including ownership of industrial and financial institutions, and sweeping social welfare legislation. Social Credit also proposed a redistribution of wealth, but from the opposite swing of the political pendulum. Social dividends would be paid by government so that each household could have enough food and goods to function. Social Credit also took Alberta into virtual legal revolt against Ottawa by passing several bills aimed at changing the monetary system. All were later ruled unconstitutional and disallowed. Although Premier William Aberhart failed to deliver his election promise of $25 a month to every Albertan, his magnetism, a powerful combination of evangelical fervour and partisan zeal, kept the party in power, and there it remained for 35 years.

In his foreword to Morton's study, Professor S. D. Clark noted that such social movements always lost their steam. "They shifted from being movements of revolt to become movements of reform. In doing so, they inevitably lost the support of great masses of western people. . . ." Preston Manning knows this danger very well, since his party already faces it with expansion into Ontario and the Atlantic provinces, but he hopes to leap past the whole western pattern of explosive protest movements which make a big splash, effect a few changes, and then die.

From the start, Manning has wanted his party to express a positive national agenda for reform, not just a sense of regional anger.

Only with national support, he feels, can the federal system truly be changed. That support will not come unless the party has a full range of policies on national issues as well as a set of regional demands. Because of Manning's zeal and preparation, no western party has ever marched onto the national stage as well prepared as the Reformers.

Above all, Manning does not want Reform to become just another party motived only by self-interest and self-preservation. He claims that he would rather see it die first. The party's constitution contains this remarkable provision: "This constitution shall become null and void, and the Party shall cease to exist, on November 1st, 2000 A.D." It can be saved, however, if the constitution is re-enacted by a two-thirds majority of delegates to a party Assembly held on or before that date. Manning is trying hard to ensure that his party does not become an instrument for ambition and power, but his solution is not foolproof. If the party is highly successful by the year 2000, Reformers might be just as reluctant as Tories or Liberals to vote themselves into oblivion.

Preston Manning and his father have always tried to fan the populist flame. After Social Credit began to fade, they spent much of their time striving to encourage other groups they found congenial. They tried hard to reform the Conservative Party to their designs. In the late 1960s, Ernest Manning played a part in creating the National Citizens' Coalition, a conservative lobby group founded by Colin Brown, the late insurance executive from London, Ont. After meeting Brown in London, Manning encouraged him and became a founding member of the board when the NCC was chartered in 1975: anything to keep alive the idea of small government controlled by the people.

Today many NCC members are very active in the Reform Party,

lobbying relentlessly, and often successfully, for the NCC's policies on balanced budgets, direct democracy, and many other issues. "The Reform Party has cribbed probably two-thirds of our policy book," laughs David Somerville, now president of the NCC. The backscratching is mutual: in 1990, the NCC named Reform Party Senator Stan Waters the winner of the Colin M. Brown Freedom Medal and Award. Waters had first met Ernest Manning when they were on the NCC's advisory board in earlier years. The NCC's motto, "More freedom through less government," could suit the Reform Party equally well.

While his father was encouraging the early NCC, Preston Manning was employed by the National Public Affairs Research Foundation, a fledgling conservative think-tank funded in part by Alberta's oil industry and based in Edmonton. The elite group of directors included many friends of the premier. From this base, Preston Manning researched and wrote the books and papers that carried his father's name. (Some writers have concluded that this group was a forerunner of the NCC, although Somerville says there was no connection. In a real sense, however, both organizations were ideological testing grounds for the Reform Party.)

The Mannings carefully set out their credo in three major documents produced from 1967 to 1970. There is hardly a thought in the dense prose of these works that is not reflected in Reform Party policy today. Every word shows the influence of Preston and his group of Young Turks. Very few Canadian politicians have left such a complete record of their political thinking, mostly, perhaps, because few have done so much of it.

The Mannings' book *Political Realignment* (1967) explained their philosophy for creating a new party system in Canada. Earlier that year, the premier had tabled in the legislature *A White Paper on Human Resources Development*, a course of social action intended to regenerate his tired Socred party. During the provincial election later in 1967, Calgary South Conservative candidate Joe Clark said that the document "was the first time in history a government had gone to battle clad only in a white paper." (In a riding where "Nobody gave him a snowball's chance in hell," in Peter Lougheed's words, Clark came a close second to Socred Arthur Dixon, the Speaker of the Legislature.)

In 1970, a year after Manning retired as premier, he and Preston Manning published *Requests for Proposals and Social Contracts* under the name of their new company, M & M Systems Research Ltd. This paper fully explained the mechanism (extensive privatization) for making the political blueprint work in the real world.

In *Political Realignment*, the best-known of the three, they lamented the bankruptcy of the federal system and urged the creation of a reformed Tory Party on the right, to be called the Social Conservatives. The Mannings defined this movement as "A new political ideology which will harness the energies of a free enterprise–private economic sector to the task of attaining many of the social goals which humanitarian socialists have long advocated. . . . The final product must successfully weld the humanitarian concerns of those with awakened social consciences to the economic persuasions of those with a firm conviction in the value of freedom of economic activity and enlightened private enterprise."

Today, some see this thinking as evidence of Preston Manning's moderation, his willingness to reach out and make peace with the left. Ray Speaker argues: "When Preston says he wants to have the NDP and the Conservatives in the [Reform] party, he means it. The two should co-exist. The two can work together. . . . The government shows compassion for those in need, that's why the NDP can belong to his Reform Party. Anybody who thinks in terms of left and right, and doesn't understand that there is a melding of the two in Preston's philosophy, that's where they misinterpret Preston."

Yet *Political Realignment* shows that the Mannings themselves think very definitely in terms of left and right, and see the organized Canadian left as the enemy. The book contains this typical blast: "It is imperative that we avoid the error of those who define their political utopia in collectivistic and socialistic terms (in terms of the ideal society rather than ideal individuals) and who are then committed to the use of coercive measures in order to direct individuals into prescribed paths." The alternative is Social Conservatism, which always emphasizes the "free and creative individual" over society as a whole. The responsibility for developing both the economy and human resources rests with "private citizens and associations of citizens." Government plays only a supporting role. Ultimately, Social Conservatism "regards as ideal whatever kind of society emerges from a free and creative citizenry." Crucial to this thinking is a denial of collective responsibility, the very foundation of the early CCF, and central to NDP philosophy.

Yet there is also a genuine social impulse behind this style of individualism. In the Mannings' view, social support would be supplied by citizens freely choosing to help themselves and others. They believe that the goals of the "humanitarian socialists" (quality medical service, universal education, and all the rest) could be reached more efficiently by individuals working singly and in private groups for the society.

The Mannings saw Social Conservatism as part of a new two-party system that would embrace all Canadians, offering a clear choice between collectivism and individualism. They seemed confident that with the field uncluttered, the majority would choose their option. The NDP would become the choice of Canadians who favored socialism, while the Progressive Conservatives, they hoped, would re-create themselves as the party of caring individualism, the Social Conservatives. Ernest Manning pleaded with the Tories to take this step because an entirely new party was not, in his view, the best thing for Canada. Then he made a political prediction that has proved more accurate than the religious prophecies that he delivers on his radio show: "If the Canadian political situation continues to degenerate, and if the cause of conservatism continues to suffer and decline . . . the idea of establishing a wholly new political party committed to the social conservative position will find an ever increasing number of advocates and supporters." That is exactly what began to happen 20 years later, in 1987, when his son founded the Reform Party of Canada.

Political Realignment received some national attention because Ernest Manning was the premier of Alberta, but it had little impact on the political scene. Alberta Social Crediters, after being told for a generation that the old-line parties were corrupt and evil, thought it strange that the Mannings suddenly wanted to join forces with one of them. Some federal Conservatives misread the book as Ernest Manning's attempt to jump to the front of the national campaign then being waged for the Conservative Party leadership.

The *White Paper on Human Resources Development* was an attempt to apply all of the Mannings' principles to everyday government in Alberta. Some of the rhetoric is almost identical to parts of *Political Realignment*, especially the passages about the evils of collectivism. Again, the parallels with modern Reform Party ideals and tactics are precise.

The Mannings, fearing that their Alberta party was seen as too right-wing and too business-oriented, placed great stress on the development of "human resources." All government was to join this campaign to raise the standing of people, especially the disadvantaged and those living in economically depressed areas. "Human resources will be treated as intrinsically more important than physical resources," the paper said. However, "Prior consideration will always be given to human beings individually (persons) rather than to human beings collectively (society)." Free enterprise would supply the engine, and the state would have "a supporting function rather than a domineering function." To provide this support, the government announced the creation of a Human Resources Development Authority (HRDA). It would be responsible, among other things, for eliminating "deficiencies in values and aspirations." The

Mannings also called for "more explicit social concern and action on the part of those who believe in private ownership and freedom of economic activity."

The White Paper is packed with organization charts and the peculiar argot of systems analysis, Preston Manning's great enthusiasm of the day. This belief that reality can be pinned down to a theory and a chart carries odd echoes of Social Credit monetary thinking, with its attempt to explain all economics through a simple formula (the famous A plus B theorem invented to explain the shortage of purchasing power). It is also tempting to suggest that the Mannings, who believe so deeply in a divine religious order, are always trying to find its reflection in earthly systems.

The *White Paper* was not well received, even by Ernest Manning's own government. Some Socreds feared (wrongly) that it was a foray into socialism, while others saw it as airy-fairy intellectualism from Preston Manning and his band of uppity Young Turks in Edmonton. The old-line Socred politicians did a bad job of explaining the emphasis on human resources, itself a vague and bureaucratic catch phrase that excited few people. Within two years the whole initiative was moribund, except, as will be seen in Chapter Five, for a peculiar business venture by Preston Manning that continued until 1988.

The oddly named *Requests for Proposals and Social Contracts*, co-authored by the Mannings in 1970, is a straightforward description of the kind of society they want. The language is far clearer, perhaps because Ernest Manning was no longer premier and could afford to be direct. This document is nothing less than a blueprint for the privatization of most services provided by government, including health care, education, regional development, and various head-start programs. "There is nothing contrary to sound principles or sound economy in government making it profitable for private enterprise to get involved in social action projects," the Mannings state. Government would be limited to a management role: defining goals, setting standards, awarding contracts, allocating money, and checking results. The rest would be done either by profit-making companies or by "non-profit organizations of the private sector," such as universities, research foundations, service clubs, labour groups, and student bodies.

The model for this radical program was purely American and came directly from Preston Manning's experience before 1968, when he took a six-month leave from the Research Foundation to work with TRW Systems of Redondo Beach, California, an aerospace contractor. (In the same period he travelled to Southeast Asia to see for himself if the United States should be involved in the Vietnam War, and concluded that it should.)

Manning was captivated by the American method of getting military and aerospace jobs done by contracting work to private companies. Under this system, the U.S. federal government published a "request for proposal" that outlined the project; companies responded, and the best bidder won. (That was the theory, but the same system later led to huge swindles and cost overruns by U.S. military contractors, and to manufacturing defects which caused a Space Shuttle explosion that killed seven astronauts.) Manning described with admiration the challenges met by the American method, including "building a missile to carry an H-bomb, putting a variety of satellites and space vehicles into orbit, and landing men on the moon." He felt that the same method could be used to achieve social goals in Canada.

According to the paper, those goals included privatization of both health care and education. To test the strategy, governments would pay companies to provide health care clinics for employees and their families. Industries would take over vocational training in their own field of expertise, often by building schools in or near their factories. "The private sector is going to pay the bill either by providing such services directly or by paying taxes to the goverment," the paper says. "In many cases it would be more cost effective for industry to provide needed development services directly. . . . "

The document does not say where this "test" would end, but it leaves the impression that all medical care and schooling could well pass into the private sector. The Mannings claim that a vital role would remain for government and the civil service, but when they list the functions that could never be privatized they name only three: "The administration of justice, the conduct of foreign affairs, and the organization of the Armed Forces."

Some commentators have noted how similar this sounds to the all-out free-enterprise dream of former U.S. President Ronald Reagan. Ernest Manning's remarks in the archival interviews lend some weight to this connection. He said in 1981 that although Reagan's success or failure had yet to be decided, "He has given his people the impression of strength . . . there's an upsurge of public confidence in the future of the economy of the States today that is fantastic, compared with what it was a couple of years ago, and compared with what it is in this country." The Mannings felt then, and still do, that their similar solutions can provide the same results for Canada.

The *Request for Proposals* plan is, like the *White Paper*, systems language for government tendering of contracts. This is what already takes place across the country, especially in public works and road construction. The system also serves, however, as a rich source of patronage for the friends of whatever government happens to be in power. The Mannings' proposal would extend this system into many services now provided by government. Thus, the local hospital, besides being built by a well-connected contractor, could end up being run by another one. Governments would still pay the bill, including the profits, with no guarantee that the ultimate cost would be lower, the service better, or the standards comparable from one region to another. The Mannings were aware of some potential problems, such as resistance from civil servants, and discussed them in the paper. Nevertheless, they concluded that the benefits would outweigh the drawbacks.

Ernest Manning certainly knows about such problems and pressures of dealing with the private sector. Gordon Taylor says that when he was Alberta's highways minister, the premier once encouraged him to ease the terms of a road contract because the contractor made large contributions to the Social Credit Party. After studying the contract, Taylor told the premier there was nothing he could do. Manning accepted the decision with good grace and the contractor was out of luck, Taylor says. Manning-style privatization would create such situations every day, and the decisions might not always be so magnanimous. (Indeed, historians such as the University of Alberta's Bob Hesketh question whether Social Credit was quite that noble.) In any event, Preston Manning's own venture into social contracting, as president and chief executive officer for 20 years of Slave Lake Developments Limited, was not free from problems, politics, and bitter accusations.

The *Requests for Proposals* document is probably the best single guide to how Preston Manning's ideas translate into everyday politics. Its proposals would stop the growth of government and centralized decision-making. They would create a highly decentralized society of local power centres that, in Manning's view, would serve people better. Most of all, they would leave a great deal more power in private hands, thereby strengthening the individual in the eternal struggle against the state. Ultimately, these ideas rest on the deep faith that individual enterprise can do the job, whether it be delivering the mail or delivering babies. The system meets all the Manning requirements for a Christian social order.

The tracks of his early thinking are evident in nearly every page of the Reform Party's 1991 *Blue Book* of principles and policies. At the 1991 Assembly held in Saskatoon, Reform delegates voted to adopt the *Blue Book*. Although the agenda is suitably dressed up in modern language, it still sounds very familiar to any reader of the earlier

Manning documents. (This is hardly surprising, since Manning wrote the entire opening Statement of Principles, the Leader's Foreword, and probably much else besides.) His ideas are obvious in the party's policies toward Quebec, the American tone of the constitutional proposals, the treatment of ethnic minorities, and many other areas. All these are examined in detail in other chapters. For now, several direct comparisons of general policy will make the point.

In *Request for Proposals*, the Mannings said: "The overall purpose and objective of government and of the economy should be to facilitate the development of human potential – to provide individuals with the opportunity and the means for self-development and achievement." Preston Manning wrote in the *Blue Book*: "We believe in the value of enterprise and initiative, and that governments have a responsibility to foster and protect an environment in which initiative and enterprise can be exercised by individuals and groups."

The role of government outlined in *Request for Proposals* is to be strictly limited. In the Reform Party policy guide, Manning states: "We believe that the legitimate role of government is to do for people whatever they need to have done, but cannot do at all – or do as well – for themselves individually or through non-governmental organizations."

In social policy the parallels are even more striking. The *Blue Book* approves the idea of a guaranteed annual income, a point that sounds out of place until one remembers Social Credit theory on missing purchasing power. The guaranteed annual income would be an efficient way of making payments ("social credits") to people according to need. These people would then be able to buy the services they require, including social services, on the private market. The *Blue Book* also recommends study of a security investment fund and negative income tax, devices that could have the same result.

Like Social Crediters of a generation ago, the Reformers want to make individuals responsible for their social needs. "The Reform Party opposes the view that universal social programs run by bureaucrats are the best and only way to care for the poor, the sick, the old, and the young," says the party *Blue Book*. In a prescription straight out of *Request for Proposals*, the *Blue Book* adds: "We would actively encourage families, communities, non-governmental organizations, and the private sector to reassume their duties and responsibilities in social service areas."

There is also a strong hint of user-pay requirements for those who can afford social services. "No citizen should be denied access by reason of financial status or inability to pay," the *Blue Book* states. "Likewise, this does not necessitate the full subsidization of those able to pay all or part of the costs themselves."

Besides shifting as much responsibility as possible to the individual, the *Blue Book* calls for vast transfers of power from Ottawa to the provinces. For social programs, it says, there should be "unconditional transfers of the tax base from the federal government to the provinces" so that "provincial policy would be set provincially by provincial governments clearly accountable to the electors of each province." Ottawa would have no influence over social programs, just as it would lose all power to enforce medicare standards. This, too, is in keeping with Manning's belief that centralized power is evil and destructive. One of the few strong roles for Ottawa would be in environmental control, and even that would be largely a co-ordinating and regulatory function with the provinces.

It may seem odd, therefore, that Manning does advocate national standards in one unexpected area: education. The *Blue Book* makes no statement on education, but Manning has said in public that he favours standardization of schooling across the country. This is likely to be a popular stand: the Spicer Commission, for instance, heard from many people fed up with the difficulty of comparing degrees from one province to the next, or even within a province.

Although the Mannings do not believe in the formal union of

church and state or of church and education, they do have a personal preference for schools that instill Christian religion. Manning's boys are at Glenmore Christian Academy, and for years he was on the board of Regent College, a post-graduate theological school on the campus of the University of British Columbia. It specializes, he says, in "the integration of the Christian faith with other aspects of contemporary life." Ernest Manning took much of his formal education at Aberhart's Prophetic Bible Institute.

In an archival interview in 1981, Ernest Manning expressed his views forcefully. The church should not be directly involved in education, he said, but "Education, to my mind, lost one of its most important ingredients when the spiritual aspect was put away on the back burner. I don't think you have to have the schools run by the church to have a spiritual dimension in education. . . . The idea of abolishing all respect or recognition of spiritual verities from the classroom on the grounds that this might be treading on somebody's toes in the matter of religious convictions – we've paid a terrible price for it. Society wouldn't be in the mess it's in today if we hadn't taken that course."

Like many populist leaders in Canadian history, the Mannings believe themselves to be religiously inspired. The charismatic Louis Riel thought that he was on a divine mission from God. Progressive politician Rev. William Irvine wrote in 1920 in *The Farmers in Politics*, "The line between the sacred and the secular is being rubbed out." Fellow Progressive Rev. J. S. Woodsworth, who went on to become leader of the CCF, predicted in 1915 that religion "Will become the every day life of the common man – that or nothing." The Almighty influenced other Depression-era populist leaders such as Rev. Tommy Douglas of the Saskatchewan CCF. Maurice Duplessis of the Quebec Union Nationale took William Irvine's prophecy to heart and hired the clergy to administer the hospitals and schools. Yet it was William Aberhart who provoked W. L. Morton to write: "That propagandist genius compounded out of fundamentalism, enthusiasm, and a gloss of economic literacy, a gospel of evangelistic materialism which carried over the air the promise of secular salvation."

Preston Manning believes, as his father does, that the role of government is to make people free so they can find God in their own way. All forms of bigness, in government, unions, and business, tend to be "collectivist" and to suppress this vital freedom to make a religious choice. Ernest Manning made the point with vivid clarity in a radio broadcast during the Second World War, when he argued that Canadians faced "a choice between Christian Democracy . . . and the materialistic and pagan doctrine of state socialism."

Nevertheless, Preston Manning bristles to this day when anyone suggests to him that Alberta's Social Credit government was a theocracy, a union of religion and government. "There was nothing to compare with the links between the Duplessis government in Quebec and the Catholic Church," he said in an interview. "Nothing could touch that. Baptists are terribly independent. Put five of them in a room and you'll probably end up with three churches." The Mannings have always argued that their radio ministry is unconnected with politics, even though Ernest Manning often expressed political judgements on the show.

While the Mannings may not advocate the official linkage of Church and state, they certainly prefer to have people of their own religion running the state. Manning Sr. has stated firmly that in politics he prefers to be surrounded by Christian believers. When asked in the archival interviews in 1982 how he selected his cabinet, he replied:

"If I had a choice between two people with comparable qualifications other than the spiritual dimension – experience, knowledge of the area, and so on – and one was a committed Christian and the other was totally disinterested in it, I would take the committed Christian every time. . . . I would pick him first every time because he has the additional dimension that the other one lacks." Christian denomination is not the prime concern, he added. "What's really important is, what is the individual's relationship at heart with God and Jesus Christ?"

Today, Preston Manning's lone Reform Party MP is Deborah Grey, a fervent evangelical Christian recruited to run in a 1989 byelection in the Alberta riding of Beaver River. Manning and his father have tried to recruit other evangelicals to the cause. Most members of the party's executive council are Christian believers.

The family's deep suspicion of socialism springs in part from Social Credit conspiracy theory, itself rooted in a complex mix of prophetic religion and Social Credit economics. There is a plot to take over world finances, the reasoning goes, so all centralized planning is susceptible to control by the members of this conspiracy. The conspirators (often the "money lords" in collaboration with international Communism, both manifestations of the anti-Christ) caused the Depression and inspired plans for universal social programs after the Second World War.

Ernest Manning showed clearly that he believed this conspiracy theory when he said, just before the war ended: "Social Crediters contend, backed by evidence, that this defective system is being deliberately imposed on the people by men who control our monetary system for the purpose of gaining supreme power – that their objective is world dictatorship."

The prime role of government, in the Manning view, is to preserve the individual's freedom to find salvation. The result will be a humane, well-ordered Christian society where more and more "free and creative individuals" are able to find salvation. A genuine impulse to public service emerges from the Mannings' religious thought, but it rests upon a foundation of self-interest. Done in the proper spirit of humility and devotion to God, politics will help to get them into heaven.

The natural way of achieving such Christian freedom, the Mannings believe, is to place as much power as possible in private hands, safely out of the reach of any bureaucrat. Preston Manning's religiously inspired political agenda, like his father's, is profoundly anti-government and anti-centralist. He will take as many functions as he can manage away from government, and shift as much of the remaining power as possible from Ottawa to the provinces. There are many vivid examples of these thrusts in Reform Party policy today, but two of the most striking are the party's stands on medicare and privatization.

The Reform Party, as Preston Manning often says, is not stupid. Therefore it does not openly propose to dismantle medicare. But the party's official policy could very well bring exactly that result. This policy calls for Ottawa to turn over all authority for medicare to the provinces. Federal funding "should be unconditional and recognize different levels of economic development in the provinces," the policy states.

Preston Manning freely admits that this policy will lead to checkerboard medicare. Under the party's system, he says, Alberta might choose to have user fees for medical service, while Saskatchewan, the first home of medicare, would probably decide against it. When Manning made this point during a town hall meeting in Calgary Southwest in June 1991, he did not suggest that there was any problem with such differences.

Furthermore, nothing in the wording of Reform Party medicare policy precludes an eventual return to private medical insurance. It speaks only of "ensuring that adequate health-care insurance and services are available to every Canadian" – wording that applies just as well to private insurance as it does to today's government-run systems.

It is worth remembering that Ernest Manning fought a fierce battle against the introduction of all national social programs, including medicare. In 1965, with Ottawa preparing to act on medicare, he declared: "To those who want to see a free society preserved in Canada, the proposed . . . program is a direct challenge to individual liberty and responsibility." As an alternative to a state-run plan, he proposed that governments subsidize private insurance policies. Individuals, he noted, would be responsible for buying those policies – just as they are in the United States today. At the time Ernest Manning fought those battles, his son was already deeply involved in shaping his tactics and goals.

The Reform Party's 1991 privatization policy shows equally clear marks of Preston Manning's deep devotion to trimming government and ending centralization. It states that all Crown corporations should be placed where they can work best, and "We believe that there is overwhelming evidence that this would be the private sector in the vast majority of cases." The policy *Blue Book* calls for total privatization of Petro Canada and Canada Post, adding that "there should be no restrictions on private competition in the delivery of mail."

Preston Manning's political goals are very clear. He wants a society of widely dispersed power centres with most institutions and functions in private hands, safe from any collectivist conspiracy. He wants each individual to be free to find the Mannings' Christian God. Ideally, he would like each person to provide for the major part of his or her basic needs, including key social services and medicare. He wants the influence of Ottawa drastically cut and transferred to the provinces. Ultimately, even much of that decentralized power would devolve into the private sector. Elected politicians would oversee small governments whose role would be to manage publicly funded enterprises, but not to operate them.

Manning's basic political ideas have not changed since those days of intellectual ferment in the late 1960s. Like his father, he feels that political values are rooted in the eternal order, the struggle between good and evil. The mechanics of policy may change, but the vehicle is universal and serviced by the Almighty.

CHAPTER FOUR

SOLDIER OF GOD

"There stands in your midst one whom you know not."
– Ernest Manning on "Canada's National Bible Hour."

IN PRESTON MANNING'S life, evangelical Protestant religion is the first thing of all things, the source of his attitudes, beliefs, goals, and dreams. Politics is not an end in itself, but the road God has set him upon in this world: his calling, his path to personal salvation, his way of serving the Almighty. He is here on earth to earn his place in heaven and to take as many of us with him as he can manage. This religious impulse lies behind everything he stands for, from his fierce belief in capitalism to his deeply conservative views on welfare and the role of women. That fundamentalist religion has often led some adherents (although not him) into dark and nasty side alleys of intolerance, especially anti-Semitism.

Preston Manning, alone among Canada's major political leaders, believes that the world can end at any moment with the physical return of Jesus, that every corpse in every grave on earth will rise up, alive again, to face Christ and hear His judgement, that the saved will go to heaven and the damned will burn forever in hell. These truths are not laid down in any earthly constitution, but in the Bible – and the entire Bible, as his Calgary church insists, is "verbally inspired by God" and "a complete revelation of His will for the salvation of men."

Manning learned this religion during a peculiar time in western and Canadian history, when his father held power in Alberta through a potent mix of Christianity and Social Credit politics. The elder Manning became premier in 1943 following the death of his mentor, Premier William "Bible Bill" Aberhart, a thundering preacher who made little distinction between Alberta's secular and religious thrones, and occupied both for eight years.

Growing up as the son of a premier who was also the most revered religious leader in western Canada, the young Manning learned respectful obedience and acceptance, not rebellion or independent thought. He did not kick up his heels even in the rebellious 1960s, his time at the University of Alberta in Edmonton. Today there is virtually no dividing line between his religious views and those held by his father.

For many years, in fact, Preston Manning repeated and supported his father's views on "Canada's National Bible Hour," the fundamentalist radio show (begun by Aberhart in the 1920s as the "Back to the Bible Hour", and continued by Ernest Manning). Until 1988 Preston Manning preached on such subjects as faith and business, faith and politics, faith and science, and faith and conflict resolution. Many listeners found that they could barely distinguish the son's nasal voice from his father's.

The show is still on the air with Ernest Manning preaching twice a month. In a typical radio sermon in July 1991, the elder Manning warns listeners to prepare for an age of the anti-Christ "for which secular humanism and apostate religion even now are preparing the way." Then he adds: "The people of a distressed and perplexed world society will mistakenly think he's the superman they need to resolve the world's problems and bring in a new world order of stability and peace.

"It won't bother them that he's a Satanist, and that Satan is the source of his wisdom and power. By that time Satanic New Age philosophy will have conditioned people to regard Satanism as progressive thinking, and they will willingly join the anti-Christ in his idolatry."

The Canadian signs of this looming disaster, in Ernest Manning's telling, include much of the Reform Party's list of national problems: "A quarter of the people want to separate from the rest of the country. Government costs, both provincially and federally, are out of control. Crushing debt and taxation are stifling our economic growth and threatening the social security of our people. Regional alienation, political instability, and public disenchantment are destroying our national unity and national pride. We are in many respects a nation in distress."

With a final, emotional appeal, Ernest Manning tells his listeners how to find peace from these woes and many worse: "O men and women, be wise. There is only one person in whom you can put your trust with absolute confidence that He will do exceeding abundantly above all you can ask or think. There stands in your midst one whom you know not. That one is the Lord Jesus Christ, the divine resurrected Son of God . . . He loves you. That's why He died for you on the Cross."

Ernest Manning has been forecasting the end of the world for years, often with courageous precision. In 1937 the elder Manning told a meeting of the Edmonton Prophetic Bible Conference to be ready for the Second Coming very soon. "Surely it can't be much longer before the Lord himself must descend from heaven," he said. "This is what I say may take place in the coming year. The stage is so completely set that surely it can't be left longer." The evidence leading to this apocalyptic conclusion was "world-wide deception, social and moral degeneracy, centralization of power, worldliness, and despising of God's provenance." The inaccuracy of the predictions did not appear to disappoint much.

Whether the world was in a depression or a world war, Manning's mostly rural listeners well understood natural disasters beyond their control. At any time an "act of God" could destroy a promising farm crop and bring a farmer to ruin. Reassurance of a happier world beyond was a powerful comfort. Today listeners all across Canada still tune in to hear the prophecies of this remarkably powerful preacher.

Ernest Manning implanted these views in his two sons, Keith and Preston, from the earliest age. He said in the archival interviews in 1982 that he used to tell them: "Your number one concern in life should be your personal relationship to Jesus Christ. He's the sovereign Lord of everyone. Settle that matter to start with. It'll do more to change your life and stabilize your life than any single thing you can do. When you've done that, when you want to be something or do something, that's good. Ambition's a wonderful thing – feed it, nurture it, use it, apply it. But in the process, don't barge off on your own. Just keep that other factor in mind: Is this what God wants me to do?"

As a model Christian son, Preston Manning took the advice deeply to heart. He now seems to see himself as a kind of Christian guerrilla working in a corrupt, secular world. Reflecting in 1989 on the role of a Christian in modern politics, he told Alberta journalist Paul de Groot for an article in *Faith Today* magazine:

"There's a continuum. At one end is to be completely out of it and isolated. At the other end is to be unequally yoked with corruption and unbelievers, and all of the rest. Somewhere in between is to be in the world but not of it, to be in the system but not swallowed up by the system. I really think that is the scriptural position, the position to which Christians are directed, to be the salt and the light. It is possible to function in the system, in the business system, the political system, and not compromise your beliefs or your values or your integrity to the degree that you can't be effective and shouldn't be there."

Preston Manning grows guarded and suspicious when asked to discuss his beliefs with people whose Christian credentials are suspect. Asked about his faith in an interview with one of the authors, he said only: "It plays a role, not in setting policy, but it plays a role personally. What you are is a lot of what you believe. My own personal life is affected by those beliefs." He was equally vague when he responded to the party's questionnaire for candidates. Describing his values and motivation, he says that "relationships constitute the essence of life", and the most important of those is "one's relationship with God."

Ernest Manning was more revealing in the unpublished 1982 interviews when he described a series of talks his son gave on "Canada's National Bible Hour." Preston Manning used the symbol of the cross, "A vertical shaft and a horizontal shaft. . . . Your vertical shaft – man's relationship with his God – [is] the up and down relationship . . . The horizontal one reaches out to the neighbour on either side." In the theology of the Manning family, there has always been an obligation to help people on earth so that they can find their way to heaven.

Those beliefs are utterly clear in the Calgary church now attended by Preston Manning, his wife, Sandra, and their five children: the imposing First Alliance on Glenmore Trail. "We believe the Bible," says executive pastor Gerald Fowler, one of eight pastors at First Alliance, which has an average Sunday attendance of more than 1,100. "We believe it is inerrant, that it was inspired by God through the superintending of the Holy Spirit, and that it was written by men, but it was written under the inspiration of God, and that it is without error. . . . We believe in Christ, we believe that He came, that He lived on this earth, that He died, that He rose again, that He ascended to be with his father, and we believe that He will return."

A Statement of Faith issued by the Christian and Missionary Alliance is more vivid. It states that "The Second Coming of the Lord Jesus Christ is imminent and will be personal, visible, and premillennial. . . . There will be a bodily resurrection of the just and of the unjust; for the former, a resurrection unto life; for the latter, a resurrection unto judgment." The statement also endorses faith healing through "prayer for the sick and anointing with oil."

The church began in the U.S. in the last century, and until 1981 its Canadian wing was run out of the U.S. headquarters in Colorado Springs, Colorado. Federal government pressure to pay Canadian missionaries with Canadian funds prompted the administrative split, but there are no doctrinal differences. "We have exactly the same beliefs," said a spokesperson at Canadian headquarters in Willowdale, Ont. Teams of Canadian and U.S. missionaries often head overseas together.

This church divides the world clearly into two classes, the saved and the unsaved. One U.S. brochure targets for early salvation seven million Asian Americans, whose "Inventiveness equals Yankee ingenuity; their work ethic matches hard-driving, honest-working American values. . . . But they share a common characteristic: non-Christian religions. More than 95 per cent of Asian Americans have absolutely no knowledge of Christ." To make a difference, the literature advises, "PRAY that the Lord will lead you to contact Asian people. LOOK for Asian restaurants and shops."

Another pamphlet focuses on the lost souls in the Mediterranean Basin countries, including Spain, France, and (with less geographic precision) England and West Germany. The people in these lands "know little about Jesus. Instead they embrace humanistic philosophies, Communism, materialism, and pleasure-seeking ideologies. Demonic influence through thousands of mediums is prevalent. Superstition is rampant. Eastern cults and Islam spread."

The Gulf War was a fine model for the church, suggests the president of the U.S. Christian and Missionary Alliance, one David L. Rambo. In his 1991 annual report, Rambo likens his church to the military coalition that won a decisive victory over Iraq. "The coalition stood firm, its cohesion consisting of one basic ingredient: a common cause. . . . [The church's] common cause continues to this very day, embedded in our very name: The Christian and Missionary *Alliance*. . . . While the world heaps honors on the victorious allied nations of the Gulf War, we sing God's praises and express thanks to His people for what our coalition of faith has achieved." The only tragedies Rambo mentions in his report are not those of war, but "the continuing tragedy of closed or non-growing churches."

Preston Manning's branch of this church, housed in a sprawling, modernistic brick building, features relentlessly upbeat services and messages. Elders and ushers, all male, greet families at the front and rear doors with friendly handshakes and welcomes. Even the huge parking lot is part of the determined marketing effort; it has special spaces for "first-time visitors." Inside, husbands lead wives and children down the aisles to the pews. Every important public function, it seems, is performed by men, and virtually everyone in the congregation is white. At one service in July 1991, the only non-white in evidence was a black woman who strode to the front to sing Gospel hymns, her powerful voice booming through a sound system as crisp and professional as anything at a rock concert. The backup came from a skilled little band with guitar, piano, and drums. In the choir most Sundays is Sandra Manning, known to her friend Ingrid Speaker as "a beautiful vocalist and musician."

The highlight of the July service was a talk by Kevin Jenkins, the Calgary-based president of Canadian Airlines International. Jenkins, an energetic, confident man, described how he began to find Christ when a business friend gave him a book by Chuck Colson, the U.S. Watergate conspirator who found born-again religion while he was in jail. Jenkins said he was impressed and began to take Bible study classes one day a week. He was truly convinced later when he heard Colson speak in Edmonton, and now he finds "abundant life by surrendering to Jesus."

The whole operation at First Alliance is high-powered and high tech, the farthest thing possible from a little neighbourhood church with a lone aging pastor and an amateurish organist. This production would fit nicely into a U.S.-style mega-church. (Indeed, one pastor speaks admiringly of his visit to a Chicago church with a congregation of 16,000.) Yet there is also the unconditional warmth and friendliness of people who intend to love their neighbours, all of them, against any odds.

The Christian and Missionary Alliance is an evangelical denomination with 1,856 churches and 279,000 members in the U.S alone. Around the world, including Canada, there are 12,438 churches and congregations which support 1,246 missions in 38 countries. The Calgary First Alliance is one of the biggest. Many congregations number fewer than 100, and in some areas the church is concerned about declining attendance.

It isn't quite what Manning grew up in; he had always attended Baptist churches in Edmonton. But when Manning moved in 1990 to Calgary, the Reform Party headquarters, the choice of a new family church was important, and perhaps not entirely spiritual.

"They searched out where there was an active youth group and where there were things that would be best for their kids," said Ingrid Speaker. They were also looking for a school for their two sons, Nathan and David (they were 13 and 11 in the spring of 1991). The Mannings hit upon Glenmore Christian Academy, a private school controlled by the First Alliance Church with participation by other fundamentalist denominations. The school teaches the Alberta school curriculum to Grade 9, supplemented by a heavy measure of evangelical theology.

The First Alliance Church is also one of the largest in the sprawling area of Calgary Southwest, where Manning will run in the next federal election, probably against hapless Tory incumbent Bobbie Sparrow. His presence at First Alliance certainly isn't making him enemies among influential parishioners such as Jenkins and Bob Kinnie, who is chairman, president, and chief executive officer of Canada Safeway Ltd., the supermarket empire. (The Reform

Party's 1990 disclosure of contributors shows that a Robert Kinnie, CEO, gave $3,000.)

Manning attends as often as his schedule allows and speaks when he can, says Pastor Ray Matheson. At one breakfast talk, the pastor recalls, "He spoke about how so much of his life had been as a mediator in disputes in regard to the oilfields. He saw Christianity as human beings and God being in a dispute and Jesus Christ as the mediator. He did a beautiful job of giving the core of the Gospel message." The pastor offered to send a tape of the talk to the authors if Manning approved, but it never arrived.

Manning made much the same point in a 1990 interview with Ian Pearson for *Saturday Night* magazine. "The evangelical Christian's understanding of the Gospel was that it was a story about reconciliation of conflicting interests on a profound scale," he said. "How do God and man get reconciled? I studied that from a theological standpoint. I tried to see if there's any application of those principles that are in the Christian Gospel to conflict resolution in other areas. Ultimately, it's a story of conflict resolution on a much more profound level than politicians will ever be able to do. Compromising isn't enough." Ernest Manning has often made this point, that humans need divine help to reconcile their differences.

Nobody who knows Preston Manning doubts that his religious beliefs are sincere. He is not obvious about them; he does not drop his head to say grace at business lunches or try to win a convert every day. In his party disclosure statement he said: "I do not seek to impose my religious or political views on others, although I defend the right to hold and express one's deepest convictions and to seek to persuade others of their validity and relevance."

That is a fair statement of how Manning conducts his spiritual life in public, but it doesn't begin to reflect the overwhelming importance of religion to his whole being. A man who believes Christ may return to earth at any moment cares a great deal about God's opinion, perhaps not so much about that of the voters. His values are eternal, or so he believes, and his policies (although slightly more flexible, being worldly) are based upon those values. Reformers like to say that they will do exactly what their constituents demand or they will resign from office. Preston Manning, however, is governed by God, not by Gallup. Dr. Charles Hobart, a University of Alberta sociology professor who has worked with Manning, says it best: "For the Mannings, the bedrock at the deepest level is religion."

The roots of these beliefs go back a long way, to one powerful man. The Manning family owes its politics and religion largely to William "Bible Bill" Aberhart, an Ontario high-school teacher who moved from Brantford to Calgary in 1910, and became Premier of Alberta in 1935. All his life, Aberhart was querulous, dogmatic, and difficult, a man who left discord and division behind him at churches and schools and in government. "Aberhart was involved in more religious controversy, strife and schism than any other person in western Canada," say David R. Elliott and Iris Miller in their recent biography, *Bible Bill*. Even John Barr, a friendly chronicler of Social Credit, called him "a strong leader but a poor follower, a confident pilot but a fractious, quarrelsome and sometimes rebellious crew member."

He did not pass his early life in the warm religious cocoon some writers have portrayed. Elliott and Miller report that soon after Aberhart arrived in Calgary he received word that his father had died by accident. It happened because William Sr., a bit of a drinker, was in the habit of visiting his son Charles' hardware store in Seaforth, Ont., for a nip. Huron County was officially dry at the time, so the son always left a bottle on a certain shelf to ensure that his father could get a drink whenever he liked. This time, though, a new clerk had switched the bottles, and William Sr. downed a swig of deadly carbolic acid by mistake. (He could not have read the label because he was illiterate.) He ran across the street to the doctor's office, but was dead within minutes.

William Jr., who was awaiting the arrival of his wife and children in Calgary, did not return to Ontario for the funeral. His father's bizarre exit from the world probably cemented Aberhart's distaste for alcohol and sinfulness of all kinds. His absence from the funeral also suggests that the young man, who had been keenly religious since his teens, must have felt deep conflicts within his family.

Aberhart had many qualities of genius. His memory and powers of organization were astounding, and few who met or heard him escaped the pull of his magnetic personality. One school colleague called him "a great noise and a great light. In his presence, one felt as if one were near a magnesium flare." By the 1920s his religious radio show, an entirely new form of home entertainment, was attracting zealous converts to Aberhart's crystal-clear revivalist religion. His booming delivery and bombastic oratory suited the new medium perfectly. Thousands of Canadians still remember that nasal voice reaching out of the radio as if to grasp the listener's very soul. "You had to have your guard up or he could get you; he was a marvellous speaker," recalls Rev. Ed Checkland of the University of Alberta.

One of the listeners was young Ernest Manning, a Saskatchewan farm boy who first heard an Aberhart broadcast in 1925. By the fall of 1927 he was the first pupil lined up to enroll at the master's new Prophetic Bible Institute in Calgary. In the 1982 archival interview, Manning Sr. described how he fiddled with a new radio and found a new life.

"You'd sit up often till 2:00 o'clock in the morning with a set of [headphones] clamped on your head, twirling these dials, trying to see how many stations you could pick up. . . . On a nice clear winter night you could get them all the way down to California and all over. So tinkering around this way one Sunday, I picked up this broadcast from Calgary that Mr. Aberhart started that fall of 1925. That was responsible for changing the whole course of my life. I had no particular plans in life up to that time; I certainly had no intention of coming to Alberta. . . . Our home was a nominal Christian home, but I had never realized the reality of a Christian conversion and there being more than just a religious theory or religious belief – something that made a vital change in your life.

"Well, it was through listening to Mr. Aberhart's Biblical expositions that I realized that . . . the whole core of genuine Christianity was that Christ had in very truth been resurrected from the dead, that He was alive, that He was divine and was prepared to enter into a relationship with people if they were prepared to receive him . . . which I did to the best of my knowledge at the time, and brought about a complete transformation in my life."

If Ernest Manning had been a bit aimless before that, afterward he would be Aberhart's loyal earthly disciple until the older man's death in 1943. In religious matters Manning still follows Aberhart as if his imposing mentor, a huge man, were still at his side, towering over him.

At school and church Aberhart was often a hard master. Elliot and Miller say that he ran his classroom "much like an army camp. He assigned each of his students a three-digit number by which he addressed them rather than by name, and stamped their assignments with a rubber stamp that read 'checked by Wm. Aberhart.' Some students appreciated Aberhart's teaching methods, but others hated them. With recalcitrant students he had no patience; for slight misdemeanors he is said to have doled out strappings on Monday, Wednesday and Friday." He would sometimes strap his two daughters, Ola and Khona, for violating household rules, after giving them a stern lecture. Yet he was inspirational too. In 1922 he told his students at Crescent Heights High School: "Remember, where one man succeeds through Pull, there are ninety-nine who succeed through PUSH."

Aberhart was almost unbelievably energetic. Besides raising a family, playing soccer, and devoting long hours to his job as principal at a succession of schools, he spent much of his extra time at an even longer string of churches. He finally settled on one, Westbourne Baptist, that he was able to control (although there was controversy there, too, about his dogmatic beliefs). Remarkably, Aberhart dominated every church he passed through even though he never became an ordained minister.

As a young man he hit upon a peculiar theology called "dispensationalism." To make sense of the inconveniently complex Bible, this system neatly divides human history into seven eras called dispensations. As Elliott and Miller explain: "In each dispensation God made a covenant with man, man broke the covenant, and judgment followed. Each time, man's failure to keep the covenant was of increased magnitude. In each period the regulations were somewhat different; therefore the key to understanding the Bible was to know which verses applied to which dispensation."

This must have appealed to Aberhart's urge to organize, categorize, and memorize. It also led him to the Scofield Bible, named for American preacher Cyrus Scofield, who produced a controversial annotated text that explained Scripture as dispensations. Aberhart wrote: "It was Dr. Scofield who started me on my Bible study. He advertised a Correspondence Course of some fourteen lessons for $5.00. I sent for it and his first four lessons started me off so that I knew how to study. . . . He placed me on a path that has proved more bright as the days go by." Aberhart was a self-educated theologian who trained himself by absorbing ready-made answers. This may explain why he had so little knack for debate and even less for compromise.

By 1926, with his radio show booming, Aberhart was determined to create a Bible college dedicated to his beliefs. He raised money zealously, and in 1927 the Prophetic Bible Institute opened in downtown Calgary. The students, including Ernest Manning, were exhorted to lead lives "of separation from all harmful and spiritually degrading pursuits and worldly affairs such as the moving picture show, the theatre, the dance, and any similar carnal institutions which tend to lower moral standards and destroy the Christian influence of a pure life."

The official doctrine of the college included the "absolute supremacy, infallibility and efficiency" of the Bible, as well as: "The creation of man in holiness, by the direct act of God and not by an evolutionary process; the historicity and terrible reality of the fall of man and the resulting total and universal depravity of human nature. . . . The everlasting happiness of the righteous and the awful and everlasting misery of the unbelieving wicked, in a literal lake of fire, prepared for a real, personal Devil and his angels. . . . " Institute textooks reviled modernism, Roman Catholicism, and all forms of skepticism. Humans in general (even the Institute students, one presumes) were "vile and detestable and lustful." The Institute promised to answer the great questions of the day, including whether the whale really swallowed Jonah, and if the world truly began on Oct. 23, 4,004 B.C., at 9:00 a.m. (Eastern Standard Time), as Bishop Usher had calculated.

John Barr reports that Ernest Manning, the most devoted student of all, had a sense of humour about this. "For years, when vexed by another driver cutting him off in traffic, he would say dryly, 'There goes the accumulated consequences of 6,000 years of human depravity.'" Aberhart, however, had little sense of humour and there is no evidence that Manning, laugh as he might, rejected any of his teachings.

Aberhart's fierce crusade for absolute and total belief in the Bible was part of a much wider conflict, and an extremely bitter one. At that time many Protestant denominations were sending college-educated "modernist" ministers to head churches all over rural Canada. According to William E. Mann in *Sect, Cult and Church in Alberta*, these new preachers deeply offended farm folk by talking over their heads most of the time, and saying things considered blasphemous the rest. The modernists questioned the literal truth of the

Bible by arguing that science casts new light on Scripture, and by hinting that Christ was a mere man who did not rise from the dead. They suggested that the Bible was not an infallible road map to life and the universe, just a series of helpful hints for living a worthy life.

The debate raised furious emotions all across Canada and the U.S., especially in rural areas. This was the time of the famous 1925 Scopes Monkey Trial in the U.S., which pitted William Jennings Bryan, a former candidate for president, against famed defence lawyer Clarence Darrow. Half the world turned its attention to the ordeal of a Tennessee teacher, John T. Scopes, who had taught evolution on a dare to test a new anti-evolution law in the state. Bryan offered his services as prosecutor, calling the trial "a duel to the death" between Christianity and evolution. It turned instead into a tragi-comic showdown between Bryan, the unswerving fundamentalist, and Darrow, the wily atheist. Bryan fell into a trap by agreeing to appear on the stand as an expert on the Bible, and by the last day even his followers in the courtroom were laughing derisively at his contradictions. Scopes was convicted, but fundamentalism lost the symbolic struggle.

The same battle was being fought day by day in church halls across Canada. It was a struggle between modernism and fundamentalism, between skeptical science and unquestioning faith, between the more sophisticated city dwellers and unschooled rural people, between young city-trained ministers and older rural congregations. In Alberta, the Jehovah's Witnesses even organized marches to express hostility against townspeople, and several of these strange parades reached the town of Leduc, south of Edmonton.

Aberhart aimed his Institute straight at the modernists. One of its goals was "to use every legitimate Christian means of combatting and resisting Modernism, Higher Criticism, Skepticism, and Secretarianism in all its forms." An Institute bulletin charged that "many of the theological seminaries or colleges are disseminating modernism and infidelity. . . ."

The two sides of this dispute, modernism and fundamentalism, were to spawn the most vital Canadian political movements of the 1930s. The Co-operative Commonweath Federation, led in Manitoba and Saskatchewan by J.S. Woodsworth (a Methodist minister) and then Tommy Douglas (a Baptist preacher), would spread the Social Gospel, which gave religious significance to erasing the ills of society. Social Credit, led first by Aberhart and then by Manning, Baptists of another kind, would battle this "socialism and modernism" with all their force. They believed that the world is just a temporary thing. Their role, in religion and politics, was to snatch souls from the jaws of hell and send them safely to heaven.

Today most Canadians have forgotten these battles or consider them less relevant than they were. Not Ernest Manning: He fights with the same vigour, using the same arguments and slogans, as he did 50 years ago. To those with long memories, even his voice is an exact echo of Aberhart's. Preston Manning reflects every thought of Ernest Manning's so precisely that his public voice sounds almost identical to his father's, and very much like Aberhart's, even though the great man died when he was less than a year old.

Aberhart was in some ways an accidental politician. Although a very political animal, he was for many years almost oblivious to political life outside the church. He was interested only in the education of children and the saving of souls for Christ. Again there is no evidence that Ernest Manning, in his eight years as student and then employee at the Prophetic Bible Institute, differed in any significant way. Manning says even today that he was never very interested in politics, only in solving people's problems.

John Barr notes: "As a single-minded religious activist and school principal on secure tenure and salary, Aberhart was slow to personally feel the Depression's pinch." Nevertheless, as the 1930s began, "Students and former students began to come to him and tell him about their troubles at home, and their difficulty finding work. Many out-of-work men came to Aberhart for personal loans. Several children fainted in class at Crescent Heights; they admitted to Aberhart it was from hunger . . . one of his young Grade 12 pupils became despondent and committed suicide."

Through an acquaintance in Edmonton, Aberhart heard about a doctrine called Social Credit developed by a Scottish engineer named Clifford Hugh Douglas. The ingenious Douglas argued that enough goods were produced in capitalist society to satisfy every need, but people did not have the means to purchase those goods. This shortage of buying power was the cause of the Depression: and the reason for the entire problem, in Douglas's view, was the exploitation of the international banking and credit system dominated by a Jewish conspiracy.

Aberhart rode Social Credit doctrine and his own immense popularity to victory in the 1935 Alberta provincial election. Ernest Manning, at 26 the youngest person elected to a Canadian legislature, became his deputy premier. Aberhart's version of Social Credit, especially his promise of a $25 monthly credit dividend for most Albertans, was irresistible at a time when thousands were going hungry in the midst of plenty. For many years Alberta was famous around the world as the only home of a Social Credit government. One day in 1937, news wire services sent out 35,000 words about Aberhart and his movement. Aberhart's radio show often attracted 300,000 listeners in Canada and the U.S. Social Credit, which began as a genuine populist storm, would run Alberta until 1971, when Peter Lougheed's Tories finally chased it from office.

As Elliott and Miller recount in *Bible Bill*, controversy followed Aberhart everywhere because of his authoritarian actions. The premier's first attorney-general, as he resigned from the party and his cabinet post, called the premier "a Teutonic dictator," a megalomaniac and the most sadistic man he had ever met. Aberhart responded by cancelling the minister's expense account for a recent government trip. The premier so feared open debate that he did not speak in the legislature for his first three and one half years in office. Instead, he spoke directly to the public through his radio broadcasts.

Aberhart's most famous and controversial move was to pass the Accurate News and Information Act, which required every newspaper to print verbatim any statement issued by the chairman of the Social Credit Board. Papers could be made to reveal in writing the names and addresses of all sources and of journalists who wrote articles or editorials. Any newspaper that refused could be shut down or fined $1,000 a day. Don Brown, a reporter for the *Edmonton Journal*, was arrested on a charge of misquoting a backbencher, subjected to trial on the floor of the legislature, convicted, and sentenced to jail. By this time, however, public outrage at the government's measures was growing and the sentence was dropped just before Brown went to jail. The government quietly backed away from regulating the defiant papers. A Pulitzer Prize, the only one ever given in Canada, was awarded to the *Journal*, and citations went to the *Calgary Herald*, the *Calgary Albertan*, the *Edmonton Bulletin*, the *Medicine Hat News*, and 90 weekly newspapers. During the dispute many papers compared Aberhart to Adolf Hitler.

Aberhart always justified such actions by saying they were counter-attacks on the eastern banks and their lackeys. This attitude led to one of the darkest episodes of the whole Social Credit era.

One day in 1937, Conservative leader David Duggan told the legislature that he had seen a pamphlet calling him and other prominent government opponents "banker's toadies." It read in part: "My child, you should NEVER say hard or unkind things about Bankers' Toadies. God made Bankers' Toadies just as He made snakes, slugs, snails and other creepy-crawly, treacherous and poisonous things. Never, therefore, abuse them – just exterminate them!"

Elliott and Miller recount that after complaints were lodged, police raided the headquarters of the Social Credit League and seized 7,000 copies of the pamphlet. Party whip Joe Unwin and George F. Powell, Major Douglas's personal representative, were charged with defamatory libel and counselling to murder. At the sensational trial which followed, it was revealed that the government had paid for the pamphlets through order-in-council. They were then distributed under a fictitious party name, the United Democrats. Both men were eventually sentenced to six months at hard labour. Aberhart, by now his own attorney-general, often criticized the sentences on his radio show and urged people to appeal to Prime Minister Mackenzie King for clemency. The only checks on dictatorship in Alberta, it sometimes seemed, were the institutions that Aberhart came to hate: the Supreme Court, the office of the lieutenant-governor, the federal justice system, and the free press.

Social Credit had another persistent dark side. For a very long time – far too long – the provincial movement, as well as the national Social Credit party that sent many MPs to Ottawa, was tainted by virulent anti-Semitism. Fundamentalist religion, combined with a conspiratorial theory of economics, gave rise in many followers to a deep suspicion of Jews.

Douglas's anti-Semitism, relatively dormant in the early 1930s, became rampant with the rise of Nazi Germany. He accepted the forged "Protocols of the Elders of Zion" as true and claimed that Jews were "protagonists of collectivism in all its forms." In 1946, with millions of Jews already dead in Europe, his British *Social Crediter* newsletter argued for a solution to "the collective problem of racial and political Judaism," which was defined as "an occult, pyramidal organization more nearly resembling the ruling party in Russia at the moment than anything else visible." The *Canadian Social Crediter*, published in Edmonton by the Alberta party, repeated and amplified many of these absurd claims. In the issue of December 11, 1947, for instance, one writer railed against "American-Jewish finance, said to be the most powerful arm of Jewish finance."This anti-Semitism was fomented by loyal followers of Major Douglas in the Canadian movement, and it produced deep discord.

Aberhart and then Manning, to their credit, fought the more vicious strains of this poison. They held the fundamentalist Christian view that the Jews are God's chosen holy people whose reassembling in Israel will signal the return of Christ. Both made public gestures of tolerance and denounced anti-Semitism. When Douglas called Jews "parasites" in 1938, Aberhart disowned him in a statement to the Alberta press. In 1947 Manning lost patience with the Douglas-inspired anti-Semites on the board of the *Canadian Social Crediter*, and sent in one of his lieutenants, Drumheller MLA Gordon Taylor, to fire the whole lot.

In the archival interviews in 1982, Ernest Manning gave a fascinating account of the conflict:

"In Douglas's assessment of the world monetary monopoly, he argued in his books that these were mostly Jews. Jews have had a prominent role in the financial field. One of the things, for example, that used to be talked about quite a bit in those days by so-called Douglasites was the Protocols of the Wise Men of Zion. . . .

"This is a thesis that purports to be a world plan by the Wise Men of Zion, the Jewish leaders, for taking over the control of the world. . . . I've read them; I've never felt they were authentic myself. But this kind of thing was quoted. And among the Douglasites, even in the Social Credit Party, there were quite a lot of them that used to put a lot of stock in these Protocols of the Wise Men of Zion.

"One time in the House I made a speech repudiating this thing. I said, 'This is the viewpoint of individuals; it is *not* the position of the government, it is not the viewpoint of the Social Credit movement in Alberta. It never has been, and it never will be.' And I pointed out that in any political party you could find anti-Semites. There was nothing peculiar about the Social Credit party . . . there isn't a political party in existence that doesn't have somebody that's anti-Semitic, or anti-Catholic, or anti-something. But it's grossly unfair for somebody to say that that is the position of the party."

And yet, undeniably, there *was* something very peculiar about Social Credit. Alone among successful elected parties of the time, its main publication spouted anti-Semitism. Some of the movement's MPs in Ottawa, notably Norman Jaques, made anti-Semitic declarations in the House of Commons. (In 1943 Jaques tried to read parts of the Protocols into the record, but was stopped by the Speaker.) Aberhart, although he disavowed anti-Semitism, did not put a halt to its expression in the movement's publication. And Ernest Manning was premier for nearly four years, from 1943 to 1947, before he moved against the Douglasites.

Scholars have spotted in some of Aberhart's utterances the very attitude he claimed to oppose. In a letter to a Jewish Social Crediter, for instance, he said: "You will really see that I am bitterly opposed to anti-Semitism. . . ." Yet later he added: "What surprises me is the inability of some splendid fellows, who are Jewish by birth, to discern the people who are opposed to them. . . . You must surely be aware that much of the persecution in other lands is due to the oppression by members of your own race."

Some of Ernest Manning's statements carry an equally peculiar flavour. He told the Alberta legislature in a speech in 1939: "The public utterances of men directly associated with the inner working of financial affairs are being pondered by a thinking public today as never before. People are wondering just what the noted Baron Rothschild meant when he said, 'Permit me to control the credit of a country, and I care not who makes its laws.'"

In the 1982 archival interview, Manning made the connection more directly. When the interviewer asked why the issue of anti-Semitism kept coming up, he said:

"I think the reason for that is that so much of the Social Credit philosophy zeroed in on monetary reform. This takes you right back to who controls the monetary system of the world. There's no denying that the Rothschilds and others were prominent Jewish bankers. . . .

"The old-line parties, for example, that hardly ever talk about anything monetary, have no association with things of that kind. If any of the parties were zeroing in on international finance, they couldn't help but say, somewhere along the road, 'The Rothschilds are a good example of the families that control the monetary system of the world.' And immediately someone would say, 'Oh they're Jews. This is anti-Semitic.'" Manning went on to speak of his many good friends in Alberta's Jewish community, and how they never took the anti–Social Credit "propaganda" in the media seriously. The fact is that many Jews, although they trusted Manning personally, were deeply concerned.

At the very end of Social Credit's era on the national stage, anti-Semitism hounded the dying movement into oblivion. Jim Keegstra, not long after he was fired as a teacher in Eckville for telling his high-school students that the Holocaust never occurred, was elected a second vice-president of the national party. The leader, Martin J. Hattersley, fired Keegstra from this job too. Hattersley then dismissed two of Keegstra's supporters, Thomas Erhart and James Green. But at a later executive meeting the dismissals were overturned and Hattersley himself was forced to quit. As David Bercuson and Douglas Wertheimer observed in 1985 in *A Trust Betrayed*, "There is not much left of the federal Social Credit Party in Canada or in Alberta today, but what there is seems to be as anti-Semitic as Douglas Social Credit ever was."

Keegstra, whose conviction for spreading hatred was overturned by the Supreme Court of Canada, has been ordered to stand trial once more by the Alberta government. He once attended Aberhart's Prophetic Bible Institute in Calgary.

Without question, some of these attitudes have been handed along to the modern Reform Party, and some Jewish leaders are deeply suspicious of the party. Ron Ghitter, a former Alberta MLA, says he sees many of the same attitudes that he encountered when he chaired a provincial inquiry into Alberta's school system following the Keegstra affair.

"Basically what the Reform Party stands for makes me very nervous," says Ghitter, now a Calgary businessman. "I've seen the past practices of the Social Credit Party. I found [during the Committee hearings] that the same people kept coming forward with the same narrow-minded rhetoric which was based somewhat on evangelical religion, and based on a black and white notion of what the answers to the world really are. As a result I find groups of this nature very harsh on minority groups, on Jews, on people other than those who adhere to their beliefs. This type of attitude is implicit in the Reform Party. They see the world in black and white, they often see it in religious terms. . . . Implicit in their policies are attitudes which are negative to minority groups, certainly negative to Quebec, and certainly on the fringe of racism."

Preston Manning is so sensitive to these charges that in 1991 he began meeting Jewish groups to ease their fears, just as his father did many years earlier. He told one of the authors: "There's suspicion of a new party, particularly if it's one the media labels as right wing and extremist and populist, [that] it might have anti-Semitic or racist positions. . . . I understood their concern about that. I went through the steps that were taken to prevent that from ever happening to us. I go through the parts of our platform that might have some special appeal to Jewish people, like knocking racism out of the Canadian constitution.

"I have knowledge of this from my father's experience in the 30s, of the difficulty of once it ever takes root, of tearing it out. That's why I'm very interested in preventing it from ever taking hold or being a factor in the Reform Party. . . . I have run into people in the Jewish community who expressed this fear of anti-Semitism. When I asked them, 'Have you ever met any of the leadership of the Reform Party, have you ever read any of our stuff, have you been to any of our meetings?', they said no. I said, 'So where did you get this?' I told them, 'What you're doing is pre-judging a minority group, and isn't that what this is all about?'"

Manning does not deny that there are bigots in his party. "With a new party there's always a danger of people who hold extreme views of all kinds, including racial views, being attracted," he said. "We're taking some steps. We find the best protection against that is just our growth. The more we broaden out, the more these extreme people start to tail off. They're attracted to small open groups where a couple of strong people [can be influential]. But if you have a riding association with 1,500 or 2,000 members, well, these guys know they can't influence that so they tail off. So we're endeavouring to protect ourselves and the best way we can is through growth. And we're making sure our policy statements . . . are not coloured by those types of people."

Preston Manning, to judge him by his own history, statements, and beliefs, has just one hope for Jews. It is the same hope that he feels for all other humans on earth, whether they call themselves Hindus or Muslims, Buddhists or Taoists, atheists or agnostics. He wants them to accept his Jesus so that they will go to heaven. As the Reform Party leader goes about this work, he sees himself as moving among "corruption and unbelievers . . . in the world but not of it."

CHAPTER FIVE

POPULIST ON BAY STREET

"There must be something in the Bible against making money."
– Phillip Stuffco on his brother-in-law, Preston Manning

IN THE BOARDROOMS of corporate Canada, the Reform Party is still small potatoes – and small donations. Despite its image as a friend of business and a booster of free enterprise, corporate bosses are not yet writing the hefty cheques that mean real success in Canadian politics. In 1989 the party received only $141,000 in donations from business and commercial organizations, and in 1990 the total actually dropped to $138,000. The federal NDP received more ($141,500) even though it refuses most business donations. Almost all the Reform Party's revenue of $2.2 million in 1990 came via small donations from individuals. The Tories, by contrast, received $6.3 million from companies in 1990. In total donations, the traditional parties remained far ahead of the Reformers: the Tories received $11 million, the Liberals $12 million, and the New Democrats a whopping $15.4 million.

Most of the corporate political money is stashed in company headquarters in Ontario, and the Reformers did not exist there as a party until 1991. This surely tended to discourage donations. Nonetheless, Manning made one foray to Toronto in 1990 to see if the vault could be cracked despite this handicap. Media mogul

Conrad Black and financier Hal Jackman invited Manning to a dinner of the Toronto business and political elite, an appearance that aroused much suspicion among the populist loyalists back west. Populism is never very friendly to big business, and Manning's followers are no different. His father, after all, had once campaigned with Bible Bill Aberhart against Canada's "50 Big Shots," most of them in downtown Toronto.

A slightly larger group of big shots, 54, gathered at the posh Toronto Club to hear Manning give his New Canada pitch. "We'd ask voters to choose between the Old Canada and the New Canada," he told the crowd. "Old Canada is a Canada where governments chronically overspend and where there's a constitutional preoccupation with French and English relations. In New Canada, governments would be fiscally responsible and we'd go beyond French-English relations as the centrepiece of constitutional discussion." Ian Pearson, quoting these remarks in *Saturday Night* magazine, reported that the cigar-smoking dignitaries liked this mild prophet from the West, although they managed not to be overwhelmed.

Later Manning mailed a fund-raising solicitation to all the guests. One of Conrad Black's companies, Sterling Newspapers, contributed $5,000 to the Reform Party. The amounts were otherwise paltry, as the year-end results showed very clearly. In the right frame of mind, half the people in the room could have rounded up more than the party's corporate total for the entire year. "Capitalists are not feeling very generous," one of the guests that night observed a year later. They never are unless they see an advantage, and the Reform Party has not yet shown the influential decision-makers what their money can buy.

The Reformers are also competing on the same turf as Conservative and Liberal masters of the art of fund-raising. They have nobody with the experience or connections of Leo Kolber, the Liberal money man with a pipeline into the Bronfman empire, or

Tory fundraiser W. David Angus, who started finding money for Brian Mulroney in the 1970s. The Reformers are well aware of their weaknesses, however, and in September 1991 they began to act. They launched a major corporate fund-raising drive headed by their own money man, Calgary lawyer Cliff Fryers.

As the party's chairman and chief operating officer, the trim, intense Fryers is a familiar sight at Reform Party meetings. Things are looking up in the corporate world, he insisted in an interview with *The Financial Post Magazine.* Canadian Pacific Ltd. gave the party $25,000 in 1991 and other companies have begun to donate. The problem is, the companies which Fryers named are mainly Calgary-based oil firms. His real challenge is to get the serious money flowing from Toronto, since the other major source of federal political money in Canada, Montreal, will be virtually impossible to tap. Well-heeled anglophone federalists will not see much point in giving money to a party which invites Quebec to leave Canada and does not plan to run candidates in the province.

Manning himself knows some of the key players in western business, but he is almost unknown to the major figures in Ontario and Quebec. Although he spent 20 years in business as a consultant, he always seemed more interested in the job at hand than in status or the profits to be made. "There must be something in the Bible against making money," jokes Phillip Stuffco to his brother-in-law. With his connections and background, Manning probably could have cruised into the role of wealthy, high-flying entrepreneur. Yet the Manning clan has never been preoccupied with making money. Family comfort and well-being are important responsibilities, but in their universe, significant wealth hovers perilously close to sin.

Manning has little use for those obligatory trappings of successful modern business and politics: the lavish office, the mahogany desk, the oak-panelled conference room. His office at the party's headquarters in Calgary is almost ostentatiously spartan. During the days of M & M Systems Research Ltd. (later Manning

Consultants), he and his father seemed oblivious to their small, extremely modest quarters. While interviewing Ernest Manning at the company's Edmonton office in 1981 for the weekly *Alberta Business*, journalist Randy Hardisty was startled to find the former premier in such humble surroundings. "It just seemed out of place for somebody like that," recalls Hardisty. "You'd expect something grander. It was almost like walking into a warehouse office."

Preston Manning learned frugality from his father and it is the way he chooses to live and work. In restaurants, for example, he eats sparingly and leaves a standard tip of 10 per cent. This modesty extends to the family's political accomplishments. Baptist minister and University of Alberta professor Ed Checkland notes: "There are no monuments to Ernest Manning in Alberta. Why? He knows to whom he is responsible: to God. He has a sense of identity."

For the son of a former premier, Manning led an amazingly quiet, private life during more than two decades as a businessman. He was so seldom in the news, in fact, that when he went to Vancouver in May 1987 as an organizer of the first Reform meeting, the *Edmonton Journal* discovered that it did not have a recent photo of Preston Manning in its files. An editor had to chase around to his office on a Saturday morning to pry one out of a wary employee.

"I was in the consulting business," Manning says in explaining his low profile in those days, "the type of business where you're not looking for publicity, you're working for the client. If there's any kind of publicity, the client has to get it."

Those clients included some of Canada's largest energy utilities, the Business Council on National Issues, oil companies, federal government agencies such as the National Energy Board, and several provincial governments. Preston Manning has worked on projects as varied as the ill-fated four-province western power grid and the entrenching of economic rights in the constitution. In 1981 he organized a major conference on business opportunities for native people, another one of his special interests for many years. Manning helped prepare applications for some of Alberta's energy megaprojects, including the Cold Lake heavy oil plant. His strongest areas of expertise, in all likelihood, are regulation of the energy sector and electrical utilities, and planning to improve native social conditions. "His work for native people was absolutely first rate," says Calgary consultant Ron Wallace, who often saw Manning's studies. "In a crowded field he was one of the best. He enjoyed tremendous respect."

Despite his low public profile, Manning worked very closely with his father, often in areas related to politics. Indeed, a great deal of his working life was devoted to developing political ideas that would prove useful later. Manning described how he became involved in the push for property rights: "When we first saw the [Victoria] Charter [in 1971] there was nothing in it about economic rights at all. We went to a bunch of business guys [the Business Council on National Issues] and got some money for lawyers to develop a property rights protection clause. We drafted this thing and carted it around to all the different provincial governments. Most of them were Conservative governments. We said, 'Put this thing in your bag, and when you're discussing rights, how about raising this?' The interesting thing is, we couldn't persuade one of them to do it." His fascination with this issue survives today in a Reform Party policy that calls for a constitutional change to recognize "the right of every person to the use and enjoyment of property." Manning finally enjoyed a vicarious victory on September 24, 1991, when the federal Tories surprised nearly everyone by including property rights in their constitutional proposals.

As Manning plunged into business, public memory of his politically active time in the 1960s began to fade. This seemed to suit him fine. He usually worked very much in the background, far out of the media's view. He has always seen himself as a quiet Christian conciliator, a man of good will who pulls people together and gets them working toward a common goal. He does not seek publicity and conflict or enjoy them when they come.

There may be another reason for this reticence. Early in his business career, he received some questionable publicity and all the controversy he could handle. The episode called his own judgement and methods sharply into question, and still has implications for his Reform Party today. The publicity concerned the sacred Reform tenets of conflict of interest, financial management, and the use of political influence. Indeed, his family's continued ownership of shares in the venture, Slave Lake Developments Limited (SLD), could in the future place Manning very close to the kind of controversy he deplores. The whole affair showed a young man who was naive and inexperienced at business, despite his ideological fervour and political connections.

Like so many Manning projects, this one began with the best of intentions and motives. Slave Lake Developments, incorporated in 1969, several months after Ernest Manning retired as premier, was to be nothing less than a laboratory for Preston Manning's social ideas, the testing ground that would show how private enterprise could achieve community goals. The company would do this with the greatest possible involvement by the local people.

The laboratory was to be Slave Lake, 250 km. north of Edmonton, a community with a serious housing shortage at the time. After a long period of near-poverty, the southern shore of Lesser Slave Lake was experiencing a boom based on oil exploration and forestry, but there was little private investment in the social necessities of a growing town. Many newcomers were forced to live in mobile homes, trailers, and tents. Slave Lake Developments would solve this problem by providing low-cost housing and other necessities, Manning hoped. Area residents would be encouraged to invest by buying shares. They would thus enrich themselves, help the community, and remove some of the burden from government. As a way of keeping score, Manning even instituted a system of "social accounting" to go along with the financial bookkeeping.

The whole enterprise was lifted straight out of the pages of *Request for Proposals and Social Contracts.* It fulfilled all the criteria – local control, private ownership, social purpose, and a limited supporting role for government. Preston Manning, as the son of an ex-premier whose party was still in power, had the clout and connections to turn those abstract ideas into reality. However, this reality was to be very different from the utopian ideal he envisaged. Today the details of the story are packed away in dozens of dusty document boxes sitting in the annex of Alberta's Provincial Archives in Edmonton, but they are worth digging into.

When SLD was incorporated, Ernest and Preston Manning were two of the shareholders and founding directors, and Preston became president. Another original director was Walter Twinn, chief of the nearby Sawridge Indian Band, and a local entrepreneur, who in late 1990 was named a Tory senator in the drive to pass the Goods and Services Tax.

From the start SLD dealt with the Human Resources Development Authority (HRDA), the very government body that the Mannings had created with the 1967 *White Paper on Human Resources Development* (and headed by good friend Ray Speaker). Support for the Mannings' project was approved by a Socred cabinet committee on development in the Slave Lake area. For a while there hardly seemed to be a dividing line between the cabinet, the government agency, and the company. Neil Gilliat, the area's salaried HRDA official, was an original director and shareholder of SLD, and also a member of the Canada-Alberta Joint Planning Committee that approved government funding for Slave Lake Developments.

According to company minutes, dated 20 months after the fact, Gilliat resigned from the board on March 13, 1970, because of "conflict of interest." Later, Gilliat stated that he had intended to quit "when the company was off the ground and started to consider projects." He transferred his 10 shares in the company to another director, and a second director took up a $500 interest-free loan that

Gilliat had made to Slave Lake Developments.

As a government official, Gilliat said, "I have given advice to the company, as I have to many other companies, on government programs and agencies who could assist them. I have not, or ever expected to, receive *[sic]* compensation of any kind for the advice, etc." A government investigation later found Gilliat blameless, calling his actions "the normal assistance of any Government office to a new business enterprise." Today Gilliat says he and others may have been "a bit naive" but they were only trying to get a worthwhile project off the ground. "You wouldn't believe how tough it was to get money from banks in those days," he says. "You had to get people involved."

Four other directors of Slave Lake Developments were Leo Boisvert (the board chairman), Mel Zachary, William Thomas, and Gordon Cook. Each held more than 10 per cent of SLD's shares. Yet Boisvert was the mayor of Slave Lake and the other three were town councillors. Later they would vote several times in Slave Lake council on matters of interest to SLD, including the approval of land purchases. This was a clear violation of Alberta's Municipal Act.

During all this time (and until 1988) Preston Manning was president and chief executive officer of Slave Lake Developments. He dealt with politicians, wrote proposals, and met bureaucrats. Yet he did not seem to see anything wrong with the blurring of private and public functions. When the conflict-of-interest charges arose, he remained mostly silent. In his 1971-72 president's report he shrugged off the whole matter by saying: "On the negative side a needless controversy generated by critics of SLD concerning the motives and concept of SLD has produced some community disruption." The man who considers himself an expert at resolving conflicts chose to ignore this one.

The words have an odd ring from a leader who now asks Reform Party candidates to fill in a huge questionnaire to prove that they have no conflicts of any kind. Manning was not in conflict himself, since he was not elected or employed by government. Nor does anyone claim that he was on the take. Nevertheless, he worked with people who were in a very doubtful position.

The Slave Lake controversy simmered in the community for a couple of years, raising doubts and eyebrows but little publicity. During that time the company pursued its goals, which Manning stated as:

"To earn profits for its shareholders through the development of the physical and human resources of the Slave Lake region. . . .

"To achieve social as well as economic development . . . through the exercise of private enterprise and initiative."

All this private initiative was possible because of a good deal of public help. The first project, a 90-unit apartment and townhouse complex called Woodland Place, was built largely with a $1-million low-interest mortgage from Canada Mortgage and Housing Corporation. (Another $50,000 came from a bank loan, $50,000 from private companies, and the shareholders kept their control through a $50,000 subscription.) In the same period, SLD applied to the Alberta and federal governments for $40,000 a year in operating grants. (On its 20th anniversary, the company showed how history can fade into myth by boasting that SLD "was established by the residents of the community itself, without government handouts or loan guarantees.")

Meanwhile, Bruce Thomas, the local newspaper publisher, had been poking into all these connections. On November 10, 1971, he published his startling allegations in his feisty little local newspaper, the *Port of Slave Lake Oiler* (motto: "Good to Wipe Your Wet Boots On"). "Four councillors may be involved in a severe case of conflict of interest," Thomas wrote. He described how the councillors who were also SLD board members had voted to accept the company's bid to buy five town lots. (SLD wisely had "second thoughts" and later decided not to buy the land.)

The odour in Preston Manning's social laboratory was finally out in the open. It quickly wafted to Edmonton, where Peter Lougheed's Progressive Conservatives had been in office for only a few months after defeating the Socreds in the provincial election on August 30, 1971. Many of the new Tories had little interest in the Mannings' human resources thrust, and even less stake in protecting the pet project of the two most important men of the old regime.

The Tories' new Minister of Municipal Affairs, Dave Russell, soon sent two senior municipal inspectors to investigate the charges. On November 24 they wrote a memo to their deputy minister stating that the four councillors on the SLD board had violated the Municipal Act by neglecting to declare their interest and by failing to abstain from voting. Russell quickly notified Slave Lake Municipal Secretary Mrs. B. Lineton, in a letter dated November 29th, 1971. It reads in part:

"From the investigation made and as indicated in the report, it is apparent that four of your Council have contravened Section 30 of The Municipal Government Act. There are three alternatives provided in the legislation to govern a situation of this kind and I can only advise members of Council of the alternatives, as I feel that whatever decision is made should be made at the local level." The alternatives, Russell said, included voluntary resignation of the offenders, disqualification by council, or application to a judge to declare their seats vacant.

"I regret very much the events that have happened," Russell concluded. "It indicates to me, as I am sure it must to your Council, that even with the best of intentions, a member of any legislative body, be it municipal, provincial or federal, must be extremely careful to divorce himself completely from any suggestion of involvement with persons or firms that have dealings or contracts with the Government to which he has been elected."

The remarkable thing is that Preston Manning did not seem to realize how badly this controversy would damage the credibility of his project. Nor, it seems, did he or his father ever caution the mayor and the councillors. When Boisvert asked Edmonton lawyer E. J. Walter for an opinion, the attorney wrote:

"At no time from the information we have, were the Councillors or the Mayor advised by anyone of the provisions of the Municipal Government Act relating to the disqualification in matters involving a Municipal Council and contracts in which they had an interest. It should be stated here also that from our information, none of the Councillors or the Mayor had any knowledge of these provisions in the Municipal Government Act."

As premier, Ernest Manning was certainly familiar with the danger in politicians mixing private and public business. In 1964 he fired his provincial treasurer, Edgar Hinman, for investing in private companies. The treasurer's activities had encouraged people to pour money into those companies in the belief that nothing could go wrong, and this made them doubly angry when things did. Ernest Manning barely hesitated: when people began to complain, the treasurer was gone in a day. Arthur Hailey, writing for *Maclean's*, concluded after investigating all this that the premier had a keen sense of political ethics. Ernest Manning, of all people, should have been aware of conflict provisions in the Municipal Government Act.

When Preston Manning finally responded in some detail in 1973 to Thomas's critical articles in the *Oiler*, he did not mention the conflict-of-interest furor. He was far more eager to refute charges that he was enriching himself at the community's expense. First he noted that it was absurd to say SLD was "Manning's company," or that the housing and office building projects were "Manning's projects." Eight of the nine board members were locals, he said (his father had by this time resigned). The "projects are locally owned and controlled undertakings. And there is still opportunity for any and every resident of the area to participate in this ownership. . . ."

Then Manning came to the point that really irritated him: the charge that the family was making money at the expense of the locals. He wrote: "For the past four years, M & M Systems Research

Ltd. – the consulting firm through which I make my living – has provided approximately $10,000 worth of services per year to SLD to help it get started. These services have been donated without charge. In addition, M & M Systems, my father, and myself, have signed bank guarantees totalling thousands of dollars to secure the initial borrowings of Slave Lake Developments." His only "vested interest," he claimed, was in the success of the company and the development of the area.

Leo Boisvert to this day doesn't see much wrong with what happened. "We had come through a tremendous boom in Slave Lake, and things had to get done," he said in an interview. "Town council had forward-looking people who planned for needed developments, so we left ourselves open to conflict-of-interest charges. We had meetings with the Municipal Affairs Minister [Dave Russell]. He said we were a bit careless in council meetings. But most political people are vulnerable." Asked what Preston Manning thought of the conflict charges, Boisvert said: "You know, I never asked him."

Today, *Oiler* publisher Bruce Thomas calls Boisvert "an honest, good person who was basically naive at that period in time." Boisvert never did have to quit the town council. Nor did the other three who violated the Municipal Act. Their lawyer, E. J. Walter, came up with an ingenious technical argument to get them off the hook. The Act required them to resign, he said, but they had already quit in order to be candidates in the municipal elections of October, 1971. They were re-elected. Therefore they should not have to resign again because of something they did in the previous term. Walter also advised them strongly not to mess with the Municipal Act again. The Tory government did not press the issue, and life in Slave Lake went on as before with the same men involved in both council and SLD. Boisvert, in fact, remains chairman of the SLD board today.

Nevertheless, life was not at all happy for the company. The Tories showed their annoyance on another front by stalling payment of further SLD operating money. A flurry of memos revealed that the Conservatives, mindful of the bad publicity, were trying hard to get clear of the Manning project. One administrator noted: "This agreement incidentally was made on the direction of the previous government's Slave Lake Cabinet Committee. It now appears that the Slave Lake Developments Ltd. have not provided satisfactory evidence that they are meeting the requirements of the contract, and for that reason I am redepositing the $20,000 [grant]."

The provincial treasurer, Gordon Miniely, quickly got into the act, writing a sarcastic memo about the project to Don Getty, who was the new intergovernmental affairs minister. Six months after the dispute began, Getty rang the death knell for provincial support in a letter that said: "The attached cheque [for $20,000] is to cover the balance of funds on the understanding that this is the final payment and no further payments will be considered."

Beyond their problems with the Slave Lake project, the Tories felt that the whole Human Resources thrust was hopelessly naive and complex. "There were all these fancy charts and diagrams," recalls Lou Hyndman, a former Lougheed minister, "but to us it looked like a recipe for another giant bureaucracy to get in people's way. Today it sort of reminds me of Bob Rae's idea for a social contract."

The Slave Lake tale says a good deal about Preston Manning. First, he was intensely idealistic and dedicated. He seemed truly to believe that he could create, through his inspiration, a new community ethic for business and government. As in almost everything else, he relied on hard work, good will, and faith. He seemed not to realize how heavily his success relied on his name and how vulnerable his project would be when Social Credit was kicked out of office. His vision of harmony between business, government, and community, however admirable, could only work smoothly within his charmed circle in Alberta. In the rough outside world, it was politics and business as usual.

Yet Manning was also a hands-on administrator who did all the important work himself, from writing reports to lobbying governments. He signed many documents "on behalf of the board." He displays those same qualities with the Reform Party today: very little happens that the leader doesn't know about or control, and nothing of importance emerges that he has not read or written. He strives to rally people behind him, but it is always Manning who keeps his hands on the strings. His goals may be idealistic and even naive, but his methods are very practical and determined.

This may explain why Slave Lake Developments survived and began to prosper modestly even after Social Credit was driven from office. The company weathered early Tory hostility, a deep recession in the early 1980s, an oil price crash in 1986, and continuing low commodity prices for area farmers. Yet SLD continued to grow slowly, and today it owns 10 buildings, stores, and housing developments, not just in Slave Lake but in other area communities. The company receives indirect government help: provincial departments are the major tenants in two Slave Lake office buildings. There is no question that Manning beat long odds merely by keeping this company afloat for 20 years.

It is not so clear, though, that Manning achieved many of his social goals. SLD today looks pretty much like any other real-estate development and management company out to make a profit. About 70 per cent of the company's 300 or so shareholders live in the area, but prairie co-ops had even more local participation half a century ago. Manning's lofty systems analysis seems to boil down to an old formula for success in Canadian development: spot something people need, build it with government help, and then sell it or rent it, often to the very government that helped build it in the first place. His laboratory was involved more in old-fashioned business than in idealistic social improvement.

Manning made many friends in Slave Lake, people who admired his selflessness and devotion to the project. Boisvert knows him as "a tremendous fellow, very sincere in his concerns about people. At SLD he wanted to do the right thing. He was never one to push ideas without advice and consultation." Then Boisvert adds: "And his father always came into the picture somewhere along the line."

Yet the question remains: how could Manning have been involved with a board that got into such a jam? He tried to harmonize government and business through good will, but in the process the line between the two somehow became blurred.

There is some evidence that Manning still has trouble defining that line. In mid-1991, his family holding company still owned 4,200 shares of Slave Lake Developments – worth about $22,800, according to SLD's latest estimate of book values. This brings Manning very close to violating the spirit of his own strict guidelines for Reform Party candidates. The party questionnaire asks potential Reformers if they hold shares in any company that has a contract with the federal government "for the building of a public work." SLD does not have that, but in late 1991 it landed a contract to lease office space to Canada Manpower. This places the party leader uncomfortably near the line he drew in the sand for other Reformers. Yet in his own disclosure statement Manning insists that "the assets of our family holding company represent no potential for conflict-of-interest for an MP."

Another point from the Slave Lake days casts some doubt on Manning's statements about his career. In response to the question "Have you ever experienced a business failure in the last 20 years," he replies, "no." Then he adds a note saying that there was one exception, sort of: a General Motors dealership taken over by Slave Lake Developments went bankrupt in the early 1980s.

The name of the GM dealership was Gilliat Motors, and it was run by the same Neil Gilliat who by then had left the Human Resources Development Authority. According to Leo Boisvert, Gilliat Motors "needed an infusion of capital, so Slave Lake Developments went into a minor partnership with them." It was a doubtful investment:

during the 1981-82 recession, Gilliat Motors went into bankruptcy. SLD directors did not want this failure to jeopardize the rest of the company, Boisvert says. Since Manning was president of SLD, and one of SLD's associated companies went under, this seems to qualify as a business failure.

There is no suggestion, however, that either Manning or his father was involved in SLD for the money. Indeed, he has probably taken less out of SLD than he put in over 20 years. His brother-in-law, Phillip Stuffco, who has done much of SLD's legal work for the past 10 years, told one of the authors: "I'm quite mad at Preston because I think he could be a rich man. This guy is a complete do-gooder. A lot of the ideas that he's had have turned out really well, and he could have done that privately. For instance, Slave Lake Developments is a small community-owned public company. Preston started it, it was his idea, he went out and found financing. It has turned into a very successful operation with small shareholders. That company's done very well. It probably has $12 million worth of assets.

"He took some small hourly stipends but they are a joke. We always had to do it [the legal work] real cheap; there were always these budget constraints. There was never any big money. The company's done real well because of that type of fiscal management. I've often thought Preston could have done that all himself, or he could be working as a consultant and earning $250,000 to $300,000 a year."

Leo Boisvert recalls that Manning was never in Slave Lake Developments for the money. "Good heavens, no! He'd be lucky If he got his expenses out of it." Then Boisvert adds, "Money never seemed to be his main thrust. I think politics was."

Although he is far from rich, Manning and his family live comfortably. He quietly abides by his principles of frugality and simplicity, the product of both his religious fundamentalism and his Social Credit distaste of indebtedness to banks. In 1991 Manning disclosed that he lived in a paid-up house worth $200,000 (he later moved to another one in Calgary Southwest). He had a car valued at $20,000, an RRSP account worth about $75,000, and equity of about $30,000 in the family holding company. He has no debts except for "monthly credit-card balances not in excess of $5,000." He seems to hate the idea of borrowing money for any reason. A few years ago, Phillip Stuffco relates, Manning and his wife sold a lakefront lot at Slave Lake because "they needed the money." Manning and Stuffco then shared the cost of building "a little guest house" on property owned by Gordon Beavis, their father-in-law.

In 1991 the Reform Party was paying the leader a salary of $6,000 a month plus a taxable monthly allowance of $1,500. His after-tax monthly income is therefore about $4,600, and he is quick to point out that if he were a member of Parliament it would be $5,900. His benefits include a car allowance, some health, dental, and insurance coverage, and a "discretionary contribution to my RRSP account."

Whatever else Manning learned from his long and private career in business, he did not gain much respect for the rights of unions or their members. As a businessman, he has employed surprisingly few people, usually just a few staff members at any one time. He is invariably considerate and polite to them, but he has little of the labour-management experience that most company presidents collect by the time they reach his age.

Nonetheless, he has strong views on business relations with unions. So does his party. They believe in the right to work, a view expressed carefully but clearly in the party's labour policy: "The Reform Party supports the right of all Canadians, particularly the young, to enter the work force and achieve their potential," the *Blue Book* states. "Union and professional bodies may ensure standards, but should not block qualified people from working in a trade or profession or from gaining the necessary qualifications." In practical terms, this means the free hiring of replacement workers during a strike and the end of the union shop. An employer would be able to hire non-union people to work alongside union members. The reference to professionals, likely thrown in to soften the blow, may appear to have less meaning. Yet it would seriously weaken licensing bodies and associations, both designed to protect the consumer as well as the professional.

The Reform Party claims to "support the right of workers to organize democratically, to bargain collectively, and to strike peacefully." Nevertheless, their labour policy reveals a misreading of union principles, which Reformers seem to interpret as a collectivist conspiracy against the rights of the individual. If ever implemented, the party's policy guarantees a collision with organized labour.

This labour policy again has roots in the Manning family history. In 1982, in the archival interviews, Ernest Manning declared that "One of the so-called rights that organized labour is very jealous of is the right to have a closed shop in an industry. Where the majority say they want a union to represent them, the minority is forced to belong to that union. They fought for that and they regard it as a right. I think it's debatable whether it is properly a right." Ernest Manning suggested that if 70 per cent of the workers voted to join a union, the other 30 per cent should still be able to work as non-union employees.

The Mannings are always consistent: in every case, they advance the rights of the individual over those of the group. For them, unions and all professional associations inhibit the individual's right to choose. What the absolute majority of a collective may desire is insignificant if it in any way imperils the will of the dissenting individual.

On these issues, the long connection between the Reform Party and the National Citizens' Coalition is worth recalling. The NCC was one of the chief supporters of Ontario teacher Merv Lavigne, who brought a suit claiming that his union (the Ontario Public Service

Employees Union) did not have a right to contribute his dues to left-wing causes even though a majority of union members voted to do so. Lavigne recently lost his six-year fight in the Supreme Court of Canada, a major victory for the group over the individual. NCC members have been active in shaping Reform Party labour policy, and Preston Manning agrees completely with that policy.

Indeed, Manning's expertise in conciliation seems to stop short when it comes to labour. The *Blue Book* states: "The Reform Party supports the harmonization of labour-management relations, and rejects the view that labour and management must constitute warring camps." This sounds highly naive in light of Reform policies that would surely result in warring camps. The policy seems to reflect Preston Manning's own career in business. It has been intense, extremely dedicated, but quite limited in scope. It is not surprising that he was a stranger to the 54 big shots in Toronto.

CHAPTER SIX

A SIMPLE PARADISE

"The Reform Party is asking some questions which some people don't want to hear."

– Calgary Reformer Ron Beer

"What we now need is a calm, rational analysis of why so many non-white people break out in a nervous sweat whenever Manning speaks of his vision of Canada."

– Activist Rosemary Brown

FOR PERHAPS the first time in his life, Preston Manning was called a racist to his face. It was June 1991, and he had just stepped off a plane in Toronto when a reporter for an ethnic television station asked him to explain his party's "racist" position. On hot-line shows and at three press conferences in Toronto he was asked about the party's association with William Gairdner, controversial author of *The Trouble with Canada*, which calls for limits on "non-traditional" immigration. Gairdner, a former chairman of the National Citizens' Coalition, which Manning's father helped to found, has been a popular figure at Reform Party rallies. At the Saskatoon Assembly in April, 1991, dozens of Reformers lined up to buy books signed on the spot by the author. Gairdner seemed to haunt the Reform Leader wherever he turned in Toronto. Manning cut short a press conference when reporters persisted in asking questions about his views on the book. Later, as Reformers streamed into the huge rally at Toronto's International Centre, a small knot of protestors chanted: "Hey, hey, men in suits, we all know your racist roots. Hey, hey, men in ties, we don't need your racist lies."

Manning seemed shocked by the uproar. His first reaction was to try to distance himself from Gairdner without actually criticizing him. "I'd rather not discuss Mr. Gairdner's work," he said. "If you have problems with it, you can give us your complaints, we can look into it." In fact, Manning had already looked into Gairdner and his views. "My wife and I had dinner with him once," Gairdner said in an interview. "I was at a Reform Party gathering in Vancouver a year and a half ago. After I heard him speak at the Empire Club in Toronto, he asked me if I would speak in Saskatoon and I said I would." Manning did not point out this personal connection during the fuss in Toronto.

The people who demonstrated against Manning, Gairdner continued, "are a lot of the dregs of society banding together to chop down old Preston, who was speaking inside to five thousand and six thousand people at a time. They're homosexual groups, they're the socialist workers' league and this and that. They're the very kinds of people with their noses in the trough, going after government money, that the public is sick to death hearing about." Gairdner was grateful to Manning for not taking the easy path by simply disowning him. Of course, he added, "About five thousand people in his party have probably read my book and they like it a lot." Gairdner was certainly right about one thing: The demonstrations were tiny compared to the crowd at the rally. But they received top play in Toronto newspaper reports and national TV broadcasts.

Is Gairdner's book racist? The author denies it vehemently, just as Reformers deny that their policies are racist. "A dislike for government-imposed 'multicultural' policies has nothing to do with disliking other cultures," he writes. "Such a response does not imply a racist or chauvinistic attitude." Yet his chapter on the subject is called "The Silent Destruction of English Canada." His basic argument is that homogeneous cultures function best, and that ethnic diversity is ruining the country. Current policies "can end only in intra-ethnic strife and militancy on our own soil," Gairdner concludes. Without question his views reflect a strong body of opinion within the Reform Party and growing sentiment outside it. Even the Spicer Commission recommended that immigrants receive more training in Canadian customs and values.

Since the Gairdner espisode, the charges against the Reformers have escalated as the traditional parties begin to turn their sights on the formidable new foe. Sheila Copps, deputy leader of the federal Liberals, attacked what she called the Reform Party's "Aryan philosophies." Reformers are promoting an "Anglo-Saxon single integrated culture," she charged during a visit to Alberta. Saskatchewan New Democrat MP Lorne Nystrom labelled the Reformers "folksy fascists" and "small-minded evangelical cranks" in a four-page pamphlet to supporters. Liberal leader Jean Chrétien accused Manning of encouraging racists. "Mr. Manning is always playing about the edges so that if you are a racist you might feel comfortable with him," he said in an interview with one of the authors. "For him it's always in the grey area. I'm not comfortable with that type of approach, because it appeals to the dark side of some people."

Attacks also came from the academic community. University of Regina sociologist John Conway told *The Globe and Mail* that the party's policy "is intended to appeal to the views of those who are concerned about the increase in Third World immigration. Of course they can't say that, but they clearly imply that when they talk about the first criterion being an economic one."

Rosemary Brown, a former NDP member of the B.C. legislature and a leading black activist for many years, wrote in the *Vancouver Sun*: "What we need now is a calm, rational analysis of why so many non-white people break out in a nervous sweat whenever Manning speaks of his vision of Canada. . . . We also need an explanation of why so many of the people who support the Reform Party think Manning is promising a return to a Canada of fewer immigrants from non-white, non-English speaking countries . . . why is he using those memory-laden phrases, 'immigrants who fit in', or 'traditional society'? Does he not know that those are the trigger words of the '50s for 'whites only'?"

Manning tried hard to fight off the charges during his Ontario tour. Two days after the Toronto ordeal he told a friendly audience in Peterborough, Ont.: "The way to combat negative labelling is not to go about saying, 'No we are not racist, no we are not racist,' but to constantly promote and affirm federal laws, positions, and policies that are neutral and colour-blind with respect to constitution or immigration or multiculturalism. And this will give the Canadian people a choice between the traditional parties that promote specific special status for some Canadians based on race, language, and culture, and the Reform position that federal law and the constitution should treat all Canadians equally regardless of race, language, and culture." This brought a ten-second burst of applause, the same reaction he gets at all his rallies from Ontario to British Columbia. Manning constantly asserts the main points of the party's policy: that everyone should be declared equal regardless or race, colour, or any other characteristic; that no ethnic groups should receive government money; and that immigration should be based solely on Canada's economic need. The critics charge that by being "colour-blind" the Reform Party ignores minorities and thus is inherently racist.

Nothing annoys Preston Manning's friends more than suggestions that he is a racist. They react furiously to the very notion. "A lot of the papers say Preston and the Reform Party are racist," fumes Phillip Stuffco, Manning's brother-in-law. "How do they explain the fact that I'm a Métis and I was taken into that family and that question never arose? They welcomed me with not even the bat of an eyelash." Stuffco is also Catholic "and that's never been a problem either," he says. "Preston's the exact opposite of a racist."

Manning also spent a good deal of time during his business career trying to help natives better their lot. In 1981 he organized a successful conference that brought native business people into touch with officials from resource companies, utilities, and banks. Before that, he wrote a report outlining the impact on natives of Alberta's Cold Lake heavy oil plant. As always, he was interested in helping disadvantaged people pull themselves up by their own bootstraps. The interest is sometimes personal too: Manning once befriended a destitute native woman, Ernestine Gibot, and tried to help her back on her feet. "Preston is no racist," insists a longtime consultant to ethnic minorities who knows Manning well. "It's a religious thing with him. I'm sure his father taught him that all people are equal from the time he was old enough to understand."

Phillip Stuffco adds: "Once he brought a black guy home with him. He met this guy on the plane, the guy was supposed to get off in Edmonton and he started to leave the plane in Winnipeg. Preston ended up bringing him straight to the house."

The story is famous among Manning's friends, retold so often it almost has the power of myth. It has appeared in several newspaper and magazine accounts, never with the name of the person Manning helped or any identification beyond the claim that he was an African student. The tale sounds almost too good to be true, but it is.

The man was Samuel Okoro, a young Nigerian who was travelling to study at Edmonton's Northern Alberta Institute of Technology. Today, he is a security guard at Winnipeg's Red River Community College. Married with four children, Okoro still counts Preston Manning among his dearest friends because of what happened in 1975.

"I would like to prove to people that those allegations against Preston are completely unfounded," Okoro said in an interview with one of the authors. "When I came to Canada, I didn't know anybody, I didn't have any friends, and I met Preston in the plane at Toronto. I sat beside him, he asked me where I came from, I told him, and he asked me where I was going to stay in Edmonton. I told him I was supposed to stay at the YMCA. I hadn't been to Canada at all, any place.

"When our flight from Toronto landed in Winnipeg, I thought I was in Edmonton. I picked up my briefcase and I was leaving the aircraft. I was on my way out just in the middle of the steps. He said, 'Did you tell me you are going to Edmonton?' I said yes and he said, 'Well, this is Winnipeg.' So I came back.

"When I arrived at Edmonton airport, his wife was there with their two kids. They took me straight to their home! They gave me a place to stay. I lived with them for one week, and then I found a place. Every day on his way back from work, he came to visit me. And every Friday he took me home. I was at their home Friday evening, Saturday, and Sunday. All of us attended the same church. He helped me a lot. I don't understand why other politicians are trying to damage him by calling him a racist.

"Throughout my stay in Edmonton, I spent all my Christmas Days with them. They treated me like their child; I became one of their sons. When my wife-to-be came from Nigeria to this place, they organized the wedding, and they even paid for it.

"My first year in Edmonton I was sick with ulcers, and I was admitted at the hospital. They were the only family I had in Edmonton. She [Sandra] came to see me every day with the kids, Andrea and Avryll. Even when I came out, Preston went to my house and moved all my things back to their home. He wanted me to be cared for until I got stronger." Very often in those days, he said, Manning would take him to his father's home, where the whole family would talk and play games.

Sam Okoro is in his mid-30s now, and Manning still comes to visit him whenever he is in Winnipeg and has the time. Okoro grows emotional when he tells this remarkable story of generosity and acceptance. Critics who accuse Manning of personal racism may wonder if there was some paternalistic missionary impulse behind his actions, but they cannot refute the fact that Manning and his family did something selfless and kind, something that racists could never do. To his credit, Manning never mentions the episode when people call him the name that wounds him most.

However admirable his personal qualities, Manning's policies still provoke passionate debate. Toronto author Michele Landsberg says: "It never really matters what the individual man is like. It's his policies that count, and what his policies will do is absolutely terrifying." Nothing evokes such heated responses more readily than Reform Party proposals to level the multiculturalism empire that Ottawa has built up over the past 25 years, and to alter radically the rules for immigration.

In a speech on October 1, 1990 in Calgary, Manning insisted that this would not destroy the Canadian mosaic, but would put it "on a more solid foundation. . . . Reformers say, 'Let the individual and the group, and even lower levels of government, devote their attention to the shape and form of the individual pieces that make up the mosaic. But let the national government . . . provide the common background onto which those pieces must be affixed, and the glue which must hold them together." One such bond is the RCMP, whose "traditional role" the Reform Party supports wholeheartedly. The party would preserve "the distinctive heritage and tradition of the RCMP by retaining the uniformity of dress code. Changes should not be made for religious or ethnic reasons." Nothing infuriated Reformers as much as Ottawa's decision to let Sikh officers wear turbans and native recruits wear their hair in traditional braids.

Manning's view goes back at least to 1967, when he and his father called for "the separation of race and state" in the Alberta government *White Paper on Human Resources Development.* This does not mean that governments consider racial or ethnic qualities unimportant, the paper insisted. "The basic point is that governments ought to regard these matters as rightfully belonging to the private sphere .... Governments and institutions of the state should never become vehicles for racial sentiments of any kind. Government policy should not be oriented toward any religious or ethnic group but rather should be oriented toward the basic social and economic problems of the individuals concerned. . . . " The paper backed provincial support for multiculturalism. "This mosaic approach prevails in Alberta and as a result our society has been greatly enriched by the benefits of multiculturalism."

Some very tolerant and liberal-minded people are attracted to this Reform Party policy, usually because they feel that federal multiculturalism has become a political boondoggle which helps the party in power win elections without doing much for ethnic groups. York University history professor Jack Granatstein says: "This happens to be the one area where I agree completely with the Reform Party. What strikes me these days is how many ethnics are against multiculturalism. It tends to be the organized ethnics who are in favour. Those are the people who love it, because they're on the gravy train." Granatstein is now working on a book about multiculturalism which he says will come to some of the same conclusions as the Reform Party.

Without question, though, the Reform Party's "colour-blind" immigration policy is winning support from other people who are very preoccupied with colour and non-white immigration. The policy attracts them because of their feeling that the traditional, white Canada is being swamped by immigrants, and that government-funded multiculturalism compounds the sin. The party's answer to this is simple and appealing to many: declare everyone equal and give no one special help. The Reform Party *Blue Book* says there would be no affirmative action for minorities (or women) and no government money for ethnic groups. Immigration would be based solely on economic criteria, except in cases of "genuine refugees," strictly defined. Sponsorship privileges would be limited to "immediate families, that is, wives or husbands, minor dependent children, and aged dependent parents." The constitution should be amended to deny rights to bogus immigrants; in the meantime, the "notwithstanding" clause should be used to suspend those rights and deport people immediately. All major changes to immigration policy, the party says, should be approved by a national referendum.

All this adds up to a tough immigration policy, and Manning himself has backed it with equally tough words. In the October 1, 1990 speech in Calgary, he said that Ottawa should tell new immigrants, "'Look, we made a mistake in the past when our politicians met you at the boat or the plane and offered you a grant to preserve the culture which you were trying to get away from.'" Immigrants themselves should decide how much culture they want to preserve and pay for the effort, perhaps with some help from the provinces. Ottawa's only role is to provide equality of opportunity and to promote a shared Canadian culture.

Manning's policies have already drawn a blast from the Ukrainians, one of the most powerful ethnic groups in the country and certainly the most dominant in his home province. Andrij Hluchowecky, director of the Ukrainian Information Bureau in Ottawa, noted in the *The Globe and Mail* that Ukrainian-Canadians spend many millions of their private money every year to maintain their culture. They "are pioneer settlers in Canada, and in their third and fourth and fifth generations their role in Canadian society is not a matter of privilege but of right," Hluchowecky wrote. There are a half-million Ukrainian-Canadians, many of whom vote, and few of whom are likely to agree with the Reformers that the hyphen in their identity is a bad thing. (The Party's *Blue Book* states: "The Reform Party of Canada opposes the current concept of multiculturalism and hyphenated Canadianism pursued by the Government of Canada.") The Reform challenge to multiculturalism and immigration may backfire as ethnic leaders line up against the party.

Experts in ethnic relations such as anthropologist Frances Henry, another York University professor, are apprehensive. "You can't abandon the Canadian policy of multiculturalism," she says. "Although it has its flaws, for the first time, it's an anti-racist policy. At the moment there is a strong multicultural backlash, and the Reform Party has gauged that public opinion." Henry is equally concerned about the party's immigration policy. "It simply doesn't make sense with Canada's needs. Demographically we need strong immigration to maintain our population momentum. If not, we'll have less than zero population growth."

Manning himself now appears worried by the explosive energies the party's policies can unleash. Just after the Ontario trip, in a remarkable statement to immigration reporter Estanislao Oziewicz of *The Globe and Mail*, the leader almost seemed to deny that the party has any right to dabble in immigration policy. "I actually discourage our assemblies from getting too deep into this," he said. "I don't believe in a bunch of white guys making policy for Indians, a bunch of settled citizens who have never come near a refugee – however well intentioned and all the rest – trying to come up with policy. On immigration we've hardly got very far, and on refugees even less."

This statement is flatly contradicted by the party's detailed eight-point policy on immigration and refugees. Reformers know exactly where they stand on these issues, and no subject riles them more at their meetings.

Manning himself, before the Ontario trip, showed that his own thinking is usually very clear. In an interview, he said: "If you take this business of Canada as this meeting of French and English, and you carry that into immigration, what you get is slightly racially flavoured immigration policy. Despite all the euphemisms, Quebec wants their immigration to support the French fact. Then you get this reaction in English Canada, that we ought to preserve the balance, preserve the English fact. . . . If you drive that down to the street, and you drive it into areas like immigration, it's racist, it's got racist connotations. . . .

"Our main reform on immigration was to say, get away from that, to base immigration on Canada's economic needs and requirements. If Canada needs computer programmers, and the best place you can get them is in India, well, go get them in India. Don't ask, 'Now what does this do to the French-English balance?'" Manning denied that a policy based on economic need will discriminate against non-white immigrants. That might have been true 20 years ago, he said, but today such immigrants are as likely to come from Asia as anywhere else. "We argue that what we're talking about is less racially oriented than the current official version. So our problem is to communicate that."

Some Reform officials state the case much more bluntly. Lee Morrison, a party council member from Eastend, Sask., says: "This might sound crass or cruel, but you've got three billion people out there who could better their lives by coming to this country, and probably several millions at any one time who would jump at the chance. Since we can't help them all, why shouldn't we be deliberately and cold-bloodedly selective? Call it enlightened self-interest. The only exception I would make would be bona fide refugees."

Ron Beer, the former policy director of Manning's Calgary Southwest riding association, wrote in the association's newsletter, *The Informer*: "The Reform Party is asking some questions which some people don't want to hear. Questions like 'Is the current Canadian immigration policy helping or hindering Canada?' 'Should our laws be tougher on illegal entrants to Canada?'" Later on Beer answered his own questions: "With most of our immigration occurring on humanitarian grounds as opposed to economic grounds, the current policy limits the economic benefits of immigration to Canadians."

Manning tries hard to keep such official party views from shading into racism. In 1988, for instance, he showed that he is not willing to accept a certain kind of candidate. He rescinded the nomination of Vancouver newspaper columnist Doug Collins, whose views are considered racist by some. Manning asked Collins to endorse parts of the party's platform that repudiate extremism. When Collins would not, Manning refused to let him run under the Reform banner.

The party's policy on aboriginal people is also quite radical on the surface. In essence, the Reformers say the same thing to natives that they say to Quebec: go off and decide what you want, then come back and talk. Native people should form their own constituent assembly, states the party *Blue Book*, to "consider their position on such matters as the nature of aboriginal rights, the relationship between aboriginal peoples and the various levels of government, and how to reduce the economic dependence of aboriginal peoples on the federal government. . . . " The Indian Affairs Department should be replaced "with accountable agencies run by and responsible to aboriginal peoples." Land claims should be settled and "aboriginal individuals or groups are free to preserve their cultural heritage using their own resources." Ottawa should allow native people to assume "full responsibility for their well-being by involving them in the development, delivery and assessment of government policies affecting them."

From the native perspective, a couple of crucial points are missing. There is no mention of self-government or the constitutional recognition of aboriginals as first peoples in Canada. (The latter omission is hardly surprising, since the Reformers are not willing to give it to anyone else either.) Native-rights advocate and college professor Harold Cardinal, author of *The Unjust Society*, is pessimistic. "If the party is against any recognition of aboriginal self-government in the constitution, if that is the party's position, it seems that the initial openness indicated by Manning is meaningless," he said in an interview. "Unless there is specific recognition of aboriginal self-government, there is no basis for aboriginal government to operate anywhere in the country. That negates any possibily of talking between native people and the Reform Party, because there'd be nothing to talk about." The idea of a constituent assembly for natives, Cardinal added, "is a practical approach, and the right one, but if at the same time they mean there will be no constitutional recognition, they're really saying, 'Go waste your time in some sand box and when you're finished wasting time come talk to us.'"

The Reform Party's stand on women's issues is consistent with its refusal to recognize special rights, or needs, for any groups in society. In the party's *Blue Book*, there is no mention whatever of programs for women. The reason is that the Reform Party rejects the very idea that any problems are specific to women. In Reform country women are simply considered equal. This worries many feminists. "I'm sure they do have a policy on women," says Michele Landsberg. "It's just not written down. There's a whole set of traditional values they're trying to return to."

This would suit the party's lone member of Parliament, Deborah Grey, very well. The model Reform Party woman, Grey does not like feminism, affirmative action, or anything at all that smacks of special treatment for her gender. That is why she opposes laws to enforce equal pay for work of equal value. Women are different but equal, she says. They should not try to be like men or to pull men down in order to feel that they are gaining ground. Grey summed up her feelings in an interview in her Parliament Hill office.

"I had supper with a very nice young couple here in Ottawa," she said, "and the fellow said he was at the point of feeling guilty for being a white male. For me, that says it all. Women are just trying to lift themselves up to the detriment and at the expense of men. We have different gifts. We are different biologically. I don't care how much the National Action Committee on the Status of Women tries to talk about equality, women are still the birthgivers, and I suspect it will go on in that way for a long time. We just have to accept that and celebrate it, that that's the way it is."

This attitude, which puts women's biological and spiritual calling above all else, permeates the Reform party. Indeed, the party hierarchy in 1990 decided at a special seminar on women's issues that there really aren't any. Danita Onyebuchi, the only woman on the party's 17-member executive council, remembers being uncomfortable with the very topic.

"I was invited to this convention on 'women's issues,' quote unquote, with the party in Calgary," she said, "but I don't feel there is such a thing as women's issues. If it affects women it affects society, period. I mean, we are half the society and influence the other half greatly. It wasn't only me that was feeling that way. Most of the women at the meeting said, 'These are not women's issues, these are people issues, these are societal issues.' It's not like we're a little minority group or something."

Yet women are definitely a minority group in the Reform Party's upper echelons. Besides Onyebuchi on the executive council and Grey as the high-profile MP, the only other really influential woman is Diane Ablonczy, the party's dynamic first chair and now Manning's executive assistant. Ablonczy and Onyebuchi are also sisters. Onyebuchi describes how she was almost pestered to run for the executive council as her sister was about to step down.

"First they asked me to be a director of St. Boniface riding, where I live. That was pretty noncommittal so I could do that. Then because of a dearth of perceived – oh, I guess I shouldn't say that – I was approached by the nominating chairman here in Manitoba about running [for the council]. I bounced it off my sister and she didn't say anything; I took that to mean I couldn't contribute anything, so I wrote and said I didn't want to run.

"They kept bothering me, kept phoning me. I said, 'You need five names on your nomination papers, I don't think five people know me.' They said, 'You're wrong, and if you say you'll run we'll get those five names in a heartbeat.' So I phoned my sister again and said, 'Do you think I could contribute anything?' She said, 'I didn't want to pressure you or influence you in any way, but yeah, I really think you could.' When they phoned again I said, 'Well yeah, what the heck.' I didn't really known anything about anything, if you want to know the truth."

Despite this, Onyebuchi insists that she was not invited as a token woman because her sister was leaving the board. Certainly there is a small pool of women to choose from for executive positions: Only 28 per cent of Reform Party members are women, according to an internal party survey taken in 1990.

"Unless the Reform Party broadens its appeal to more women, it won't come to power," says Doris Anderson, author of *The Unfinished Revolution* and former president of both the Canadian Advisory Council on the Status of Women and the National Action Committee. "They won't do anything to ease women's woes. Women carry a double load with child care and work, and parties like the Reform Party have no accommodation for that. Women's position has been backtracking all through the 80s in Canada, the United States, and the United Kingdom. This is not the trend in Europe generally, where conditions are much better for women in everything from longer maternity leave to day care. Most governments in Europe . . . are not as right-wing as we've been. If it doesn't change here, women are in for a long rough time, and the government won't do much for women, certainly not Preston Manning."

Feminism, especially the type expressed by the National Action Committee, is anathema to most Reformers. Asked if his evangelical religion might present difficulties in politics, Preston Manning said: "The problem's not going to come from evangelical, fundamentalist Christianity. In the States it might. . . . But in Canada you have to be more concerned about secular fundamentalism – feminism and a certain strain of ideological environmentalism.

"And I don't speak about that negatively," he continued. "These are people with a strong ideological orientation who want to influence the political process. I don't disparage them. But somehow your political system has got to on the one hand accommodate these people. On the other hand it's got to protect itself from value-oriented people who would impose the minority view on the majority." Such people feel very strongly "about so-called women's issues and that sort of thing," he added.

Onyebuchi, a Winnipeg businesswoman, says she appreciates some of the things feminism has done, but now the movement goes too far. "I disagree with a lot of their tactics. For example, I attended a rally, it was called 'Take Back the Night' or something, and they got up and they were all a bunch of men haters. Well, I'm sorry, I happen to love men. It's terrible that women and children can't go out at night, but men feel the same way about their wives and daughters. You can't say that men are at fault and they're just a bunch of vultures and that poor women and children are no longer safe. . . . I mean, some women are killing their husbands and our fathers too. People in general have become depraved."

William Gairdner's book *The Trouble With Canada* includes this unrestrained tirade against feminism: "The radical feminist movement constitutes a fundamental attack on the whole idea of a free society as it has painfully evolved over the past five centuries, from principle to practice. In future our society will look back at its own crumbling walls and wonder how it so blithely allowed the Trojan horse of radical feminism within its gates." Moderate feminism can be just as dangerous, Gairdner asserts, "because it alters social structures without this expressed intention. After all, whether the trigger be pulled by a sleepwalker or a revolutionary, the same damage is done."

Women's rights have no place in the constitution or federal policy, Preston Manning believes, although provincial governments can play a part in equalizing treatment for women if they wish. By creating a strong economy, he feels, the party can bring about equality for women in the workplace. Manning does not explain how the party will rectify the extreme imbalance of wages in Canada. One survey after another shows that women earn about two-thirds of men's wages, whether the economy is weak or strong.

Deborah Grey considers this unfortunate but probably unavoidable. "If I choose because I am the birthgiver, to take five years or six years out of my occupation," she says, "then the man in that position is going to keep going through the [salary] grid and I'm not. So I guess decisions need to be made. . . . You can't change that fact that women are the nurturers generally."

The real issue in Reform Party policy is not the rhetoric about equality, but the long-term implications for those who are seriously disadvantaged by the system. According to *Women and Poverty Revisited*, a report released in 1990 by the National Council of Welfare, "By the time most women return to full-time paid work, it is too late for them to catch up. They become the prime victims of the built-in injustices of our labour market, which excludes women from the best positions, pays them less than they are worth and segregates them into a narrow range of low-wage occupations with few fringe benefits and limited chances for advancement. The only safeguard which stands between most married women and poverty is their husbands' incomes."

This fragile balance is reflected in the report's distressing figures. Fully 57 per cent of all single-parent families headed by women live in poverty. "What we found was that women are still extremely vulnerable to poverty for reasons almost totally beyond their control. The main causes are child care responsibilities, labour market inequities, marriage breakdown and widowhood." Again, elderly women are twice as likely to live out their years in poverty as elderly men (22 per cent to 11 per cent).

Few things have annoyed Reformers more than the federal NDP's decision in June 1991 to set aside a certain number of ridings for women. "To me that's just so patronizing," fumes Deborah Grey. "It's just as far from democracy as you could ever get. And yet they say this is wonderful for women. It's going to be a joke. It's anti-democratic. It's pathetic. I will then be seen as a member of Parliament who is a woman, rather than as someone who is competent and able."

NDP leader Audrey McLaughlin reacted sharply to Grey's remarks in an interview. "One of the things I find offensive is when women in elected positions like myself just say, 'You can do it too.' I find that terribly offensive. I think we have a greater responsibility to assist women, and particularly visible minority women, women of colour, aboriginal women, disabled women, who have two strikes against them. We have said in our party that we're going to work toward gender equality. We don't just say it. We want to make it happen, we're going to do it. I think we'll get a better result for society – and not by demeaning men. We just want half. We're not asking for 100 per cent."

Other women who are not exactly popular with the Reform Party, including Sheila Copps, deputy leader of the Liberal Party, do not care for the NDP quota system. Nevertheless, Copps charges that the Reformers are hypocritical to claim that they want more women in politics when they favour changes to election financing that would discriminate against women. Copps refers to Manning's insistence that tax credits for political donations be ended. "This would discourage far more women than men from running," Copps said in an interview, because women have less financial independence and thus need donations more.

On a whole range of issues that affect women in particular, the Reform Party simply applies its usual panacea: privatization. The party's 1991 *Blue Book* states flatly: "The Reform Party opposes state-run day care." It wants no more child-care initiatives from Ottawa because of "the current fiscal situation." Any government programs, federal or provincial, should be based on need and follow the "children and parents, not institutions and professionals." The main role for government would be to regulate standards. All these measures favour private day care over publicly funded, non-profit centres, and most are now being used by Conservative provincial governments to whittle away the non-profit area.

Ernest Manning, the eternal battler against universal government programs, made his feeling about child care very clear in 1980 in one of the archival interviews. He spoke of "the conflict between the sophisticated highly trained professional social worker's approach to the thing, as compared with the far less professional approach by people who, when the children's interest was at stake, would go to bat for them day or night, anywhere, any time." Manning Sr. implied that professionalism is incompatible with "the care of kiddies by women who just naturally have a motherly instinct for them and love them."

The Social Credit women of Ernest Manning's cabinet knew exactly where they stood. Ethel Wilson, minister without portfolio in his Alberta government, once wrote an historical fashion pageant to celebrate the 50th anniversary of women obtaining the franchise. The script reads in part: "Thousands of young mothers forgo the urge to become involved in public, business or professional life and devote themselves to providing a domestic oasis, a well protected launching pad for future generations. Who is to say that they have not chosen the better part?" Wilson further laments those things that "subtract from moral standards and enduring faith in GOD *[sic]*. It is into the hands of the women of this century, life has dropped its most spectacular challenge, its greatest responsibility. It is an historical fact that since time began, women have established the moral standards of Nations. Nations have risen, they have fallen, because of moral standards. This is perhaps the greatest challenge of our time."

In those days, Preston Manning's mother sometimes wrote articles for *The Busy Bee*, the newsletter of Alberta Social Credit. In the mid-1950s she penned pieces such as "What about the Reserves?" (about money and party membership), and "No Time to Slump" (this was about the need to organize). Always the pieces were signed by Mrs. Ernest C. Manning or Mrs. E. C. Manning. There was a special section for women in *The Busy Bee*, called the "Queen Bee." It consisted entirely of recipes. There was even the "Teen Bee" for young people. (In the mid-60s, Owen Anderson helped refurbish the Socred newsletter. He added "Alberta's Young Socred" to replace the "Teen Bee." Very soon the "Queen Bee" was gone and the women's pages presumably buzzed off with it.)

Unlike her mother-in-law, Sandra Manning does not appear to contribute publicly to Reform policy, nor has she penned any articles for the party's *Reformer*. At the Calgary Women's Show in 1990, she did help with the Reform Party's booth, where volunteers explained that the party has no position on women's issues.

The Manning family's view of women 30 years ago was fairly close to that of society at large. National leaders of the day, after all, were hardly advocates of women's equality, and their wives were expected to be traditional. Today, however, most politicians at least pay lip service to women's issues. Political wives such as Maureen McTeer and Mila Mulroney are recognized as strong people in their own right. Nevertheless, Preston Manning and his wife remain unashamedly traditional in their separation of political and domestic roles.

With their strong opposition to abortion, key Reformers continue to find themselves on the far side of the pendulum from most women's groups. Preston Manning told a rally in Peterborough: "I am on the pro-life end of the spectrum, and my views on that come from my evangelical Christian perspective." Grey, another evangelical, feels the same way. "I'm pro-life," she says flatly. "I made that very clear in my riding. I did a referendum in the riding and it came back about 60 to 40 on the pro-life end of it, saying they could make exceptions when the mother's life is in danger or in case of rape or incest. I don't have a big problem with that, although I wouldn't just draw a flat line. I had a woman come to me recently who said, 'I am 47 years old, and when I was 14, I was raped.' She said, 'I had that baby and he's the most beautiful 33-year-old son now, and I've got grandchildren.' So she said she's really glad that she didn't [have an abortion]. But I think each case would need to be decided one by one."

The party's policy regarding abortion does seem to leave some room for compromise. MPs would be expected to state their views on abortion clearly, ask their ridings to debate the matter, and try to find a consensus. Members are to "faithfully vote the consensus of the constituency." If there is no majority opinion in the riding, MPs are free to vote their conscience. Grey and Manning both feel that an MP forced to vote against his or her deep conviction should resign before the next election. Grey says she would have quit if her constituents had not supported her against the Tory abortion law, Bill C-43. When the religious beliefs of key Reformers collide with their policy on the right of the individual to make choices, religion wins.

All this appeals powerfully to Real Women, the organization of conservative women who oppose "radical" feminism. "Knowing that Deborah Grey and Preston Manning are pro-life certainly gives us more personal confidence in them," says Judy Anderson, co-president of Real Women. "That doesn't mean we're all going to vote Reform or anything. But for me, as the president, I like to see politicians who are pro-life, and who are willing to stand up and not be brow-beaten out of it.

"We don't tell our members how to vote," Judy Anderson continues, "but I'm very enthusiastic about the Reform Party. We're both against equal pay for work of equal value, we're against so much government intervention into family and private life, which is what the radical feminists want. If they got their way, there'd be no private life left. The Reform Party seems to support many of the philosophical ideas that we have."

Without doubt, the party is strong on traditional family values. Its policy on family law comes down hard against "child abuse and family violence as acts which attack the very foundations of organized society." The policy supports laws to protect the victims, as well as therapy for both abusers and abused. There is no contradiction in this, since the party sees the family as the fundamental unit of society. One of its principles calls for "strengthening and protecting the family unit as essential to the well-being of individuals and society."

Nevertheless, suggesting that violence against women is a separate problem within the family can get a Reform country MP into deep trouble. This may explain why Bobbie Sparrow, the Tory member for Calgary Southwest, voted against a report called "The War against Women," tabled by her own government in June 1990. (One of the others was her Calgary Centre cohort and Government House leader, Harvie Andre.) Sparrow, who has the unenviable job of running against Preston Manning in the next election, said she did not like the title of the report, or its appeal for tighter gun control. (It also recommended the Royal Commission that is investigating violence against women.) Sparrow's Tory mate, Barbara Greene, who steered the report through committee, promptly accused Sparrow of trying to "out-reform the Reform Party. . . . She's running against Preston Manning . . . and I understand the Reform Party is quite anti-woman." The two Tories had an unseemly battle on a province-wide talk show in Alberta, with Greene claiming that Sparrow had promised to support the report, and Sparrow trying desperately to defend herself against callers and her own Tory colleague, Greene.

This Reform attitude overlooks the fact that many Canadian women do not live in the comfortable, traditional family so idealized by the party. One in eight women is battered at home, says a 1987 report by the Canadian Advisory Council on the Status of

Women (*Battered but Not Beaten: Preventing Wife Abuse in Canada*, by Linda Macleod). The violence often begins when a woman becomes pregnant. Income has no bearing on whether women will be beaten by their partners, although those from middle and higher income families are not as likely to admit the assaults. Of all the women murdered in this country, 62 per cent die as a result of domestic abuse. Equally chilling is the degree of assault against children. Before they are 18, one in four females and one in ten males will be sexually abused, according to the federal government's 1984 Badgley Commission report.

Whatever her motives, Sparrow's stand was certainly in tune with the Reform Party's aversion to interference in social matters. Its entire social policy, in fact, is aimed at reducing the role of government in the lives of individuals and families (except, it seems, in the case of abortion). According to the party *Blue Book* the Reformers would abolish "Family Allowance, Child Tax Credit, Spousal Exemption, Child Exemption, federal contributions to social assistance payments, retirement plans, federal social housing programs, day-care deductions, and minimum wage laws." All these would be replaced with a new social-security system based on the family or household but utilizing the federal taxation department. The Reform Party has not yet decided how to do this, but promises to "explore options from among existing proposals such as the guaranteed annual income, security investment fund, and negative income tax."

Unemployment insurance would return "to its original function – an employer-employee funded and administered program to provide temporary income in the event of unexpected job loss." In other words, government-funded UI would be abolished, and those who worked for companies too small to support UI plans would presumably be out of luck.

Where the state must be involved, the Reform Party much prefers that it be the provincial rather than the federal government.

In medicare, as noted elsewhere, the provinces should receive both federal money and full authority to set their own standards. In other areas of social policy, Ottawa should transfer not just money but the very means of raising it – the tax base – to the provinces. Thus "the content and particulars of provincial policy would be set . . . by provincial governments clearly accountable to the electors of each province."

The emphasis is always the same: to return responsibility as directly as possible to individuals and families, and to set the same rules for everyone regardless of gender or any other distinguishing quality. At no point does the Reform Party actually suggest abandoning anyone, but critics see its approach as at best naive, and at worst an excuse for ignoring people in trouble. "You can jettison people out of the car as you go along the road to this New Canada," says Audrey McLaughlin. "You jettison the sick, and you jettison the poor, and you'll get to your destination. Is it going to be worth getting to?" Nevertheless, Reformers believe that their social ideas are common-sense tools for saving Canada from bankruptcy and putting power back into the hands of the people. They want the country and all its institutions to run in the simple, uncomplicated way they believe families once did, before society began to fall apart.

CHAPTER SEVEN

SOLITUDES IN BLACK AND WHITE

"New Canada must be a balanced federation, not an unbalanced federation where one province has special status or a special deal."
– Preston Manning

"We know perfectly well that we are causing a lot of problems for Canada," says Gilles Duceppe, the only Member of Parliament to be elected under the Bloc Québécois banner. "If I were a Canadian, I would be fed up with Quebec too."

Many Canadians are certainly fed up, and this more than any other fact explains the phenomenal rise of the Reform Party. Its rapid climb in the polls started as debate over the Meech Lake Accord heated up in 1989 and early 1990. Across the country, Canadians who disliked the deal could find no federal party to agree with them. They grew ever more disgusted as the federal Conservatives said that the agreement was good for the country and that opposition was virtually un-Canadian. Mainly they came to resent the constant focus on Quebec, the result of the "no-linkage" deal struck by the provincial premiers at a conference in Edmonton in 1986. The message heard across the nation was taunting but clear: "Quebec first, the rest of you later." Because the Conservatives, Liberals, and NDP were all part of the deal, the dissenting voters had no "national" party to turn to. Waiting in the western wings was the Reform Party, fully formed and ready to go. Its regionally inspired Quebec policy was perfectly suited to the psychological mood of the West, just as the new Bloc Québécois responded to Quebec's emotional nationalism in the post-Meech era. Within a year, Reform's hard-line stand on Quebec was winning support in Ontario too. Burdened by a recession and record job losses, fed up with Quebec's demands, Reform enthusiasts from Ontario swarmed to greet Preston Manning and his party at a series of rallies in June 1991.

The mood at those meetings was remarkably angry. In Toronto, Peterborough, and other centres, the crowds cheered Manning's demand for economic reform and his attacks on the Tories. They also lustily applauded his call for taking all references to French out of the constitution and making Quebec an equal province with all the others. As always, his tone was mild and unemotional, but the audiences got the idea: here was one leader who refused to kowtow to Quebec.

Manning's stand on Quebec attracts many people who have no use for other Reform Party policies on economic and social issues. "I need a political therapist," says Edmonton lawyer Jerome Slavik, a longtime New Democrat. "I can't stand the Reform Party's position on things like medicare and other social programs, including immigration, but I like what they say about Quebec. I'm not prepared to make any more economic or constitutional concessions just to see Quebec stay in the country." Like many other people on the left, Slavik is still angry at Quebec for supporting free trade with the United States.

Despite Manning's low-key rhetorical style, the Reform Party's support on the Quebec issue is often motivated by anger as much as by logic. This anger is mainly the western type, the natural product of many years of feeling left out of Confederation. In this mood westerners do not usually consider Quebec's feelings and demands, just as Quebec rarely considers theirs. Some westerners, including more than a few in the Reform Party, would be happy if Quebec did leave Canada. In this view, the party can make its case freely because the result of Quebec's refusal, independence, is one legitimate option for Canada.

Liberal leader Jean Chrétien likes to call the Reform Party and the Bloc Québécois "Siamese Twins," in reference to their common parent: regional anger with the federal system. On one level there is a good deal of truth in the observation. People in both Quebec and the West feel that "national" parties have failed them by making too many compromises with the other side. Party discipline kept MPs from saying what their constituents felt about Quebec or English Canada. By trying to speak for all Canada, MPs angered voters in all parts of Canada.

It is a mistake to push the similarities too far, however. In fundamental philosophy, the Reform Party and the Bloc Québécois are mutual poison, parties so different and naturally hostile that they can never meet except for momentary convenience on a tactical level. The very heart of the Reform Party, its fervent individualism, is the born enemy of modern Quebec collectivism. These two political forces, the rawest expression of the deep split in the Canadian political psyche, can never be reconciled in such pure forms within one country. The Reform Party, despite its optimistic noises about striking a deal with Quebec, is the strongest expression of individualism Canada has seen in many years. Indeed, the logical result of the Reform Party's opposition to any form of collective rights, including those demanded by the Québécois, is the separation of Quebec from the rest of Canada. Preston Manning likes to tell Quebec to go off and define itself, then come to the bargaining table and see if it wants to live in his "New Canada." But Quebec has been saying "No!" to the Reform Party's kind of Canada for more than a century. Manning's mild tone when he responded to the Conservative constitutional proposals in September 1991 did not change this fact: his party insists that if Quebec wants special status of any kind, it must leave Canada.

In late 1989, at a party meeting in Edmonton, Manning stated the party's policies as a blunt series of ultimatums to Quebec. "If Canada is to continue as one undivided house," he said, "the government . . . must ask the people of Quebec to commit to three foundational principles of Confederation. . . . That the demands and aspirations of all regions are entitled to equal status in constitutional and political negotiation. That freedom of expression is fully accepted as the basis of any language policy. That every citizen is entitled to equality of treatment by governments, without regard to race, language or culture." The party then passed a resolution inviting Quebec to negotiate separation if it could not accept the demands.

After the speech Manning said: "We think it's time somebody stood up and said, 'No, we want to put some demands on you. . . . We do not want to live, nor do we want our children to live, in a house divided against itself, particularly one divided along racial and linguistic lines.'" The leader himself was saying clearly that Quebec should go if it could not accept his party's demands. From this vantage point, it takes only a small twist of the lens to see the Reform Party as encouraging Quebec separatism. It is worth recalling that at about the same time, an internal party poll leaked to the *Edmonton Journal* showed that 94 per cent of Reform members wanted to scrap the Meech Lake deal entirely even if this caused Quebec's separation from Canada.

There are several bedrock positions in the Reform Party's New Canada policy: the absolute constitutional equality of all provinces, a Triple E Senate with an equal number of senators from each province, and a national referendum to endorse any new constitution. All this adds up to the old One Canada formula returned with a vengeance, and with some additions. This may be a legitimate dream for English Canada, but Quebec is unlikely ever to accept it.

The policy is stated in the party's policy *Blue Book* with absolute clarity. "The Reform Party supports the position that Confederation should be maintained," it says, "but that it can only be maintained by a clear commitment to Canada as One Nation, in which the demands and aspirations of all regions are entitled to equal status in constitutional negotiations and political debate, and in which freedom of expression is fully accepted as the basis for language policy across the country."

From Quebec's viewpoint, this means that the province is forever one among ten, not one of two equals, and could never enforce language laws to its own liking. ("Freedom of expression" is Reform Party code for allowing English signs in Quebec.) The Reform Party also calls for removing all references to French and English from the constitution and from federal policy. The party "opposes the conception of Canada as a meeting of two founding races, cultures, and languages," the *Blue Book* says. Many Canadians want this change, Manning insists, especially the nine million or so who are not of French or English extraction. Such people have a point too: but once again, Quebec is not likely to agree to watching its heart and soul being carved out of the constitution.

On one point after another, in fact, the Reform Party's positions boil down to English Canada's ancient dream of how the other partner in the Canadian marriage should behave. The Plains of Abraham is still a high point of Canadian history for many Reformers. This dream has a great attraction for them, but Quebeckers have never shown the slightest interest in sharing it.

After outlining the party's demands on Quebec, the *Blue Book* says: "Should these principles of Confederation be rejected, Quebec and the rest of Canada should consider whether there exists a better political arrangement which will enrich our friendship, respect our common defence requirements, and ensure a free interchange of commerce and people, by mutual consent and for our mutual benefit." To this Manning adds that the Reform Party would negotiate strictly with New Canada's interests in mind. The pill is sugar-coated but the prescription is very simple: Quebec must agree with the Reform Party view of Canada or check out.

Manning is using against Quebec the same sort of hardball tactics Quebec has employed for years against the rest of Canada, to the disgust of so many people. This is emotionally pleasing to those who feel the urge to blow off the steam that has been building ever since the Official Languages Act was passed in 1969. The tactic is responsible for much of the party's popularity. Manning continues to insist that his party is the only one that does not take as its starting point a reaction to Quebec. Yet it is clear that the Reform Party, from its creation in 1987 to its startling popularity today, is in large measure a hostile reaction to Quebec: to Quebec's impact on the constitution, its influence in Ottawa, its contribution to the debt, and its language policies. The Reform Party was the only federal party that opposed Meech Lake from beginning to end. Manning owes his current employment to the very province the Reform Party claims not to consider as its starting point. Without Quebec, the Reform Party would not exist in its present form, just as the Bloc Québécois and Parti Québécois would not exist without English Canada.

The Bloc Québécois and other Quebec nationalists see the Reform Party in a revealing light, as a convenient wedge for prying the country apart. The power brokers in the Bloc would love to negotiate with Preston Manning in the prime minister's chair. Since that is not likely to happen, they will settle for seeing him with as much influence as possible over the process, either before or after a federal election. They like to prop him up by saying flattering things about his party, even though ideologically they have virtually nothing in common with the Reform Party. Bloc Québécois MP Gilles Duceppe made all this clear in June 1991 when he discussed the Reform Party in his House of Commons office:

"If they form a minority government, we'll tell them, 'Govern as you want as long as you negotiate with Quebec, and make the best deal possible for two sovereign countries collaborating, just as in the

[European] Common Market'. . . . If we have proud people, tolerant people, in two independent countries dealing with each other, things will be fine. . . . They say, 'Well, we'll have to decide what kind of Canada we want, and if Quebec likes it okay, but if not they may go.' In a way it's very democratic of them. They're respecting self-determination."

Duceppe likes the idea of negotiating with either the Reform Party or the NDP because neither is really competing for seats on Quebec turf. (The Reform Party will not run candidates in Quebec and the NDP is no threat.) "Those people represent the rest of Canada more than the Tories or the Liberals will do. They are not squeezed between Quebec and the rest of Canada. We have to be very respectful of what they want." However, the Bloc Québécois MP makes it absolutely clear that his party can never accept the Reform Party's One Nation formula. "We've always said we can't be a province among 10 provinces. Not because we're better, not because we're worse. We're just different. We have to decide by ourselves what we want."

Then comes the inevitable conflict over language and minorities. "The English minority of Quebec should have their rights in the [Quebec] constitution," Duceppe says. "The same for the First Nations and the same for the racial and cultural minorities. I don't hear him [Manning] saying what kind of rights he wants to give the minorities in Canada. . . . We must have the collective rights of minorities respected. In a sovereign Quebec, I'm sure we'd have that in our constitution." Nothing could be further from the Reform Party's individualistic view of language and minorities. The Reformers' solution is to declare all humans equal, delete references to language from the constitution, give full authority over language to the provinces, and hope that real-world equality will somehow flow from the words themselves.

Duceppe himself illustrates the vast gulf between the Bloc and the Reformers. There probably is not a single member like him in the entire Reform Party, even if we set aside language and culture. Duceppe was a Communist student organizer in the 1960s in Montreal, and now represents the riding of Laurier Ste.-Marie in the city's East End. One of the riding's best-known features these days is the Gay Village, a five-by-twenty block area inhabited mainly by homosexuals. It is hard to imagine the typical Reformer even setting foot in the place.

Yet there are some striking similarities between Manning and Bloc Québécois leader Lucien Bouchard. Both are intensely religious and they sprinkle their speech with religious references. They are deeply serious, almost tortured by their sense of mission and duty, highly intelligent, but not very cosmopolitan. Each feels a responsibility to represent large numbers of people who have no other voice. "They lead political movements representing a huge segment of the population that feels excluded from the institutional process," says Michel Vastel, the perceptive Ottawa bureau chief for Quebec City's *Le Soleil.*

Most of all, perhaps, the two leaders share a deep sense of place and belonging. From his twangy speech to his ambling walk, Manning is a man of the prairie, Canada's last bastion of frontier individualism. Bouchard was raised in the Saguenay-Lac St. Jean region, the most nationalistic area of Quebec. In an article in *L'Actualité,* Vastel reported that when Bouchard's American-born wife went into labour, he rushed her from Ottawa to Hull in the middle of the night to make sure his child was born on Quebec soil.

There the similarities end. While Manning seems almost afraid to use emotional language, Bouchard stirs up nationalist feelings with his explosive talk of "humiliation" by English Canada. Manning created his party from scratch, while Bouchard's fell into his hands through defections from Tories and Liberals. Some Quebec observers feel that Bouchard does not really want to be the leader of a party at all. Manning has never wanted anything else. As he told Vastel in 1987, "I'm building a kite and I need wind for it to fly." To this the journalist adds: "Lucien Bouchard built a kite because the wind was already there."

Their vast mutual differences collided in October 1991 in a debate between the two leaders taped in Montreal for the CBC "Morningside" radio show. As usual, Manning insisted that the Reform Party is trying to find "the four or five minimum conditions" on which all Canadians, including Quebeckers, can agree. He warned that separation would be an economic disaster for both Quebec and the rest of Canada. Then he hinted that there might be retaliation against Quebec.

"In the past, the reason people have made concessions . . . was for the sake of keeping Canada together," he said. If separation comes, "aren't you going to have self-interest against self-interest?" He argued that western Canadian natural gas producers would try to steal away Hydro Quebec customers in New England. And Manning raised the spectre of higher gas prices and delayed shipments – "everything western Canada could do to screw things up."

Manning's official line on the Bloc is not friendly. "The one thing we have in common is a profound dissatisfaction with the status quo," he said in an interview. "But the fundamental difference is, we're federalists. We want Quebec to remain in Confederation and we do not want anybody else to secede, whereas those guys are not federalists and they want out. On constitutional issues you couldn't get further away than that."

Manning added a few comments that come very close to classic English-Canadian stereotypes of Quebec. "The other thing about the Bloc Québécois is that they, like a lot of the French-Canadian separatists, aren't too strong on economics. They haven't thought through their stuff and don't really care to. . . . Their head is on nationalism and the more traditional sense of culture and language, not clearly thought out economic plans." This will come as news to modern Quebec economists, many of them separatists, like Parti Québécois leader Jacques Parizeau, who have studied in great detail how the province can survive as an independent state.

Manning also shares the standard view outside Quebec that Quebec politicians tend to be corrupt. Defending his party's elaborate questionnaire for candidates, he says: "You can talk to us now or you can talk to a judge down the road. That's what happened in Quebec. Half of these guys who ended up in court, a first year law student could have spent half a day in their ridings and found out what they were up to. Some of them had a track record up to 20 years long of doing it at the municipal level. It's not like it couldn't have been detected, it's just that it never was. Particularly in Quebec, it's almost part of the provincial culture." He seems to feel that when a Quebec politician is crooked it is because he is a Québécois, but when a politician somewhere else is crooked it is because he is a crook. This deeply offends Québécois who can point with discomfiting ease to many cases of corruption in the rest of Canada.

Given all this, it is hardly surprising that Manning believes that the relationship between Quebec and Canada should be more separate, not closer. He feels that all attempts to integrate Quebec more tightly with the rest of the country have led to one disaster after another. Bilingualism and biculturalism were a fiasco, he says. The national relationship has survived only because, at crucial moments, wise people had the sense to pull the warring parties apart again. This is why Manning wants to give Quebec and all provinces much more power over their own affairs, including language.

"I don't like legislating in the language area at all," he told one of the authors. "I don't like this concept of official and unofficial languages, are you a founding one or are you one of the others. I don't like that whole classification system. Our view is that language and culture should be essentially a provincial responsibility, and in the case of Quebec you're going to have essentially a French province, and you would expect their direction later would be to develop and preserve the French language."

Asked if there remains any role for Ottawa, Manning said, "Just to protect people from abuses. . . . If the province started doing stuff in the language area or the cultural area that interferes with basic rights – like say freedom of speech – I think the federal government has a responsibility to enforce basic rights. Our view is that that's how you should have handled the culture and language thing, to make it essentially a provincial responsibility."

Manning wants Quebec to have more freedom, he claims, but then proposes to control the most sensitive areas of all in order to maintain the integrity of One Nation. Quebec would be granted only as much "distinctness" as the rest of the country saw fit. Bill 178, the controversial language law that prohibits the use of English on outdoor signs, would be impossible under such a system. Even many Québécois seem increasingly uncomfortable with this law, but they would not react favourably to Ottawa delaring it null and void.

This is the heart of Reform Party policy on the eternal conflict between English Canada's individualism and Quebec's collective goals for the French majority. As a policy for Canada, it cannot work: it is only logical, in fact, when viewed as a policy with the ultimate goal of Quebec separation. Most Reformers do not seem to want this on a conscious level (although some do), but in expressing their anger at Quebec they could encourage that result.

The traditional parties wrestle almost tragically with the problem, declaring on the one hand that Quebec is free to separate, then promising on the other to make sure it never happens. Efforts to reconcile the logical extremes of Canada have divided the Tories, the Liberals, and the New Democratic Party. Nevertheless, the traditional parties at least try to include the Canadian contradiction within their party platforms. They believe that without Quebec there can be no Canada, so in order to win votes and assume power, each must deal with the national dilemma. The Reform Party is under no such handicap. This is perhaps the real meaning behind Preston Manning's assertion that his party does not take Quebec as its starting point.

His father has always believed that the French-English conflict is a regional problem, not a national one. In the 1960s Ernest Manning was the only Canadian premier who spoke against the formation of the Royal Commission on Bilingualism and Biculturalism by the Liberal government of Lester Pearson. When his opposition became known, the Quebec government had to lay on extra security for Premier Manning as he arrived for a national premiers' conference. Ernest Manning explained the episode with some pride in an archival interview in 1981.

"That was a very, very serious mistake ever setting up that Commission. . . . We happened to be the only province that opposed it at the time. And we opposed it, not on the grounds of anything anti-French or anti-Quebec, but we said, 'What you're going to do is make an issue which is a local issue [into] a national issue. You're going to give the hassle over language in Quebec national status by putting this before a national commission. And it isn't a national issue. If you get outside Quebec, and maybe a few people in New Brunswick and a few in Ontario, you'll find people who yawn when you talk to them about bilingualism. . . . If you make it a national commission on a local issue, you're going to open a Pandora's box that you'll never get closed.'"

Ernest Manning said he expressed this view forcefully in letters to Pearson. When the federal opposition pressed Pearson, the prime minister released the correspondence with all premiers after obtaining their permission. The revelation of Ernest Manning's position caused an uproar in Quebec. He recalled in the interview: "I remember the security people getting in touch with me wanting to give me a few special security fellows down there because we weren't too popular! . . . Quebec of course was pretty much in turmoil at that time, and we were driven by armed services people with a personal security guy with us all the time, even stationed outside our hotel room. . . . They treated us [premiers] all the same, of course. I remember this fellow coming – I said, 'Is it necessary?'

and he said, 'Well, I think it is in your case.'"

Preston Manning shares this belief that language is a local problem that should be contained within Quebec. The whole issue of French-English duality, in fact, he sees as a central Canadian problem, not as a national one. He outlined the basis of his Quebec thinking in a long speech to the Reform Party Assembly held in Saskatoon in April 1991. Packed with historical references, the speech is the best single guide to his fundamental view that Quebec's relationship with Canada should be more separate, perhaps entirely separate, because more closeness means more strife.

"Is it not true," he asked the audience, "for both Quebecers and the rest of Canada, that it has been attempts to more tightly integrate the institutions, languages and cultures of the English and the French by political and constitutional means which has been the greatest single cause of political disunity . . . over the past 200 years?" In each case where such attempts have produced a national crisis, he asked again, has it not been solved "by establishing a more separate political relationship between the two within a broader political framework?"

"The testimony of history," Manning responded to his own question, "is that it hasn't worked, for the same reasons that the attempt to govern Canada today as an equal partnership between two unequal groups isn't working." Manning sees Confederation not in the traditional light, as an attempt to accommodate English and French within Canada, but as a sensible effort to pull them further apart. "It is sometimes said that the concept of Canada as an equal partnership between two founding nations is embedded in Confederation and the BNA Act of 1867. This is not only false, but the very opposite is true. Confederation came about in part due to the failure of the 'Two Nations' concept." The Maritime provinces were brought into Canada, Manning contends, but Quebec and Ontario were actually separated from each other. In that sense Confederation was an Act of Union for English Canada, but also an

"Act of Separation" of French and English Canada.

Preston Manning believes later years were largely a battle between politicians of the "old Two Nations school," who wanted to ensure rights for francophones outside Quebec, and noble westerners who resisted this but "fully embraced the new vision of One Nation from sea to sea." Today's crisis arose in the 1960s, said Manning, the echo of his father, "when Lester Pearson established the Royal Commission on Bilingualism and Biculturalism and revived the concept of Canada as an equal partnership between two founding races, languages, and cultures – the English and the French. Future historians will no doubt refer to this as 'the Great Leap Backward.' A fateful decision was made to make the federal government, not the government of Quebec, the primary guardian of the French fact in Canada, and, in effect, to 'nationalize' the very issue which the Fathers of Confederation had 'provincialized' in 1867."

Everyone was dissatisfied with this even in the 1960s, Manning claims. (He seems to forget the great outpouring of affection for Quebec, French, and Pierre Trudeau in the late 1960s, perhaps because many people in Alberta failed to share the enthusiasm.) "Outer Canadians, especially western Canadians, were beginning to fully realize the real significance of the 'Two Nations' theory of Canada. A Canada built on a union of the English and the French is a country built on the union of Quebec and Ontario. And in this union the other provinces are, in a fundamental sense, little more than extensions of Ontario."

The way to break this cycle, the Reform Party argues today, is not to guarantee the rights of more groups in the constitution, but to remove all reference to language and minority groups. Every Canadian, regardless of language, ethnicity, colour, or any other group criterion, would simply be declared to have equal rights. Ottawa's role would be to ensure that those rights were not violated. The preservation of French and ethnic identity would become a purely private matter unless provinces decided to get involved.

"The traditions and languages and institutions of the French and the English are to be valued and preserved as part of our Canadian heritage," Preston Manning says. "Let that be done by individuals, families, organizations, and even provincial governments if they so desire. But efforts to go beyond that – to politicize and institutionalize and constitutionalize French-English relations on a national basis and as a raison d'être for the nation itself – have led again . . . not to unity but to crisis."

Then Manning comes to the definition of New Canada that he preaches in various forms on platforms around the country. "New Canada must be a balanced federation, not an unbalanced federation where one province has special status or a special deal; not an unbalanced federation where all the provinces have special status and Canada has no status; not an unbalanced federation where one generation centralizes all the power in Ottawa, and the next generation centralizes it all in the provincial capitals. . . . " The "balance" means equal provinces, equal rights for all citizens, and more power in the provinces, checked by a federal government with the authority to protect human rights.

After arguing with considerable persuasiveness that Quebec and the rest of Canada get along best when most separate, Manning goes back to the One Nation formula. First he virtually declares that Two Nations works, then decides that it is unacceptable because it began with a pact between Quebec and Ontario. Therefore the solution to our current dilemma is One Nation. What if Quebec cannot accept? Manning deals with this in a few quick paragraphs that amount to a simple message: take it or leave it.

"If the vision of a New Quebec within a new Canada cannot be realized – if the two visions are too different or if the political judgement and will to reconcile them is not present – then the focus of the great Canadian constitutional negotiation should turn to defining mutually advantageous terms and conditions of a more separate relationship." And Quebec should understand that "Whoever is negotiating on behalf of New Canada is unlikely to be attracted to the concept of Sovereignty-Association as currently advanced by some Quebec politicians." In words echoing Abraham Lincoln, Manning warns that the impasse must be resolved in the "next several years. We cannot stagger into the 21st century still fixated on English-French relations, a house divided against itself, foolishly hoping to survive or prosper as a first-rank industrial nation." A federal election should be held quickly to determine "who really speaks for the New Quebec, and who should be entrusted to negotiate on its behalf with the representatives of New Canada."

Today, when he tries to explain why Quebec might accept any of this, Manning offers only a vague populist faith in the people. In his 1991 speech to the party Assembly he said: "The more the people of Quebec and the people of the rest of Canada are involved in the defining of the New Quebec and the New Canada, the higher will be the probability that the two visions can be reconciled. . . . Conversely, the more the visions of the New Quebec and the New Canada are the pet projects of intellectual elites, or self-serving politicians hoping to ride either Quebec nationalism or Canadian panic to political power, the lower will be the probability that the two visions can be reconciled."

In order to let the people speak, Manning proposes that delegates be elected to constitutional assemblies from Quebec, Ontario, the Atlantic Provinces, the Prairies, and British Columbia. The handiwork of all these bodies would then be presented to Ottawa and the provinces for negotiation, and the results ratified in a national referendum.

This is a democratic notion, but the fact remains that poll after poll shows vastly different views of the country among "rank-and-file" Québécois and other Canadians. These differences were not invented by politicians, and they will not go away just because ordinary people debate them. Nor will Québécois submit to a national referendum on their place in the country. Manning's idea sounds like a poisonous recipe for five duelling Spicer Commissions that would voice once again all our mutual hostilities. In any case, Manning himself does not seem very hopeful. Immediately after outlining his "solution," he said that if the talks fail, attention should turn at once to negotiating "a more separate relationship."

The leader is a keen student of history, especially the constitutional development of Canada and the succession crisis leading to the Civil War in the United States. His reading tends to weighty tomes such as Canada's Confederation Debates and the American Lincoln-Douglas debates (which his wife gave him as a Christmas present). Given his detailed knowledge of our past, some of the things he does not mention are striking in their absence.

Most notably, he does not point out how important Quebec is to western Canadians as a balancing mechanism against Ottawa and sometimes Ontario, even though Ernest Manning, as Alberta's premier, more than once used this alliance for his own benefit. As the authors noted in *Breakup: Why the West Feels Left out of Canada* (1990), Quebec has often been a western ally at crucial moments. The late René Lévesque backed former Alberta Premier Peter Lougheed's battle against the National Energy Program. For a generation the western provinces and Quebec have supported each other in the struggle for provincial rights against Ottawa and occasionally Ontario. In 1989 and 1990, the premiers of Quebec, Saskatchewan, and Alberta agreed not to criticize each other as they passed laws limiting minority language rights in their own provinces.

An official with Alberta's Federal and Intergovernmental Affairs Department during Lévesque's time remembers how shocked she was when she realized just how deep the alliance ran. "Maybe I was naive," she said, "but I had no idea this link even existed. Right from my first meeting in Quebec City, though, I sensed the deep feeling between the provinces. The Quebeckers really wined and dined us, treated us like true friends. Later on I realized that this alignment was based on a common respect for provincial rights and incredible mistrust of Ottawa and Ontario." Resentment over language was never a factor, she recalled, even when it was an issue in the media. The results of this natural Quebec-West alliance are not always admirable, but they have been vitally important to the West over the years.

The Reformers, when they invite Quebec to leave, ignore the implications for the West of losing this ally. They forget that without Quebec, Ontario would suddenly have half the Canadian population, nearly half the seats in the House of Commons, half the Supreme Court judges, and one-third of the senators. Preston Manning talks constantly about the need for a "balanced federation on the northern half of the North American continent," but it's hard to conceive of a less balanced federation than Canada would be without Quebec.

Ontario would dominate his New Canada, not out of malice or greed but by irresistible force of numbers. During a visit to Alberta in August, 1991, Ontario Premier Bob Rae gave a hint of things to come. He supported the concept of both an elected and an effective Senate, but could not endorse provincial equality. After all, he noted, "we're not greedy. It's just that we're 10 million people." With Quebec gone, Ontario leaders would be certain to consider their province even more important, and they would be right. The Reform Party's goal of equal provinces would be even harder to achieve.

Nevertheless, there is no benefit to the Reform Party in stressing these points. Noting Quebec's value to the West would tend to diminish western anger. That would in turn reduce support for a party that has become the main carrier of the anger. Also, emphasizing the natural strains between Ontario and the West would not be helpful as the party expands from the West into Ontario. These disconcerting realities would blow some large holes in the Reform Party's Quebec policy, which depends so heavily on emotion, stereotypes, and hostility. For tactical reasons that seem obvious, Reformers do not talk about possible compromises. If the party began to discuss real solutions, it might quickly be branded a party like the others and lose the "we'll-fix-Quebec" vote.

The party also rejects entirely the aspirations of French-speakers in the West and elsewhere in English-speaking Canada. Indeed, it proposes to complete, through neglect, the destruction of the French heritage outside Quebec that began with the hanging of Louis Riel in 1885. The Reformers would abandon French-speaking communities across the country (and also the English in Quebec) to the mercies of provincial governments. Ottawa's only role would be a negative, passive one, to protect against denial of personal freedom of speech.

In late 1991, Preston Manning's Quebec policy did not reflect his father's earlier call for flexibility in dealings with Quebec. In 1980 Ernest Manning said, "If there's one thing we need in Canada today if we're going to resolve our constitutional problems, [it is] flexibility. The biggest stumbling-block is going to be the federal government and the provinces which are taking such rigid positions."

The Reform Party has become a new example of the same problem. Flexibility on Quebec is not popular with Reformers who insist on their simple solution, or none at all.

CHAPTER EIGHT

BORN-AGAIN CANADA

"In a democratic country, it is inconsistent that the voices of established parties are so favoured . . . and the voices of small or new parties are effectively stifled."

– Reform Party statement to a Royal Commission

MANY CANADIANS see the Reform Party as no more than a brash, noisy voice of protest for venting anger at the Conservative government. They regard it as essentially negative, forever attacking rather than proposing, devoid of concrete proposals for Canada's future. This is a serious underestimation of Preston Manning and his party. In fact, the Reformers present a very clear and detailed vision of Canadian federalism and politics, complete with clear formulas for turning the vision into reality. Taken together, these are the most radical proposals ever presented to Canadians by a party that could hold the balance of power after a federal election. If all were to take effect, Canada would be a vastly different federation, and in some ways almost unrecognizable.

Of the many ideas about federalism in Reform Party policy, one above all forms the cornerstone of the party's New Canada. This is the call for a Senate in which all provinces would have the same number of senators, in which all senators would be elected, and in which the body would have effective powers "in safeguarding regional interests." Many westerners find compelling logic in this "Triple E" idea. It would get rid of the quasi-colonial mentality that clings to the Prairies, a legacy of Ottawa's policy of settling the region as a subordinate territory. It would give small provinces some protection against unfriendly federal policies such as the National Energy Program, which many westerners believe was an unfair attack by Ottawa on a western industry. It would make the two largest provinces, Ontario and Quebec, equal to all the others at one level of government, although they would still dominate the House of Commons because of the number of seats dictated by population.

The Reformers clearly have the American system of government in mind when they push this formula. (All 50 U.S. states, no matter how big or small, send two senators each to Washington.) As Preston Manning points out, there are plenty of examples in other countries as well. Australia, a British parliamentary democracy like Canada, also has a Triple E Senate. Switzerland recognizes the equality of its cantons, and Germany has an upper chamber that effectively represents its states (though not through equality). Canada, arguably the biggest country in the world since the collapse of the USSR, is the only large western federation that does not recognize some form of effective regional balance in the central government. Reformers consider this to be the single most important reason for Canada's eternal disunity: when eight provinces out of ten are always underrepresented, they argue, any other result would be astonishing.

Several studies have proposed models for a Triple E Senate that might work in Canada without undermining the parliamentary system. Most suggest that the authority of the House of Commons should be preserved by allowing it to override Senate vetoes, and by permitting only the Commons to initiate money bills. Also, the cabinet would be chosen entirely from the Commons. The Senate would be able to initiate some types of legislation, but would serve mainly as a check on unfair legislation forced on small provinces by large ones. By recognizing provincial equality, the Reformers say, Canada would finally shed the last remnants of colonialism and become a mature democracy. The federal Tories recognized some of these points when they proposed an elected Senate in their constitutional package of September 24, 1991.

The Triple E Senate solution, appealing as it is to Reformers, does not translate easily from the U.S., or even Australia, to Canada. The great stumbling block is always Quebec, with its well-founded anxiety at becoming the equal of nine other provinces. Quebec has never shown any willingness to give the Senate real power or to reduce the proportion of senators from Quebec. (In normal times, when the Red Chamber does not include special temporary senators like those named to pass the GST, Quebec has 24 of 104 senators.) Nor is Quebec moved by offers of "double majority" provisions or other devices to protect its culture and language. None of that changed after the Tories released their constitutional package. The Reformers, in turn, show no readiness to dilute their demand for a pure Triple E Senate. In part this stems from their disgust at unending compromises with Quebec. Some Reformers feel, too, that a Triple E Senate will be easier to achieve with Quebec out of Canada, but they are probably wrong. Ontario has always had major objections to the Triple E idea as well, for the obvious reason that, as Canada's largest province, it would lose significant power. Ontario officials have sometimes conceded that the Senate should be elected and even that each province should send an equal number of senators to Ottawa. Nevertheless, Ontario politicians have never shown any real willingness to make the body effective at the expense of the House of Commons. If Quebec leaves Canada, giving Ontario proportionately more population and influence, this argument will be even stronger.

The second building block of the Reformers' New Canada is the absolute equality of all Canadians without reference to language, culture, race, religion, or any other group characteristic. Beyond that simple declaration, most references to French and English, and all mention of two founding groups, would be absent from the constitution. Individual rights would be paramount while group or collective rights would have no standing. Most Reformers firmly believe that the individual is paramount in society and that all group rights tend to infringe on individual rights. Preston Manning's own belief in individualism, in turn, springs from his deep religious convictions. If any one idea expresses the Reform Party's core ideology, it is this pure individualism with its strong echo of the western frontier.

Such undiluted individualism is light-years from Canada's current constitution, which over the years has become a patchwork of individual rights, collective rights, and language rights. The 1982 Charter of Rights and Freedoms promises equality under law "without discrimination based on race, national or ethnic origin, colour, religion, sex, age or mental or physical disability." Nonetheless, the very next section, headed "affirmative action programs," says that the equality statement does not preclude any law or program intended to help disadvantaged groups. The Reformers would dump all such "collectivist" notions. They would also delete a long section of the Charter dealing with official languages and minority-language education rights. Minority education rights would be protected "possibly by interprovincial agreement," says the party's *Blue Book.* There would be limited bilingualism in the federal civil service. French would be the language of Quebec and English of the rest of Canada. The Reformers, in short, would try to simplify both the constitution and the country by defining Canada as a land of equal citizens living in equal provinces.

The country's French and English heritages do not fit into this vision, so the party states its opposition to "the conception of Canada as 'a meeting of two founding races, cultures and languages.'" This notion, it says, is "an inappropriate description of the reality of the regions outside Central Canada" and "unfair to the vast majority of unilingual Canadians." The trouble is that, while Canadians of British and other backgrounds usually do not feel threatened by such policies, Québécois certainly do. To them, it is hardly possible to remove the recognition of French as a founding culture without also removing Quebec from Canada. This policy is completely safe from theft by the other parties as long as they seek to win seats in Quebec.

The provinces would be far more powerful in the Reformers' New Canada. There should be a clear division of powers between levels of government, and "legislative authority should rest with the level most able to effectively govern in each area, with a bias to decentralization in cases of uncertainty." This closely resembles the American notion that undefined powers belong to the states rather than the federal government. John A. Macdonald's vision of Canada, embedded in the British North America Act of 1867, contained the exact opposite concept, because Macdonald and many of his contemporaries believed that the American system caused decades of strife and finally the Civil War.

The Conservatives made a bow toward decentralization in their September, 1991 proposals when they offered to transfer some power over culture, immigration, and other matters to the provinces. They stopped far short of the Reform Party's plan for massive and radical decentralization, however. As already noted, Manning's party would transfer all authority for medicare to the provinces, along with the complete tax base for social programs.

Ottawa's spending power, the font of all its authority, would also be severely restricted by the Reform Party. Until the elimination of the national debt, Ottawa would be forced by law to earn more than it spends every year. After the debt is gone, the federal government would have to balance the budget in each three-year period. Funding for multiculturalism would end and the Multiculturalism Department would be abolished. Many Crown corporations and as much government service as possible would be privatized. These measures would remove power from the federal capital and place it in the provinces, or remove it from governments entirely. Yet the Reform Party proposes no limits for provincial programs or spending. There is no guarantee that the provinces would not simply take up Ottawa's wasteful habits as they expand into former federal territory. Indeed, the spending of several provinces has gone up at a speedier rate than federal expenditure.

There is one area, the environment, where the Reform Party sees a leadership role for Ottawa, both in enforcement and in co-ordination with the provinces. The *Blue Book* calls for tough penalties for companies that pollute, including "fines and jail sentences for officers and executives of companies violating environmental laws." The core of the party's policy is "sustainable development," the current buzzword for meshing environmental and economic interests. "Environmental considerations must carry equal weight with economic, social and technical considerations in the development of a project," the *Blue Book* states. Manning always presents a clean environment as part of his vision for Canada. In one speech he said: "New Canada is a place where real jobs with real incomes are created, not by the government, but by internationally competitive, financially viable, environmentally sustainable industries and businesses." As ever, the Reform Party wants business to do the job, but in this case there would be a public guidance through regulations, penalties, and "environmentally conscious" purchasing by all governments. The party would also give Ottawa more power over education and manpower training.

On the strength of these gains for the federal power, key Reform Party official Tom Flanagan insists that decentralization is not part of the party's agenda. "You have to be careful not to confuse decentralization with privatization," says Flanagan, the party's director of policy, strategy, and communications. "They're not the same thing at all.... Try to think of it as a triangle: in some areas we want to give more authority to the provinces, in others more authority to the federal government, and in some others we want the responsibility to go to civil society. We have to get away from thinking of all this in terms of just Ottawa and the provinces." Nevertheless, the *Blue Book* itself states clearly the Reform preference for decentralization.

Reformers also want to place much more power in the hands of the voters through three devices: referendum, initiative, and recall. All these ideas would force major changes in the Canadian system of representative democracy, by which we elect members to represent the interests of both the people and the country.

National referenda would be binding on the government, and would pass by a simple majority of all voters, including a majority in two-thirds of the provinces (with the two territories also counted as provinces). This would apply to all constitutional changes and to shifts in important policies such as immigration. The one certainty about this proposal is that Quebec will never accept it. Quebec leaders have said time and again that they will be bound only by Quebec referenda on any matters that affect the province.

The initiative idea, in the Reform view, means that three per cent of the eligible voters could force the government to hold a referendum on a proposal or bill. The referendum would be placed on the ballot at the following federal election. Finally, the recall proposition would give electors the opportunity to fire MPs who lose support in their ridings. (Although the party *Blue Book* supports the "principle" of recall, it fails to outline any procedure.)

All these notions of direct democracy have become quite popular since the collapse of the Meech Lake Accord. In British Columbia, former Socred Premier Rita Johnston tried to entice the voters during the province's general election with ballot questions asking voters if they wanted the right to initiate policies and recall MLAs. In effect, she rolled all three Reform ideas into one by holding a referendum on initiative and recall. Johnston's personal lack of success was stunning: she lost her own riding and her party won only seven seats. Yet the ideas were hugely popular even if they could not revive a dying government: more than 75 per cent of the voters favoured both initiative and recall. The new premier, New Democrat Mike Harcourt, has promised to bring the measures into effect. As former B.C. Liberal Leader Gordon Gibson suggested in *The Globe and Mail*, the New Democrats won the election but Reform ideas captured the voters.

The idea of recalling elected members, the voters' ultimate weapon against an MP that they do not like, evokes a peculiar echo in Manning's home province, and in the Alberta Social Credit Party his father once led. When the Socreds took power in 1935 under Premier William Aberhart, the first law the new government passed allowed voters to recall their MLAS. However, in 1937, the constituents of Aberhart's own riding, Okotoks-High River, started a petition demanding the recall of the premier himself. Soon they had signed up an astounding two-thirds of all eligible voters, the percentage needed to unseat the premier. To save Aberhart, the Socred government revoked the recall act retroactive to the date of its passage. Aberhart justified this blatant manipulation by saying that big oil companies in the riding had bullied employees into signing the petition. Recall was never heard from again in the Social Credit era, but now it finds new life in the Reform Party. Such precedents convince some experts that the Reform Party's ideas about direct democracy will never become reality. "These notions are always very popular with people who are out of power," says University of Toronto historian Desmond Morton. "But once those people are in power, the ideas look far less appealing."

Of all the party's designs for overhauling the Canadian system, plans to make MPS more responsive to their ridings might be the most appealing to voters outraged by the arrogant behaviour of federal politicians. MPS would swear allegiance to their constituents as well as to the Queen. (Her Majesty's reaction to this proposed levelling is not recorded, but plenty of Reformers love the idea.) Members would be officially beholden not to party leaders but to the voters. "The duty of elected members to their constituents should supersede their obligations to their political parties," the party *Blue Book* states. To free members from party discipline even further, the rules should be changed so that a lost vote in the House of Commons would not automatically mean defeat of the government (such a loss would have to be followed by passage of a formal non-confidence motion). Until these rules are passed, Reform MPs would vote with the party unless the riding instructed them not to. The MPs would be expected to conduct mini-referenda in their ridings on every important issue. Elections would be held at a fixed date every four years. Once again, all these measures would tend to weaken Canada's tradition of representative and responsible government. Yet public anger at the way our system works is so deep that even the governing Conservatives agree with the need for serious parliamentary reform.

This radical Reform vision of the New Canada tries to strike a balance betwen the populist surge that has brought the party to prominence and the thorny political reality of Canada. As a believer in populism (and a shrewd reader of the public mood), Manning proposes to put as much power as possible in the hands of the people. As a careful student of history, however, he knows that a party must also be united or it will be crushed in the real world of politics. The Progressives, who won a stunning victory with the second-largest number of seats in the 1921 federal election, tilted too far toward populism. Most of the members did not even believe in the idea of a party, so the Progressive members rarely acted like a unified group. Mackenzie King's disciplined Liberals stole their ideas while humiliating and tricking them in the House of Commons. By 1929, the former leader of the Progressives, Thomas Crerar, had become a minister in King's cabinet.

With his eyes on the potential pitfalls, Manning is trying to make sure that his party both represents constituents and survives in the Ottawa shark pool. All the pushes and pulls are clearly evident in this tortured *Blue Book* statement on how Reform MPs are to behave: "Until Parliamentary Reform is enacted, the Reform Party pledges that, having had a full opportunity to express their views and vote freely in caucus, with such caucus vote always made public, Reform MPs shall vote with the Reform Party majority in the House unless a Member is instructed to abstain or vote otherwise by his/her constituents." This convoluted message boils down to a simple formula: talk like a populist, vote like a party loyalist. In reality, the Reformers could not do anything else until all parties agree to hard and fast rules on such matters as free votes and confidence motions.

The Reform Party also wants radical changes in how political parties raise money and finance elections. In effect, the Reformers would eliminate all public help now given to parties through such measures as refunds of expenses and tax rebates for donations. Some of the proposals are long overdue: for instance, MPs would no longer be able to "rent" their parliamentary staff during campaigns. Also, candidates who win 15 per cent of the vote would not be paid a 50-per-cent rebate on their election expenses. As the party made clear in a submission to the Royal Commission on Election Law and Party Financing: "Private interests should be supported by private dollars. The taxpayers of Canada should not foot the bill for groups, whether federal parties or not, who seek to promote a political agenda."

Other Reform proposals, such as the end of tax rebates, could in fact hurt parties that depend on small private donations. Parties whose corporate friends have deep pockets, especially the Tories, would suddenly have a big advantage. The maximum rebate of $500 means very little to a company ready to donate $10,000 or $20,000. However, the rebate for smaller donors (75 per cent of the first $100 and half of the next $450) is a very large incentive to donate. The Reformers, as noted, have not done very well with corporate donations, but they hope to change that.

The party argues that the end of rebates would not discourage small donors from giving. "We went through our first few years of existence without rebate privileges and it had no effect on donations," says Stephen Harper, the party's chief policy officer. "The money came in just fine." Harper feels that political donations are motivated more by belief in the party than by tax breaks. Eliminating the incentives would therefore hurt the Tories and Liberals, whose donors tend to give more out of habit than out of enthusiasm.

The Reformers are pushing this issue partly because they disagree with public money being spent on private causes, but also because they believe that the rules favour the old-line parties. The same motive lies behind their court challenge to limits on the amount of TV and radio advertising time that a federal party can buy during an election campaign. The suit was prompted by an allotment of TV time for the next federal election that seemed patently unfair. A federally appointed broadcasting arbitrator decreed that each radio and TV station could set aside up to 6.5 hours of prime time for party advertising during the campaign. Of this time, the Tories could buy 173 minutes, the Liberals 110 minutes, and the NDP 71 minutes. The Reform Party would get only 10 minutes, even though it often outpolls the Tories in national surveys, and the Liberals and NDP in some regions. If the challenge succeeds, all parties will be able to buy an equal amount of time as long as they can afford it.

Once again, there are two views of the results. Critics say that rich parties like the Tories would dominate the airwaves by scooping up the time that other parties could not afford. The Reformers argue that new parties would at least have a chance to buy the advertising.

"I believe the law is sinister," says Stephen Harper. "It's not motivated to solve a problem. It's created to prohibit the formation of new parties. The only way you can justify a restriction is to keep parties from pre-emptively buying up all the time." Adds Sian

Stephenson, a Calgary lawyer and the party's vice-president of regulatory affairs: "We'd rather see no legislation at all than the current legislation."

The party made a convincing argument against these time allotments in its brief to the Royal Commission. The method "is unfair and favours established parties," it said. "In a democratic country, it is inconsistent that the voices of established parties are so favoured . . . and the voices of small or new parties are effectively stifled. . . . Allocation of broadcast time . . . on the basis of previous popularity is inherently unfair." The Reform Party proposed that each registered party be allowed to buy an equal portion of the 6.5 hours available on every station. If a party did not buy its full share, that time would be split equally among the others.

The Reform Party also wants to remove all restrictions on advertising by special-interest groups during campaigns. This would make campaigns closer to American-style free-for-alls than the carefully regulated affairs Canadians are used to. For instance, there would be nothing to stop groups like American Political Action Committees (PACS) from attacking parties and individuals. Canadians had a taste of this in 1988, when non-party groups were allowed to advertise for and against free trade during the campaign. "People put their money on the table and spoke up," says Sian Stephenson. "That's what free speech is all about."

Another view comes from Mel Hurtig, former publisher and nationalist author of *The Betrayal of Canada*. "What it meant was that big business could buy an election," Hurtig says. "They didn't have to disclose the source of their funds and they weren't even subject to the normal constraints faced by registered parties. This allowed them to advertise in favour of free trade the day before the election, when the parties couldn't advertise at all. Worst of all, the advocates of free trade were allowed tax deductions for their donations." The Reform Party's ideas would truly take the lid off Canada's election battles, but Reformers do not see any danger in this. To them there can never be too much democracy, while government control almost always leads to evil.

Many observers have noticed the American quality of many of these ideas. It is no accident that Manning often echoes the great American president, Abraham Lincoln, by repeating such famous phrases as "A house divided against itself cannot stand." Manning is a keen student of the pre-Civil War era in the United States and sees many parallels between Canada's national crisis and the American turmoil of the mid-19th century. Speaking to a group of business people in Toronto in 1990, Manning compared his party to Lincoln's Republicans. He explained how the American national parties split and the new regional party led by Lincoln rose to power. According to an account of the meeting in *Saturday Night* magazine, he then said: "Now this isn't New York and you're not Republicans, and I'm certainly not Abraham Lincoln. But the ingredients exist in Canada for that kind of development. It's my intention to bring those ingredients together in the next couple of years." He noted another parallel that seemed very personal. "One of the turning points was when a broken-down old lawyer from Springfield, Illinois [Lincoln] made a solitary trip to New York and New England and presented his feelings about a populist party which the eastern establishment bought into." Manning takes Lincoln as a personal model, often quoting such aphorisms as "A drop of honey catches more flies than a gallon of gall." Yet he does not mention that, whatever their merit, Lincoln's policies did not solve the sectional strife dividing the union. That was accomplished only after four bitter years of Civil War.

Manning bristles when anyone suggests that the ideas behind his New Canada are basically American. After a news report stated that one of his speeches favoured a U.S.-style constitution, Manning told one of the authors: "I never said that. That's what *The Globe and Mail* guy said. I object to that. If you talk about equality, somehow they think the Americans have a monopoly on the concept of equality. If you talk about referendum, they think the Americans have a monopoly on direct democracy. Haven't they ever heard of Switzerland? I just talk about a constitution in which all Canadians would be treated equally without regard to race, language, and culture. . . . You can argue that the Americans do enshrine equality, but they hardly have a monopoly on it."

Without doubt, however, Reformers look with longing toward many American features of government and federal structure, and Canada would have a much more American look if they got their way. This is partly because so many Reformers are westerners. Much of the Canadian West, with little tradition of United Empire Loyalism but considerable immigration from the U.S., is less suspicious of American ideas than other parts of Canada. The party's Statement of Principles shows this friendliness clearly if a bit defensively. "The establishment of more positive relations with the U.S. need not in any way impair Canada's national sovereignty or cultural identity," it says.

The Reformers, of course, were avid proponents of free trade with the U.S. during the 1988 election federal campaign. They remain so today, although Manning seldom mentions this in Ontario, where job losses and plant closings have made the trade pact very unpopular. (Ontario lost 75 per cent of the Canadian jobs that vanished during the recession; it's impossible to say how much of this was caused by free trade, but many Ontarians blame the pact.) When he does mention the trade deal, usually in response to a question, Manning suggests that such problems are caused by Ottawa's failure to provide retraining and adjustment programs. In general, the party strongly supports the idea of global free trade. All domestic policy would support that objective, from science and research to taxation and education.

Yet it is a mistake to dismiss the Reformers as mere imitators of American ideas, or to charge them with harbouring a secret agenda to turn Canada into a mini-United States. As a populist movement that became a viable party, Reform is in a uniquely Canadian tradition. America's rigid two-party system makes such movements virtually impossible. Preston Manning may admire great American presidents, but he takes his practical examples from home-grown reformers such as Joseph Howe, Robert Baldwin, Louis-Hippolyte LaFontaine, Frederick Haultain, William Aberhart, and his own father. Although the Reform vision of Canada is radical, its inspiration and most of its proposals spring from the party's perception of purely Canadian needs.

Behind Reform plans for massive change in the political system lies another basic Reform Party attitude: abhorrence of debt and overspending. Reformers want their candidates to have money in the bank and no debts on their ledgers. They would like their country to behave the same way, and many of their policies are aimed at making sure that it does. Given the current national mood, this is likely to win the Reform Party many friends, but it also threatens powerful interest groups. Once again, the implications of Reform policy are very far-reaching.

The party's showcase target, because it is the easiest one to hit, is the current system of salaries, pensions, and perks for MPs and senators. Salaries and expense allowances should be at least frozen until the debt is eliminated, the party says. MPs should not get extra salaries for serving as cabinet ministers and committee chairmen. In addition, the Reformers call for drastic rollbacks in the rich pension scheme for MPs. No longer would MPs be able to draw their pensions before age 60, and if they already have, further payments would be postponed for an equivalent number of years past age 60. Those pensions would be subject to the same "clawback" taxation applied to payments under Old Age Security. It is hardly surprising that the National Citizens' Coalition, with its close ideological and personal ties to the Reform Party, launched a major advertising campaign against MPs' pensions in the fall of 1991. Newspaper advertisements pointed out (correctly) that an MP with only six years' experience could collect $17,000 a year, and that a member retiring at age 31 might be paid more than $2 million in a lifetime. The NCC, after writing to all MPs, divided them by name in the ad into categories called "The Good," "The Bad," and "The Bashful." (It is interesting to note that Ernest Manning, for his 25 years' service as Alberta premier, receives $28,382 a year in provincial legislature pension. He was also a senator from 1970 to 1983. The exact pension payments for senators are not public, but based on salary averages an official in the Senate office calculated Ernest Manning's pension at just over $15,000 a year. For such long service, both these amounts are very low by today's standards.)

The pension fight is only the highly visible part of the most radical cost-cutting program ever presented to Canadians by a major national party. Manning often says the party wants to slash 15 per cent of all federal spending at once. Although the *Blue Book* does not repeat this pledge, it outlines a long order of priorities for spending cuts. First comes spending on MPs and Parliament, then "a general program of expenditure reduction or elimination" in the following areas:

Thick layers of middle management in federal administration;
Federal "pet projects" such as official bilingualism, multiculturalism, and certain government advertising;
Grants to interest groups for the purposes of political lobbying;
Foreign aid;
Subsidies and tax concessions to business;
Selling of most Crown corporations;
Any area that fails to achieve a fair regional distribution, and;
Universal and bureaucratic social policy in areas such as day care.

All this is a clear attack on bureaucracy and spending. The party's policy on the Goods and Services Tax, on the other hand, is almost schizophrenic in its confusion. The reason for this is easy enough to discern: the party hates the way the tax was imposed but likes the idea of applying GST revenue to the debt. So the *Blue Book* says flatly in one section, "The Reform Party opposes the GST," while in another it calls for paying GST revenue into a Debt Retirement Fund. As we have seen, Manning now favours keeping a revised GST despite his earlier tirades against the tax. In this case, the party's dislike of debt seems to win the wrestling match with its distaste for bureaucratic measures imposed from above.

The deep cuts that the party proposes will have equally deep impacts, but the *Blue Book* is far from clear about what they will be. It calls for a radical shift in industrial policy "through the long-term elimination of grants, subsidies and pricing policies and all federal taxes, direct or indirect, imposed on the natural resources of the provinces, other than income tax of general application." It also wants a tax policy designed solely to raise money, and opposes "the use of tax concessions as an instrument for manipulating investment behaviour and the industrial structure." In short, the party would take most tools of industrial and regional development out of Ottawa's hands. This would turn the economy over to the free market, with the likely result that poorer areas, especially in the Maritimes, would rapidly lose their industries and population. To his credit, Manning did not try to hide these policies from Atlantic Canadians when he toured the area in the fall of 1991.

The party also takes a free-market approach to agriculture, an extremely sensitive policy for Reformers because so much of their support comes from rural areas. The policy shows obvious tension between conservative ideology and the fear of alarming too many farmers. Basically, the party wants to eliminate all payments to farmers "due to the inability of governments and the community at large to finance such subsidization in the long run." There would be help during the transition and negotiations to make sure that trade partners would go along. Nevertheless, the goal is "the phased reduction and elimination of all subsidies, support programs, and trade restrictions, and the reform of supply/price controls in domestic and international agriculture." Farmers would eventually pay market prices for the things that they need, including transportation, and take market prices for their products. In today's climate of high farm costs and low commodity prices, this recipe would bring instant disaster to much of the farm community.

These agricultural policies caused a great fuss at the party's 1991 Assembly in Saskatoon, as farm delegates debated whether they were practical or simply suicidal. One Alberta delegate drew applause when he said: "As a farmer, I say let's make these cuts." The *Western Producer* reported that when another farmer said the policies went too far and would be impossible to sell in rural areas, he was greeted with a chilly silence. After that the policy was tabled to avoid a potentially embarrassing vote. Party officials decided to hold a closed meeting on the convention's final day at an hour only farmers could love, 5:30 a.m. Two hours later, they emerged with the party's current policy, which was then adopted by the delegates with no discussion. Some denied that they were trying to bury a difficult issue, but Marv Moore, a delegate and former provincial Tory cabinet minister in Alberta, got closer to the truth. "Agriculture is the most divisive debate there is if you really get into it," he said. The new farm protest movements, with their demands for federal money, suggest that the party is out of touch with a large number of farmers.

The episode showed several of the party's qualities very clearly. Like many populist groups with a mission and a clearly defined enemy, Reformers have an aversion to showing disunity in public, and a deep mistrust of the media. They can be as closed as any party when they sense a threat. Behind all this is the hand of Preston Manning, a leader who knows how to rein in the party's populist enthusiasm when he has to.

Ultimately the Reform Party will have to face intense public scrutiny of all its cost-cutting policies. They threaten scores of economic groups in Canada, from western farmers to Maritime fishermen and Ontario manufacturers and unions. The Canadian system, wasteful and expensive as it may be, has many beneficiaries who will not give up their privileges lightly, or, in many cases, without suffering. The party's other radical proposals for federalism will provoke equally strong responses.

The three major parties are already gearing up to attack the Reformers: Tory and Liberal MPs, in fact, have been supplied with long briefing books on how to discredit Reform policies. So far, the Reformers have enjoyed a fairly easy ride because of the freshness and novelty of their movement. Now the battle is about to be joined. Joe Clark gave a hint of what is coming when he said, after being asked about the Reform Party's response to the federal constitutional proposals: "You know Preston. He is against everything." The more serious questions, however, relate to what the party stands for – a long list of policies that would result in an entirely new kind of Canada.

CHAPTER NINE

THE PILGRIM'S PROGRESS

> "I always knew the Reform Party would ignite a Prairie fire, but I had no idea how far and how fast it would spread."
>
> – Quebec journalist Michel Vastel

At every stage of its growth since 1987, the Reform Party has astounded the experts. It was regarded as a crank outfit when it first emerged, and observers expected it to career blindly into a political cul-de-sac. As the curious started to fill the halls in Manning's home province, pundits spoke of a "Retread Socred" revival confined to Alberta. When interest soared in British Columbia too, Reform watchers were sure that the party would falter in the other western provinces. Certainly it would never break into Ontario. All these predictions proved to be wrong. The Reform movement has started a fire of resentment and anger among English Canadians that rages beyond mere political issues and smoulders at the very heart of Canada. In releasing this populist fury, the party challenges the foundation of our social contract, our parliamentary traditions, and the political compromises that have preserved the union.

"I always knew the Reform Party would ignite a Prairie fire," says Quebec journalist Michel Vastel. "But I had no idea how far and how fast it would spread." The analogy is profoundly descriptive of the growth and intensity of prairie protest movements. From Louis

Riel to the Progressives, Social Credit and the CCF, populist movements have seared the barricades of federal politics but have left the foundations intact. This raises the obvious question: how far can the Reform fire spread, and how much of Canada's political establishment will it raze before burning itself out?

Opinions vary widely. Desmond Morton, the University of Toronto historian, feels that Reform will begin to slide as an election approaches. "People will start to look back to the Conservatives as they realize that a vote for Reform might elect a Liberal or New Democrat," he argues. "In an election I can't imagine the Tories being as low as they are now." (Their approval rating was about 17 per cent in late 1991.)

Others are not so sure. Toronto author Michele Landsberg believes that Preston Manning "will do better at the polls than is good for the country. Women especially will understand the Reform Party agenda when they find out they're down there like Quebec." Landsberg believes the impact of Manning's policies would be "absolutely terrifying." Even if the Reform Party holds the balance of power, she says, "we'll see whittling away and chipping away at everything women have achieved."

Patrick Gossage, Pierre Trudeau's former press secretary and a sharp observer, feels that Reform could fare very well in the next election. As a Torontonian he worries that Manning and his Reformers might become "a party for frustrated whites" in heavily ethnic urban ridings of southern Ontario. It would be the first time in our history that this has happened and "a very dangerous development," says Gossage.

The example of the Progressives suggests that Gossage, and others who expect Reform to soar, may be correct. With a badly organized party and mainly rural support, the Progressives won 65 seats in a smaller House of Commons in 1921. Their regional base, like that of the Reformers, extended from Ontario through the Prairies. Yet they were not nearly as prepared or as well led as the

Reform Party is today. The Progressives had virtually no capacity for planning ahead to ward off counter-attacks. Manning, well aware of this example, often thinks of little else.

Nevertheless, it is dangerous to push the precedent of Progressive success too far. "I don't think you can use history as any kind of a barometer today," says Gurston Dacks, a University of Alberta political scientist. "The Prairies and the West have changed. They are more urban, the economies are quite diverse. The prospects for a dam-bursting kind of movement are far lower." Although he cautions that predictions are risky, Dacks places the Reform Party's highest possible level of support at about 35 seats.

Another U of A expert, Allan Tupper, notes that Manning has not yet been tested under intense political pressure. "I think he's very good," the political scientist says. "But he has not yet given evidence of being able to move out of a cocoon. He will have to do that. He needs to give evidence that he's leading more than just a loose association of disaffected Conservatives."

The "cocoon" Tupper refers to is almost palpable. Manning usually speaks to adoring crowds that ask tame questions, when they ask any at all. Even mild opposition upsets him, as he showed during the controversy over William Gairdner's book, *The Trouble with Canada.* Nobody has yet seen Manning in the kind of knock-down political brawl Canadians inflict on their leaders sooner or later. His background does not prepare him for this: the Alberta of his youth was virtually a one-party state with his father crowned for a generation. Preston Manning was schooled in the politics of consensus, not those of confrontation.

His party is also very vulnerable to policy burglary by the other parties, especially the Conservatives. The Tories have already stolen several Reform ideas for their constitutional package: property rights, the call for an economic union, Senate reform, more House of Commons free votes, and decentralization of many powers. The government and the opposition parties will snatch whatever they can in an effort to dilute Reform's support.

Partly with this in mind, Reformers have made some of their core policies virtually theft-proof. It is hard to imagine the Tories, Liberals, or New Democrats ever agreeing to scrap the notion of Canada as a union of two founding cultures. Nor are they likely to advocate that all reference to collective rights be taken out of the constitution. The Reform Party will probably remain the only option for Canadians who yearn for a savage attack on the public debt. That solution calls for massive privatization of government functions in a country where people still look to federally financed social programs with some pride.

The question is, how many Canadians really want Preston Manning's policies? Tupper suspects that, as more voters discover what the Reformers really stand for, they will be turned off. "Very few people in Canada are true free marketeers, but a lot of Reformers are," he says. "This is where it starts to come unstuck. People can move to Reform, but just as easily move away from it." They may begin to shift as they learn that Reform spending cuts would affect a child in university or a relative on pension.

Ultimately, and ironically for a party that prides itself on not taking Quebec as its starting point, Reform's fate hangs largely on the Quebec question. Most experts agree that if the constitutional debate ends in more failure and bitter wrangling, the party's support could skyrocket. It may lose adherents very quickly, however, if the Conservatives begin to be seen as the brokers who can save the nation. Anger at Quebec moves many Canadians these days, says Gurston Dacks, but so does the motto "From Sea to Sea." (Others argue that an actual constitutional settlement would bring new support to the Reform Party by displeasing many people outside Quebec.)

Whatever happens, Reform's stand on Quebec provokes strong feelings and even a measure of fear. "Manning's new Canada has obviously got very little room for *La Belle Province*," says Desmond

Morton. "I find that incompatible with Confederation. I don't have much faith in a new Canada without Quebec. I'm very concerned about people who think you can get rid of Quebec like a dirty shirt. It's just not an easy option. I think Manning knows that, but on a public platform he doesn't raise those concerns. Instead he exploits that feeling."

Manning constantly walks a tighrope between the ultra-conservatives and moderates in his party. His initial, rather tepid response to the Tory constitutional package of September 1991 caught some of his supporters off guard. They wanted unequivocal condemnation but got flaccid fence-sitting instead. Not long afterward, Manning debated Bloc Québécois leader Lucien Bouchard in an apparent effort to re-establish his credentials as a hard-liner on Quebec. Manning is bound to be caught in more of these political black holes as the national unity debate heats up.

In the end, the Reform Party's main achievement may well be gauged by its effect on public policy, rather than by its electoral achievements. "I'm not sure the measure of their success is either votes or seats," Tupper says. "That's the broader question: Is this a political party, or a movement to change our way of thinking and have a policy impact? I'm not sure what the full answer is."

Preston Manning often seems uncertain too. He is truly a strange bird in the tarnished cage of Canadian politics: a leader who relies on the power of populism but has the skills and experience of a traditional politician; an ambitious man who builds a party from the ground up, yet insists he will be content if Reform votes itself out of existence; a shy intellectual who has shunned the limelight all his life but now assumes the main stage under the glare of the cameras; a political pilgrim with the soul of a fundamentalist preacher, who has plunged into the worldliest game of all.

Ultimately, the kind of Canada that Manning envisages relies on the clear pool of pure religious faith rather than the murky marshland of traditional Canadian compromise. This New Canada has existed in his mind and in his father's mind for more than 25 years. He likes to say that he develops his platform by listening to the people, but most of those policies he first wrote down in the 1960s and 1970s with Ernest Manning close at hand.

These policies imagine a land of pure free enterprise with blissful harmony between workers and employers, where entrepreneurs are barons of benevolence who eagerly erase social ills. They call for more powerful provinces, weaker central government, citizen control of politicians, and equal opportunity for all but no special help for anyone. Above all, Preston Manning exalts the right of the individual to reign supreme over the evil forces of collectivism, which his religion equates with the anti-Christ. He asks the voters to accept a vision that runs sharply counter to Canada's history of mixed public and private enterprise, compromise between individual and collective rights, and the eternal quest to embrace Quebec within the country.

Whatever its fate, Manning and the Reform Party have already had a remarkable and often beneficial impact on Canadian politics. They have frightened traditional politicians who had grown complacent and badly needed an incentive to change. They raised to the top of the agenda many western grievances, especially Senate reform, that have now become national concerns. Most of all, they have given a voice to thousands of Canadians who felt left out and even humiliated by governments. "There are a lot of frustrated people out there," Manning said in an interview. "That's one function that I think the Reform Party can play. This stuff has to be vented. . . . It's better than leaving it to fester and stew in hopelessness. . . . That's the sort of thing that breeds dangerous extremism and separatism." Bringing such feelings into the open is perhaps the most useful function of a populist party.

One of Preston Manning's old friends paints a fascinating scenario of the leader's future. He has always been far more interested in provincial politics than he lets on, says this man, who asked not to be named. Someday he may come back to run Alberta as his father did, but with far more power if the Reform Party's policy of decentralization succeeds. He may even try to build the Christian society he so deeply desires. Yet even there the social laboratory has long since changed from the Alberta of his youth. Alberta is much like the rest of the country in its broad religious mosaic of Christian, Muslim, Jew, Hindu, Sikh, Shinto, and a dozen others.

Ultimately, Manning and his party provide simplistic reactions to the complexity of modern Canada. This is both their appeal and their failure, for their goals could only be achieved if Canada itself were suddenly simpler – stripped of ethnic loyalties, feminist hopes, Québécois dreams, and all the other collective aspirations that define the country today. Nevetheless, Preston Manning has shown for 25 years that he is above all persistent. This populist pilgrim will continue to storm the ramparts of Babylon, always hoping to convince the unbelievers that his way is the best one, not only for their country, but for their very souls.

BIBLIOGRAPHY

Primary Sources

Provincial Archives of Alberta

Bigam, J. F., Co-ordinator, Priority Employment Program. Letter to Mr. R. G. McFarlane, Deputy Minister, Department of Industry and Commerce, Edmonton. Re: 10 July 1972 Draft Letter to M. & M. Systems from Honourable Don Getty, the Minister of Federal and Intergovernmental Affairs. Draft Letter addressed to Mr. L. Boisvert, Slave Lake Developments, Slave Lake, 10 July 1972. (Discusses final payment of "seed" funds to SLD.) Accession No. 84.148, Box 11.

——. Letter to Mr. R. A. Splane, Director of Cash Administration, Edmonton. Re: Lesser Slave Lake Development Associates, 10 March 1972. (Provides history of SLD govt. funding.) No. 84.148, Box 11.

——. Director, Regional Program Co-ordination. Letter to Mr. Reg Adam, Provincial Director (Alberta) Department of Regional Economic Expansion, Edmonton. Re: Low-Cost Housing Project, 30 May 1973. No. 84.148, Box 11.

"Bulletin of the Calgary Prophetic Bible Institute." Calgary, n.d. No. 69.230/1a-1d.

The Busy Bee. Edmonton: Alberta Social Credit League. No. 82.153, Files 25 & 26.

"Facts Every Voter Should Know about Alberta Social Credit." Calgary: Provincial Liberal Association of Alberta, n.d. No. 66.6/16.

Friedman, Samuel A., Deputy Attorney General. Letter to Mr. J. E. Oberholtzer, Director, Human Resources Development Authority, Edmonton. Re: Slave Lake Developments Ltd., 17 November 1971. (States there is no conflict of interest between Mr. Neil Gilliat, H. R. D. A. Slave Lake Co-ordinator, and Slave Lake Developments.) No. 84.148, Box 11.

Gilliat, Neil. "Comments on an Editorial by The Slave Lake Oiler." No. 84.148, Box 11.

M. & M. Systems Research Ltd. (Ernest C. Manning and Preston Manning.) "A Proposal to the Minister of Regional Economic Expansion by M.& M. Systems Research Ltd. on Behalf of Slave Lake Developments Ltd." Draft. February 1971. No. 84.148, Box 11.

Manning, Ernest C. "Alberta: Home of Social Credit." Edmonton, 1945. No. 69.289/1261.

Manning, Mrs. Ernest C. (Muriel Manning). "What About the Reserves?" *The Busy Bee*, October 1956. No. 82.153, File 25.

——. "No Time to Slump." *The Busy Bee*, October 1957. No. 82.153, File 25.

Manning, Preston. "Slave Lake Developments Ltd.: A Private Enterprise Approach to Regional Development." Rough Draft, December 1971, No. 84.148, Box 11.

——. "Woodland Place Housing Project (A Joint Venture) Financial Statements for the Year Ended July 31, 1972." No. 84.148, Box 11.

——. "Slave Lake Development Limited Financial Statements for the Year Ended July 31, 1972." No. 84.148, Box 11.

——. "President's Report, 1971-72, Slave Lake Developments

Ltd." 20 October 1972. No. 84.148, Box 11.

——. Letter to Mr. Jerry Bigam, Human Resources Development Authority, Edmonton, 9 November 1972. (Lists progress to date of SLD, as a result of $40,000 funding.) No. 84.148, Box 11.

——. "Letter to the Editor of the Slave Lake Oiler and Scope." 25 April 1973. No. 84.148, Box 11.

McDonald, Currie & Co., Chartered Accountants. Letter to Preston Manning, Slave Lake Developments Ltd., Edmonton, 15 May 1972. (Discusses unaudited financial statements of SLD.) No. 84.148, Box 11.

McKinnon, R.H., Co-Chairman (Provincial) Joint Planning Committee. Letter to Dr. D. R. Campbell, Director, Plan Formulation Branch, Dept. of Regional Economic Expansion, Ottawa. Re: Slave Lake Developments Ltd., 30 April 1971. c.c. Preston Manning. No. 84.148, Box 11.

——. Letter to Mr. P. Manning, President, Slave Lake Developments Ltd., Edmonton, 28 May 1971. (Recommended, for low-cost housing, $40,000 funding by Canada-Alberta Joint Planning Committee under the Federal Minister of Regional Economic Expansion.) No. 84.148, Box 11.

Milligan, Geoff, Assistant Program Co-ordinator. Letter to Secretary, Slave Lake Development Ltd., Slave Lake. Re: Slave Lake Developments Centre, Slave Lake, 6 September 1973. (Discusses problems with the building.) No. 84.148, Box 11.

Miniely, Gordon T., Provincial Treasurer, Alberta. Letter to Hon. Donald R. Getty, Minister of Federal & Intergovernmental Affairs. Re: Slave Lake Developments Ltd., 29 May 1972. (Lists concerns about continued funding to SLD.) No. 84.148, Box 11.

Oberholtzer, J. E., Director, H. R. D. A. Letter to Hon. Donald R. Getty. Re: Contract – Slave Lake Developments, 19 January 1972. (Background information following Minister's enquiry.) No. 84.148, Box 11.

Patterson, J. L., Senior Administrator. Letter to Mr. A. E.

Anderson, Disbursements Senior Auditor, 16 February 1972. (States the $20,000 grant to SLD is redeposited until they meet the requirements of the contract. Notes that the contract was made on the direction of the previous [Mr. E. C. Manning's Social Credit] government's advice.) No. 84.148, Box 11.

Reierson, Mrs. R. "Address of Premier E. C. Manning (26 November 1958)." *The Busy Bee*, December 1958. No. 82.153, File 25.

Robinson, Mrs. J. L. "Address at the Social Credit Women's Auxiliary Convention." *The Busy Bee*, December 1957. No. 82.153, File 25.

Roy, L. J. and R. W. Thompson, Senior Municipal Inspectors. Letter to A. W. Morrison, Deputy Minister of Municipal Affairs, Re: Town of Slave Lake, 24 November 1971. (Outlines "investigation of allegations made against the Mayor and certain members of the Slave Lake Council.") No. 84.148, Box 11.

Russell, D. J., Minister of Municipal Affairs. Letter to Mrs. B. Lineton, Municipal Secretary, Town of Slave Lake, 29 November 1971. (Discusses "allegations of conflict of interest of certain Council members in their involvement with Slave Lake Developments Ltd.") No. 84.148, Box 11.

Slave Lake Developments Limited. "Contract between Slave Lake Developments Ltd., and the Province of Alberta." 17 September 1971. No. 84.148, Box 11.

——. Letter to Mr. Neil Gilliat, from General Manager Mel Leask, 12 November 1971. (States, in part, that "the Minutes of SLD records your [Mr. Gilliat's] resignation in the minutes of a Directors' Meeting held in Edmonton, March 13, 1970 and reads as follows: 'The resignation because of conflict of interest was submitted by N. Gilliat.' . . . A Directors' Meeting, held in Edmonton, February 8, 1971, records the transfer of ten shares from N. Gilliat to G. Cook.") No. 84.148, Box 11.

——. Letter to Whom It May Concern, 13 November 1971. (States "this is to certify that as of March 13/70, Mr. Neil Gilliat has had no financial involvement with Slave Lake Developments Ltd. At no time during the history of the Company [SLD] has Mr. Gilliat received, or will receive, any gratuities, share concessions, or any other form of personal gain.) No. 84.148, Box 11.

——. "Interim Report December 31, 1971." No. 84.148, Box 11.

——. Letter to Mr. G. C. Christie, Campco Ltd., Vancouver, from General Manager Mel Leask, 20 March 1972. (Concerns rental rates of SLD properties to prospective incoming Campco employees.) No. 84.148, Box 11.

——. Letter to Mr. Neil Gilliat, H. R. D.A., Slave Lake, from General Manager Mel Leask, 17 April 1972. (Concerns discussing rental agreement proposal with C.M.H.C.) No. 84.148, Box 11.

——. Letter to Hon. Donald R. Getty, from General Manager Mel Leask,17 May 1972. (Requests remainder of grant.) No. 84.148, Box 11.

——. "Public Statement: To make clear the position of the company in the light of recent editorials and articles in the Slave Lake Oiler and Scope. To make clear the role of Mr. Preston Manning with respect to Slave Lake Developments." 25 April 1973. No. 84.148, Box 11.

Walter, E. J. of Brownlee, Fryett, Walter et al., Barristers and Solicitors. Letter to Mr. L. Boivert (sic), Slave Lake, Re: Slave Lake Developments Ltd., 13 December 1971. (Legal Opinion on possible conflict of interest and disqualification from elected office.) No. 84.148, Box 11.

Wilson, Ethel. "Historical Fashion Pageant." Calgary Council of Social Credit Women's Auxiliaries, 21 October 1966. No. 86.125/134.

Wood, Cornelia. "Address to Women's Auxiliary Convention, 22 November 1944." No. 86.125/131.

University of Alberta Archives

Manning, Ernest C. "Transcripts of Ernest C. Manning Interviews 1978-1982." Lydia Semotiuk, interviewer. Box 81-32, Files 1-13, 14-26, and 27-39.

——. "The Death of a Free Society." *Edmonton Journal*, 8 October 1981. (From a 1965 address in opposition to federal medicare proposals.)

Legislative Library of Alberta

Australian Social Crediter. "The Plight of the World," (Part 2). *The Canadian Social Crediter*, 13 November 1947.

Collister, T. A. (Slave Lake Town Manager). "Guest Editorial to the Residents." *The Port of Slave Lake Oiler*, 11 October 1972.

"Crisis, Guns – and Ruin: Krupp Works Revolve on Plush and Steel by J.E.W. *(sic)* in the Christian Science Monitor." *The Canadian Social Crediter*, 9 October 1947.

Flynn, John T. "The Smear Terror," (Parts 1-4). *The Canadian Social Crediter*, 20 and 27 November, 4 and 11 December 1947.

Gillese, John Patrick, Editor in Chief. "Weeks End." *The Canadian Social Crediter*, 9 October 1947.

——. "The Money Power." (Part 2) *The Canadian Social Crediter*, 13 November 1947.

——. "More about the Money Power." *The Canadian Social Crediter*, 4 December 1947.

Government of Alberta, Ernest C. Manning, Premier. *A White Paper on Human Resources Development.* March 1967.

Government of Alberta. *Public Accounts 1987-1988.*

——. *Public Accounts 1988-1989.*

——. *Public Accounts 1989-1990.*
——. Solicitor General. "Victims of Family Violence: Information and Rights." n.d.
——. Women's Secretariat. "Fact Sheet on Family Violence." n.d.
Homer, A. "Clues to the Determination of Certain Sections of Jewery to Secure Palestine as a Jewish State." (Part 1) *The Canadian Social Crediter,* 11 December 1947.
James, N. B. "Main Street." *The Canadian Social Crediter,* 4 December 1947.
M. & M. Systems Research Ltd. (Ernest C. Manning and Preston Manning.) *Requests for Proposals and Social Contracts.* Edmonton, January 1970.
——. *A Realistic Perspective of Canadian Confederation.* Calgary: Canada West Foundation, January 1977.
Manning, Ernest C. "Financial Tyranny and the Dawn of a New Day." Text of address delivered during the Budget Debate in the Alberta Legislature, 6 March 1939.
——. "Social Credit in a Nut Shell." Edmonton: Alberta Social Credit League, n.d.
Thomas, Bruce D., Editor. "Conflict of Interests in Council." *The Port of Slave Lake Oiler,* 10 November 1971.
——. "Inquiry Needed." Ibid.
——. "Forum." *The Port of Slave Lake Oiler,* 25 November 1971.
——. "Councillors Remain." *The Port of Slave Lake Oiler,* 16 December 1971.
——. "Who Owns Slave Lake?" (Parts 1-4) *The Port of Slave Lake Oiler,* 13 September, 11, 18, 25 October, 1972.
——. "Slave Lake Group Requests Government to Investigate." *The Port of Slave Lake Oiler,* 18 October 1972.
——. "Our (?) MLA." *Lesser Slave Lake Scope,* 17 January 1973.
——. "Press Owes Keen Apology." Ibid.
——. "Principles vs Interests." *Lesser Slave Lake Scope,* 24 January 1973.

——. "Ministers Apologize." *Lesser Slave Lake Scope*, 7 February 1973.
——. "Police for Crime, Not Politics." Ibid.
——. "Slave Lake Councillors to Court." *Lesser Slave Lake Scope*, 7 March 1973.
——. "Tired of Politics." *Lesser Slave Lake Scope*, 13 March 1973.
——. "Trio Lose Round 1." *Lesser Slave Lake Scope*, 15 May 1973.
——. "One Last Word." *Lesser Slave Lake Scope*, 23 May 1973.
Webb, Norman F. "Historic Reality: A Hint to the Christian Churches." *The Social Crediter*, Liverpool, England, 14 September 1946 .

Government of Canada Publications

Canada, Committee on Sexual Offences against Children and Youth, Robin Badgley, Chair. *Sexual Offences against Children: Report of the Committee on Sexual Offences against Children and Youth.* Ottawa: Supply and Services Canada, 1984. (Referred to in text as Badgley Commission Report.)
Elections Canada. *Registered Parties Fiscal Period Returns 1990.* 2 Vols.
Government of Canada. "Canadian Charter of Rights and Freedoms." *Canada Act 1982 (U.K.)* Appendix III.
——. "Women and Poverty Revisited." Ottawa: National Council of Welfare, 1990.

Reform Party of Canada Materials

Beer, Ron. "Policy Corner." *The Informer*, Vol. 1, No. 4, Spring 1991.
Manning, E. Preston. "The New Canada." Address to a Reform Party Rally, Jubilee Auditorium, Calgary, 1 October 1990.
——. "Notes of an Address." Calgary Southwest Constituency

Association, Palliser Hotel, Calgary, 4 December 1990.
——. Letter to The Chairman, Nominating/Candidate Recruitment Committee, Calgary Southwest Constituency Association, 18 March 1991. (Re: Draft Candidate Questionnaire/Information Sheet.)
——. "Address to the Nominating Committee." Calgary Southwest Constituency Association, Henry Wise Wood School, Calgary, 22 March 1991.
——. "The Road to New Canada." Address to 1991 Assembly of the Reform Party of Canada, Saskatoon, 6 April 1991.
——. "Leader's Foreword: Building New Canada." Reform Party of Canada Principles and Policies 1991, Draft.
——. "Personal Response to Draft Candidate Questionnaire/Information Sheet." Part A, Sections I to VIII, Part B, Sections I to VII. 1991, 31 pp.
——. "Résumé." 1991.
Reform Party of Canada. "Candidate Questionnaire/Information Sheet." Draft, 1991.
——. "Constitution of Reform Party of Canada." 19 April 1991.
——. "56 Reasons Why You Should Support the Reform Party of Canada." Calgary: Reform Fund Canada.
——. *The Informer*, Calgary Southwest Constituency Association. Vol. 1, Nos. 3 and 4., 1990, 1991.
——. *Principles and Policies 1990*. Calgary, 1990.
——. *Principles and Policies: The Blue Book 1991*. Calgary: Reform Fund Canada, 1991.
——. "Reform Party of Canada." Calgary: Reform Fund Canada, n.d.
——. *The Reformer*. Vol. 4, No. 2, May 1991.
——. "Strengthening Democracy in Canada: A Submission to the Royal Commission on Electoral Reform and Party Financing." 1991.

Christian and Missionary Alliance Publications

"Africa a Thousand Times Over." Nyack, NY, n.d.
"Annual Report of the President to General Council 1991." Colorado Springs, Colorado, 1991.
"Asian Americans," Colorado Springs, n.d.
"Asia: Window of Opportunity." Nyack, NY, n.d.
"Chaplains." Colorado Springs, n.d.
"Chinese Alliance Ministry: A New Partnership." Colorado Springs, n.d.
"Christ for the Body." Nyack, NY, n.d.
"Christ for Life." Nyack, NY, n.d.
"Christ for Today." Nyack, NY,n.d.
"Christ in Us." Nyack, NY, n.d.
"Coalition: Highlights of the President's Annual Report to the 1991 General Council of the Christian and Missionary Alliance." Colorado Springs, 1991.
"Latin America: Reaching the Cities." Nyack, NY, n.d.
"Mediterranean Basin: Resisting the Gospel." Nyack, NY, n.d.
"Pacific Rim: Millions." Nyack, NY, n.d.
"Plan 2000: World Report Highlights." Willowdale, Ontario, Spring 1991.
"Sixth Biennial General Assembly of The Christian and Missionary Alliance in Canada." North York, Ontario, 1990.
"Turning Relief into Belief. . . . . . Works!" *(sic)* Nyack, NY, n.d.
"Water Baptism." Nyack, NY, n.d.
"What Is the Christian and Missionary Alliance?" Colorado Springs, n.d.
"What You're Looking For Is at an Alliance College!" Nyack, NY, n.d.

Magazines

Bergman, Brian, Glen Allen, and John DeMont. "Gaining Ground." *Maclean's*, 24 June 1989, 14-15.

Bremner, Christine Peak. "Slave Lake Developments Ltd.: A Community Development Company, Celebrating 20 Years of Achievement in North-Central Alberta." Supplement to *Alberta/Western Report*, 1989.

Collins, Robert. "Preston Manning: New Voice in the West." *Reader's Digest*, April 1991, 37-41.

De Groot, Paul. "The Reform Party: Evangelical Roots, Potent Political Platform." Manuscript to be published in *Faith Today*, April-May 1991.

Hailey, Arthur. "Ordeal by Rumor: The Skeletons in Manning's Cabinet." *Maclean's*, 16 November 1964, 15-20, 65-73. PAA No. 73.51/570.

Hardisty, Randy. "Economics Loom Large in Life of Former Premier." *Alberta Business*, 9 October 1981.

Hopkins, Stephen. "Prairie Fire." *Saturday Night*, May 1988, 14-15.

Howse, John. "The Man and His Mission." *Maclean's*, 29 October 1990, 30-32.

Hutchinson, Maryanne McNellis. "Reform's Bag Man." *The Financial Post Magazine*, September 1991, 18-26.

Irving, John A. "Social Credit in Alberta after 25 Years." *Saturday Night*, 9 January 1960, 13-15.

Pearson, Ian. "Thou Shalt Not Ignore the West." *Saturday Night*, December 1990, 34 43, 74-75.

Tedesco, Theresa. "Pushing the Envelope." *Maclean's*, 12 December 1988, 17.

Vastel, Michel. "L'Ouest Va-t-il Laisser Tomber Mulroney?" *L'Actualité*, May 1988, 64-66.

——. "La Guerre de Grande Baleine." *L'Actualité*, 15 May 1990, 32-40.

Newspapers

Newspaper reports from 1987-1991, unless otherwise indicated.
The Calgary Herald
The Canadian Social Crediter, 1947
The Edmonton Journal
The Globe and Mail
The Halifax Daily News
Lesser Slave Lake Scope, 1973
The Montreal Gazette
The Ottawa Citizen
The Port of Slave Lake Oiler, 1971-1972
La Presse
The Regina Leader-Post
The Saskatoon Star Phoenix
The Social Crediter (Liverpool, England), 1946
Le Soleil
The Toronto Star
The Vancouver Sun
The Western Producer
The Windsor Star
The Winnipeg Free Press

Interviews

Over 100 people agreed to be interviewed for the book. Those who consented to be identified are named in the text. Mr. Preston Manning granted two 60-minute interviews.

Secondary Sources

Books and Articles

Aberhart, William. *Post-War Reconstruction, First Series of Broadcasts by William Aberhart, B.A.* Edmonton: Today and Tomorrow, n.d.

——. *Post-War Reconstruction, Second Series of Broadcasts by William Aberhart, B.A. Premier of Alberta.* Edmonton: Today and Tomorrow, n.d.

Anderson, Doris H. *The Unfinished Revolution.* Toronto: Doubleday, 1991.

Anderson, Owen. "The Unfinished Revolt." In *The Unfinished Revolt: Some Views on Western Independence*, edited by John J. Barr and Owen Anderson. Toronto: McClelland & Stewart, 1971.

Barr, John J. "Beyond Bitterness." In The *Unfinished Revolt: Some Views on Western Independence*, edited by John J. Barr and Owen Anderson. Toronto: McClelland & Stewart, 1971.

Barr, John J. The Dynasty: The Rise and Fall of Social Credit in Alberta. Toronto: McClelland & Stewart, 1974.

Bercuson, David, and Douglas Wertheimer. *A Trust Betrayed: The Keegstra Affair.* Toronto: Doubleday Canada, 1985.

Boudreau, Joseph A. *Alberta, Aberhart, and Social Credit.* Canadian History Through the Press Series, edited by David P. Gagan and Anthony W. Rasporich. Toronto: Holt, Rinehart and Winston: 1975.

Braid, Don, and Sydney Sharpe. *Breakup: Why the West Feels Left Out of Canada.* Toronto: Key Porter Books, 1990.

Brown, Colin T., and David Somerville. "Who We Are and What We Do." Toronto: National Citizens' Coalition, n.d.

Cashman, Tony. *Ernest C. Manning.* Edmonton: Alberta Social Credit League, 1958.

Clark, S. D. "Foreword." *The Progressive Party in Canada* by W. L. Morton. Toronto: University of Toronto Press.

Conway, John F. *The West: The History of a Region in Confederation.* Toronto: James Lorimer & Company, 1983.

Courchene, Thomas J. *In Praise of Renewed Federalism.* The Canada Round: A Series on the Economics of Constitutional Renewal, no. 2. Toronto: C.D. Howe Institute, 1991.

Elliott, David R., and Iris Miller. *Bible Bill: A Biography of William Aberhart.* Edmonton: Reidmore Books, 1987.

Finkel, Alvin. *The Social Credit Phenomenon in Alberta.* Toronto: University of Toronto Press, 1989.

Friesen, Gerald. *The Canadian Prairies: A History.* Toronto: University of Toronto Press, 1987.

Gairdner, William D. *The Trouble with Canada.* Toronto: Stoddart, 1990.

Gibbins, Roger. *Prairie Politics and Society: Regionalism in Decline.* Toronto: Butterworth & Co., 1980.

——. *Regionalism: Territorial Politics in Canada and the United States.* Toronto: Butterworth & Co., 1982.

Hooke, Alfred J. *30 + 5: I Know, I Was There.* Edmonton: Institute of Applied Art, 1971.

Hurtig, Mel. *The Betrayal of Canada.* Toronto: Stoddart, 1991.

Hutchison, Bruce. *The Unfinished Country.* Vancouver: Douglas & McIntyre, 1985.

Irvine, William. *The Farmers in Politics.* Toronto: McClelland & Stewart, 1920 (republished 1976).

Irving, John A. "The Evolution of the Social Credit Movement." *The Canadian Journal of Economics and Political Science* 14 (1948): 321-41.

——. *The Social Credit Movement in Alberta.* Toronto: University of Toronto Press, 1959.

Macpherson, C. B. *Democracy in Alberta: Social Credit and the Party System.* Toronto: University of Toronto Press, 1953.

Mallory, J. R. *Social Credit and the Federal Power in Canada.* Toronto: University of Toronto Press, 1954.

Mann, William E. *Sect, Cult and Church in Alberta.* Toronto: University of Toronto Press, 1955.

Manning, Hon. E. C. *Political Realignment: A Challenge to Thoughtful Canadians.* Toronto: McClelland and Stewart, 1967.

Marsh, James H., Editor in Chief. *The Canadian Encyclopedia Volumes I-III.* Edmonton: Hurtig Publishers, 1985.

Morton, W. L. *The Progressive Party in Canada.* Toronto: University of Toronto Press, 1950.

Palmer, Howard. *Patterns of Prejudice: A History of Nativism in Alberta.* Toronto: McClelland and Stewart, 1982.

Richards, John, and Larry Pratt. *Prairie Capitalism: Power and Influence in the New West.* Toronto: McClelland and Stewart, 1979.

Smillie, Ben. *Beyond the Social Gospel: Church Protest on the Prairies.* Saskatoon: Fifth House Publishers, 1991.

Thomas, Lewis H., ed. *William Aberhart and Social Credit in Alberta.* Toronto: Copp Clark Publishing, 1977.

Unpublished Sources

Anderson, Owen. "The Alberta Social Credit Party: An Empirical Analysis of Membership, Characteristics, Participation, and Opinions." Ph.D. diss., Department of Political Science, University of Alberta, 1972.

Doll, Kenneth M. "'The West Wants In!': A Comparative Study of Two Western Canadian Political Parties." Master's non-thesis project, Department of Political Science, University of Alberta, 1991.

Groh, Dennis. "The Political Thought of Ernest Manning." Master's thesis, Department of Political Science, University of Calgary, 1970.

Hesketh, Bob. "The Company A, Company B Charges: The Manning Government, the Treasury Branches, and Highways Contracts." Master's thesis, Department of History, University of Alberta, 1989.

——. "The Marsh Report and the Manning Government: Social Insurance, Socialism, and the Evil Money Manipulators." Department of History, University of Alberta, Edmonton, 1988. Photocopy.

Judge, Colleen. "The Manning Administration, Municipal Finance and the Social Credit Way of Life." Master's thesis, Department of History, University of Alberta, 1990.

INDEX

INDEX

INDEX